FIC
MAS

#16

BLUE ISLAND PUBLIC LIBRARY
3 1237 00314 74
Y0-AID-465

FEB 1 4 2012

DATE DUE

FEB

**BLUE ISLAND
PUBLIC LIBRARY**

*B*itter

DANETTE MAJETTE

Life Changing Books in conjunction with Power Play Media
Published by Life Changing Books
P.O. Box 423 Brandywine, MD 20613

This novel is a work of fiction. Any references to real people, events, establishments, or locales are intended only to give the fiction a sense of reality and authenticity. Other names, characters, and incidents occurring in the work are either the product of the author's imagination or are used fictitiously, as are those fictionalized events and incidents that involve real persons. Any character that happens to share the name of a person who is an acquaintance of the author, past or present, is purely coincidental and is in no way intended to be an actual account involving that person.

13 Digit: 978-1-61793-625-8

Copyright © 2011

All rights reserved, including the right to reproduce this book or portions thereof in any form whatsoever.

Dedication

This book is dedicated to all the love ones I lost this year. My beloved grandmother, Verdell D. Majette, words can't express the sorrow I feel knowing I won't be able to get anymore of your back breaking hugs. I miss you so much! Love Nat.

Aunt Ivy Jane Delotch
Uncle Andrew Kendell Curtis (Ice)
Friend Nigel Ellison

"Trust in the LORD with all your heart and lean not on your own understanding; in all your ways acknowledge Him, and He will make your paths straight."
Proverbs 3:5-6

Acknowledgements

I just want to start off by saying I feel so blessed to be putting out my fourth novel. This has been a tough year, but God has watched over me and given me the strength to endure every trial and tribulation the devil has thrown my way.

To my wonderful mother, Nellie M. Best, thanks for helping your little girl pump her books in VA. I'm definitely my mother's daughter. Truth be told…you're the ultimate hustler!!!! Love you with all my heart. To my dad, Melvin Hester, we've finally turned the corner. I've felt closer to you this year than I have my whole life. I'm beginning to like this father-daughter thing! Love you.

To the world's best son and daughter, Bryan Majette and Marketa Salley, I just love you guys to pieces. Whenever I'm feeling down, I can call you guy's day or night and you always make me feel better. I really appreciate that. I'm so proud of both of you and wish you the best of luck in whatever you decide to do in life because I know whatever it is…you're going to be the best at it! XOXO To my late son, Marquan Andrews, there isn't a day that goes by that I don't miss you. I often wonder what you would be doing right now. I'm sure it would've been something to make me proud. You'll always be forever in my heart. Love you and RIP baby!

My brothers, Ronald and Melvin Williams and sister in law Keisha, I love you guys and thanks for making sure my nieces and nephews know who their busy auntie is. I promise I'm going to do better this year at spending time with them. Lol!! My nieces, Melkeda and Ke'azah, nephews Kaiyan and Kaon, auntie loves you! To my god brothers Kevin Levy and Equan Harley, you guys are the worst! I haven't seen you in ages. Naw...we have to do better than this. So this year we need to spend some time with each other!

To the world's cutest couple, my cousin/ sister Shelly Majette Carrington and her hubby Shawn. I'm so blessed to have you guys in my life. Shelly you are my lifeline when I just want to go crazy!!!! You're always there for me, no matter when I need you and I really appreciate that. You're the sister I always wanted. Thanks for all the help and pushes to finish this book. I Love you guys! Oh and by the way, I was thinking in my brain that you still need to move to Raleigh! Lol. To Lakeisha Majette, who knew you were so gifted? Thanks for all of the help you gave me. I know it took up a lot of your time...so I owe you one!!

To my uncles Johnny Majette, Wendell Majette (Aunt Christine), Stanley Majette (Aunt Katrina), Darnell Drummond...Aunts Lucy Bailey, Wilma Johnson (Uncle Clinton) and Belinda Curtis ...cousins Michelle (Neco), Mike, John John, Gwanda, Shawn, LaTisha, Dante, Zenobia, Toni, CJ, Shanique Majette, Allen and Wanda Bailey, Bambi Curtis, Nicole, Janise and Janae Wiggins, Felicia Taylor, Shawn and Jabria Carrington, Nina Labrador and Ebone' Scott, I love you all more than words can say and I appreciate all the support. Last year was a rough year for us after losing Dubie but we handled it with the grace and dignity she would've expected from us.

To the Hester family, especially my aunts Irene, Yvonne, and Pauline and my cousins Denise, Rashaun, and Michelle Nichols thanks for all of the support.

To Jmel aka Big Poppa, what can I say? I think you've spent more time in hospitals and doctor's offices with me this year than you've had to with anyone else your whole life and you never complained. You've been there for me and the kids, time and time again, and I'm so grateful. When Mary wrote the song "Hood Love" she was definitely talking about us!!! Lol! Love you! And just know I'll always have your back because I know you'll always have mine. Smooches...Big Mama!

To my good friend Jackie Davis (author of Love Heist and

Married to A Balla), girl we've had a hard year but we're gonna do big things in 2011 if we keep hustling our books the way we've been doing! I don't know what I would've done if I didn't have you to talk to or cry on the phone with. You've helped me through so many situations and encouraged me when I wanted to give up, so thank you for that. You're an incredible mother, person and friend! Love you Nette! Also, I would like to tell Emmanuel "Poobie" Chapman that I think you are such an incredible young man. I just love the way you dote on your mom. Keep up the good work and you'll see the results will be more than you ever imagined!

To Laron Profit, thanks for all the words of wisdom you've shared with me. Your quotes of the day really lift my spirits. To my ex-husband Marc, his wife Brandi, and Ms. Betty Hamilton, thanks so much for being there for my daughter. Carla Johnson and Michelle Parham thanks for all the laughs, and thanks Latoya Brinkley for keeping me on my toes in school! And a special shout out to Ms. Terrayne Pittman at Bowie State for all of your help this year!

Well Azarel, we've done it again. When I said I was never leaving LCB I meant it! Lol Being with LCB has been both a privilege and a honor. I know what it takes to put a book out so you don't ever have to worry about me doing my part to sell it. I admire you so much as a person and a business woman. You've gone from having two titles to now having forty-eight and that's major!!! I love you and the girls like my own family.

Leslie Allen, I'm not scared of that many people, but when I see your name come across my screen my heart nearly jumps out of my chest! Lol. I don't know why in the world people think you're so mean! Lol. No seriously, we didn't finish this project together, but we started it together. This was by far the easiest book for me to write because I took what you've taught me and applied it to every chapter. "Bitter" is definitely going to be a smash. Thank you so much!

A special shout out to the LCB crew, Carla Pennington (The Available Wife), Capone (Marked), C.J. Hudson (Chedda Boyz), Ericka Williams (A Woman Scorned), J. Tremble (My Man Her Son), Kendall Banks (One Night Stand), Mike Warren (Sweet

Swagger), Miss KP (The Dirty Divorce), Tiphani (Millionaire Mistress series), Tonya Ridley (Money Maker), VegasClarke (Snitch), Tamara (Hush Boutique), Tasha and Kellie! Thanks to Ms. Ann Joyner, Ms. Cheryl Bruce, and Kelly Fox for all of your input and support over the years. Also, a big thank you to all the test readers who took time out of their busy schedules to read my book.

    I would also like to thank the following people for their continued support: Mondell Pope (Urban Knowledge), DC Book Diva, Da Literary Joint, Black and Nobel and Afrikan World Books, Ella Curry (Black Pearls Magazine), and Alena Smith (Word of Mouth Magazine), Jeff Robinson of Dynasty Five, Sean Spencer of Velvet Entertainment, Shawn of TSM Magazine, Sabrina Wright, Miss Vay Evans, Tracey Gray (Spoiled Chicks Tees), Tra Verdejo, Joe, Larry and Vince at Patapsco Flea Market, Kim, Dominique, and Lexi Brunson, Andrea Thomas, Michelle Butler-Jacks, Elrico Collins, Erika Arndt, Tiffany Adkins, Anita Belachew, Jvawn Jackson, Sheila Snipes, Lamont Pettiway (author of "Why Men Cheat"), Martin, Davonne and Necole Salley, Huleo Evans, Attorney Butch Williams, Producer Bink Harrell, Keith Whitaker, JaKeith Johnson, Joyce Tillery, Sonya Strider, RoseMarie Reyes, Danny Harrington, Shon Majette, Carla Hinds, Karen Hodges, Sheena Smith, Jodie Adams, Bobby James, Cassandra Meeks-Payton, and Carlton Lampley (QWEEC) for the hot website. If I forgot anyone please forgive me and thanks to you, too!

    As usual, I would love to hear from you. You can contact me at: www.facebook.com/danette.majette or www.theliteraryconnection.net.

Danette Majette

Chapter 1

Driving through the prominent North Dallas neighborhood, Preston Hollow, like a Mario Andretti himself, Reese slammed on brakes and hit her automatic window when she reached the entrance to her ex-husband's estate.

"Open the fucking gate!" Reese yelled to the top of her lungs.

It didn't take much for the overweight security guard to realize that she was highly intoxicated. "Can I have your name ma'am?"

"Reeeeese...Keennedy," she slurred slightly.

"Password please."

"I...don't have a damn password fat-ass! I'm here to pick up my daughter."

When the security officer told her to wait a moment, Reese began beeping the horn like crazy. "Let me in this fucking gate!"

Instead of paying her any attention, the officer turned his head like he was used to erratic behavior and called Eric's house. After shaking his head up and down a few times, he put the phone down. "Mr. Kennedy wants to know do you have any idea what time it is?"

"I don't give a damn what time it is. Tell his ass I'm not leaving until he opens the gate!"

The officer spoke to Eric a few more seconds before finally pushing a button. "Miss, I suggest you calm down," he said as the

*B*itter by DANETTE MAJETTE

huge iron gates slowly began to open.

"And I suggest you kiss my ass, Shamu," Reese shot back before pulling off in a rage.

Her tires screeched as she sped through the upscale neighborhood, toward Eric's 10,000 square foot home. But instead of parking in the driveway, Reese drove right onto the beautiful manicured lawn, killing the freshly planted carnations.

Slamming her gear in park, Reese opened the door and jumped out. "Sydney! Sydney! Get your ass out here now!" she screamed in a deranged fashion.

When Eric heard the commotion, he immediately looked out the window and sighed. He couldn't believe Reese's car was stationed on his front lawn.

"Now, I'm convinced that bitch is crazy!"

"Who?" Melanie asked.

"My ex-wife!" When Reese continued to yell, Eric ran down the stairs and opened the front door. "Get in here! You're embarrassing me!" He looked toward his neighbor's house knowing the snooty white doctor would be peeking her head out the window soon.

"Where the hell is my daughter at?" Reese asked. She stood there with her hair all over the place like Angela Bassett in *Waiting to Exhale* when she set her husband's clothes on fire.

Eric tied up his robe and walked toward her. "What the hell are you doing?" He grabbed Reese by the arm then pulled her into the house.

Walking into the home she once shared with Eric was like Deja Vu. Reese stood for a minute taking it all in, but something was different.

"So, how do you like the new décor?" a voice sounded.

Reese turned around to find Eric's fiancée Melanie standing behind her with a big smile on her face. "I wanted to make sure there were no traces of you around here so we threw all that old, ugly furniture out with the rest of the garbage. Too bad we forgot you!"

Reese looked at the tall, model-like white girl sideways. With exotic features, Reese had no idea what her nationality was.

"What the fuck did you just say? Cause I'm handing out lollipops and ass whippings today and I'm fresh out of lollipops!"

As soon as Melanie said, "Whatever," Reese ran up on her like a defensive lineman for the Dallas Cowboys. She was so fast Eric didn't even have a chance to stop her. Reese immediately started pulling on Melanie's long, dark brunette locks, and tackled her onto the floor.

"Bitch, I've been waiting to do this for a long time!" She grabbed a wad of Melanie's hair and yanked with a vengeance.

As soon as Sydney heard her mother's voice, she knew there was going to be some drama. She ran to the banister overlooking the foyer.

"Oh, my God! Ma, stop!"

By the time Sydney ran downstairs, Eric had finally managed to pull Reese away. Melanie instantly started to wail from the pain of having her head pulled in all different directions. Eric was pissed! The fact that Reese had the nerve to come into his home and attack his girlfriend had him boiling. He also knew something like this was bound to happen so that's why he tried to keep them from ever running into each other.

"Reese, what the hell is wrong with you?" Eric asked, pushing her into the living room. "Have you lost your mind?"

"Where's my daughter?"

"I'm right here!" Sydney yelled.

Reese displayed an evil glare. "I can't believe you brought your ass over here without permission. And you had a nerve to leave me a damn note on the refrigerator while I was gone like that was acceptable. Get your shit!"

"She's better off here," Melanie managed to say from the floor. "You're crazy."

"Bitch, you want more!" Reese snapped.

Sydney knew better than to challenge her mother at a time like this, so she instantly ran upstairs to grab her bag, taking two steps at a time.

"I told your ass several times that Sydney is not your daughter," Reese shrieked, then pointed at Eric. "And she's definitely not yours." She gave Melanie an evil scowl. "Eric, I told you

Bitter by DANETTE MAJETTE

I didn't want my daughter around that bitch, but you keep allowing Sydney to come over here anyway."

"Look, don't come in my house disrespecting me and my fiancée," Eric barked.

Reese rolled her eyes. Every time she heard him use that term it was like hitting her toe on a chair. It didn't hurt instantly; it tingled for a moment, and then hurt like hell the rest of the night. "Fuck you and that white bitch!"

Eric really wanted to smack Reese across the face a few times, but he didn't need any bad publicity. "Get the hell out of my house, Reese."

"As soon as my daughter gets down here I will, but not a minute before, you sorry muthafucka."

"I'm calling the police," Melanie finally spoke. She stood up and walked toward the phone.

"Call the police! I'll just tell them you brought my daughter over here without my permission. Can you say, kidnapping charge?" Reese looked at Melanie with her hands on her hips. "Your move bitch!"

"Baby, its okay. You don't have to call anyone, she's a lightweight," Eric replied in a sarcastic tone. He then looked back at Reese. "And for the record, we didn't kidnap your daughter, she didn't come over here against her will."

"Well, I didn't tell her she could come over here either. She knows not to leave the house without me knowing." Reese pointed to Melanie. "Besides, I'm pretty sure her white ass is behind Sydney disobeying my rules."

Seconds later, Sydney came running down the stairs. "You did give me permission. I asked you last night when you were laying in the bed. Don't you remember?"

"Umm…I see somebody is throwing back a few too many," Eric said. Reese shot him a look. "Oh yeah, I know all about it. Damn, has it gotten that bad," he continued with a smirk.

"Shut the fuck up. You don't know shit about me!" Reese turned to her daughter. "What have you been telling him?"

"Nothing," Sydney mumbled, then bit her bottom lip.

"Yeah right. How did you get over here?" Reese questioned.

"Nia brought me," Sydney replied.

"I think you're lying about asking me anything last night, but I'll talk to you about that in private. Let's go!" Reese ordered.

Sydney wanted desperately to walk home because she knew her mother was going to scream and holler all the way home.

"Don't bring your ass back over here or the next time things might get ugly!" Eric shouted as Reese slammed the front door.

She didn't care what Eric said. As long as her daughter was allowed at his house...she was allowed there, too. He'd already gotten away with playing her for a fool. Reese wasn't about to let him play with Sydney's emotions. She knew as soon as he and Melanie had kids, Eric was going to push Sydney out of his life.

Sydney knows that's not her real father, so why is she trying to save the damn relationship? Reese thought as she jumped in the car, started the engine then backed out across the grass. "Step your game up bitch! I had roses in the front yard when I lived here!" Reese shouted one last time before pulling off.

As they rode down the street, Sydney tried to block out her mother's yelling, but nothing seemed to work.

"How could you do this? How could you come over here knowing Eric doesn't love us anymore?"

"Just because he doesn't love you, doesn't mean he feels the same way about me," Sydney replied.

"Are you serious? Don't let that asshole fool you. His selfish ass doesn't love anyone, but himself. I keep trying to tell you that. I also told you to stay away from him!"

"But I asked you last night if I could go over there, and you said yes. Maybe if you stop getting drunk all the time, you'd remember our conversations!" Sydney shouted.

Suddenly the car stopped right in the middle of the street. Before Sydney even had a chance to react, Reese had walked around to the passenger's side like a mad woman, opened the door and snatched her up by the collar. She yanked Sydney around like a rag doll then pushed her against the car.

"I'll fuck your ass up if you ever talk to me like that again.

𝓑itter by DANETTE MAJETTE

Besides, who the fuck are you getting loud with?" You could tell by the wideness of her eyes that Sydney didn't see that coming. "Do we have an understanding?" When Sydney's eyes wouldn't stop bulging, and she shook her head yes, Reese finally loosened her grip. "Now, get back in the car!"

    Sydney desperately wanted to run back in the opposite direction toward Eric's house. A place where she could have peace. A place where she could have one night without hearing her mother ranting about minor issues, or slurring when she had too much to drink. Sydney often told herself to have patience since she knew her mother was having a difficult time dealing with the divorce, but enough was enough. She couldn't wait to go off to college.

Chapter 2

The entire ride home was quiet. Sydney looked out of the window trying to hold back her tears while Reese sung along to an old Anita Baker CD like nothing ever happened. To keep the peace, it was probably best that they didn't say anything to each other, which ended up taking place. As soon as they walked into the house, both women walked into their bedrooms and closed the door. It wasn't the best way to handle things, but it would just have to do for now.

Needing to relax before going to work, Reese walked into her bathroom and pulled out a bottle of emergency Vodka from out her dirty clothes hamper; one of her many hiding places. Belvedere was and always would be her drink of choice, especially since it didn't carry a heavy alcohol scent and could easily be disguised. After pressing shuffle on her IPod Touch, Reese poured herself a drink in the cup she normally used for her mouthwash then downed it. Within seconds she poured another one before looking at herself in the mirror.

Reese often questioned why Eric wanted a skinny, flat ass, white girl over her voluptuous frame. At thirty-seven, her shape screamed twenty-five, and her waist to hips ratio made men stop dead in their tracks. More importantly, she was educated, and had a good sense of humor. Of course with the flip of a switch she could change up because she was still a hood chick at heart, but none of that stopped her from being sexy.

*B*itter by DANETTE MAJETTE

"What does that white trash tramp have over me?" Reese asked herself as thoughts of Eric and Melanie flooded her mind like it did everyday. Most times she could barely control her anger.

Every time she entertained the thought of Eric marrying his mistress, visions of him walking down the aisle pissed her off. He even had the audacity to invite Reese to the wedding as if she would go. Shaking her head back and forth, Reese couldn't believe that he was moving on with his life so soon; especially since they'd only been divorced six months. Never in a million years did she think he'd marry her. Besides, Melanie was only twenty-two years old...still wet behind her ears. How was she capable of being somebody's wife?

During Eric's pro basketball career for the Dallas Mavericks, Reese never had a problem with him being faithful. Despite the constant groupies that flocked to him after every game, Eric always seemed to be a respectful husband and a good step-father to Sydney. Unlike other basketball wives, Reese never found another woman's phone number in his pocket or had some crazy female stalking them. He seemed totally devoted to their family. However, once Eric got injured and was forced to retire, that's when things slowly started to decline.

For the last two years of their marriage, Eric turned into a completely different person. He went from coming home for dinner every night with a smile to not coming home at all, and with an attitude. He even picked up a bad habit of lying, which had Reese in tears most of the time. But what crushed Reese the most was when Eric sent her flowers at work one day, and accidentally put Melanie's name on the card. He didn't even deny the affair when Reese confronted him at home that night. Instead, he sat her down and told her that he was in love with someone else, and wanted a divorce. The one person on the earth, who Reese thought would never hurt her, had stomped on her heart.

To add insult to injury, when Reese found out that the woman Eric left her for was a Hooters waitress, she felt completely betrayed and embarrassed. So much that she actually thought of killing him on a few occasions. Reese dreamt of ways she could torture Eric and make him hurt the way she did. She even went to

Home Depot and bought some industrial strength tape along with an eighteen foot rope just in case she needed to act out one of her plans. It took Reese several months to get those thoughts out of her head. She was so depressed some days she wouldn't even get out of the bed. Thinking about her husband making love to another woman was too much to handle, but she finally got over it and tried to move on. Although Reese pretended to be okay, she was still broken inside.

Mumbling to herself about how fucked up men were, Reese took the second glass of Vodka to the head before pouring another one. When Kem's latest CD blasted through the speakers moments later, she began dancing with herself. Moving her hips from side to side, Reese began thinking about how happy she and Eric once were. She longed for his scent, his smile, and his touch. She reflected back to the days when they first started to date and how he sexed her passionately each and every night. She needed that in her life right now.

"Fuck this," Reese said tossing back her third glass.

Turned on by memories of their passionate lovemaking sessions, her skin started to tingle as she fantasized about him. Walking back into her room, she laid on the bed, positioned her pillows in an upright position then spread her legs full eagle before starting to explore every inch of her soft skin. A slight moan escaped her lips as Reese ran her freshly manicured hand over her breast. At this point, her nipples were hard as crystals and the moisture from her sacred place became undeniable. Reese needed to extinguish the fire that had developed down below. She took one of her hands and ran it down her center until she reached her pussy. She inhaled deeply as she softly rubbed her clit. It felt good to her, but she yearned to be penetrated. She reached over opened her night stand drawer and grabbed her best friend, *Buddy*.

Buddy was an eight-inch, hot pink vibrator that she'd fallen in love with ever since she and Eric separated. After checking the batteries, she quickly applied her favorite lubricant. Not much was needed since she was already wet. She inserted it in and out a few times before flipping the switch on. A slight purr escaped her lips as she thought about the vibrator being a real dick. At that moment,

Reese slipped the head of the vibrator into her mound which caused her to climax instantly.

Taken aback by how fast it happened, she became even more aroused and decided that wasn't enough. She then sucked the nectar off of the vibrator and turned the base until it was at a medium tempo. She ran "Buddy" down her belly button, and over her clit sending a shock up her spine. Liking how this was going, she ventured further down, and wasn't going to stop until a second orgasm was accomplished. In and out, around in circles, she continuously thrust the vibrator inside her walls, causing her body to tingle. Within minutes, she violently exploded all over "Buddy" until her body fell limp.

•••••••••••••••••••

When the On the Air sign flashed rapidly inside Studio 718, Reese was ready to unleash all her frustrations. Feeling good from the half a bottle of Vodka she'd managed to consume before coming to work along with the two shots she had in her office, Reese certainly didn't plan on holding back.

"Caller, you're on the air," Reese said in a dry tone. She wasn't in the mood to hear other people's problems at that moment.

"Hi Reese. My name is Tamara. I'm so glad I got through today. Giiirrl, do I have an issue for you tonight!"

"What issue can I tackle for you tonight Tamara?"

"Here's the situation. I've been dating this guy for almost a year. He's very sweet. Likes to wine and dine me. Has taken me to Jamaica and says he wants to marry me."

"Okay, so what's the problem?" Reese asked.

"The problem is his dick is the size of my pinky toe." There was a loud burst of laughter from Reese and her co-host, Joi, in the background. "For real, Reese! I don't know what to do. I have true feelings for him, but the sex is just not there," Tamara continued.

Instantly, Reese perked up. Whenever she was in a bad mood, her callers always seemed to turn things around. "Your pinky toe? Now, I've heard it all. So, this muthafucka is making up for his lack of size by wining and dining you? Hoping you'll forget

Bitter by DANETTE MAJETTE

about his lil' baby dick?"

Tamara chuckled. "It's not really that small, but he is lacking in that area. I find myself not being completely satisfied."

"Well, Ms. Tamara, if he can't put it down in all areas, what good is his ass? There are plenty of men out there who have the entire package. Leave his ass. Why waste your precious time on a man who can't satisfy you in all areas? He's spending that type of money on trips, when he should invest in the most premier package a woman would ever want, his dick!"

"So, you think I should leave him? Can't I maybe just slip some Viagra in his food?" Tamara asked with a chuckle.

"Girl, I don't think Viagra's gonna help that brotha if it's as small as you said. Just go out and find you someone else, honey. I'll tell you right now it couldn't be me. I would've been gone the first time I saw that little baby dick," Joi said laughing.

"Sweetheart, money doesn't last long and the only thing you'll be able to look forward to is great sex. If you can't get great sex out of him, then his ass is useless. If you didn't perform in bed, what do you think he would do? He would do what they all do...find one who will. Men aren't good for anything but giving us a wet pussy. Once they get what they want, they're out the door and on to the next young thing willing and ready to do any and everything without standards. So you have to play them at their own game...leave his ass Tamara!" Reese yelled.

She was so grateful to be on satellite radio where her show wasn't the least bit watered-down. Reese had the liberty to be herself and talk shit, which regular FM stations would've never allowed.

Reese proceeded to the next call. "Caller, what's your name?"

"What up, Reese, this is Marcus."

"Marcus, what can I help you with tonight?"

"I just relocated to the area 'bout a month ago and been tunin' in to yo' show since I got here."

"Okay so what the hell do you need help with?" Reese asked. She became extremely impatient when callers didn't get right to the point.

*B*itter by DANETTE MAJETTE

"I really don't need help. I think you the one needin' the help. Every night I tune in, you're going in on men," he spat. "What's yo' problem with men? Are you a lesbian or just bitter about somethin'? Bitch, you breaking up happy homes." Marcus spoke sharply.

"Excuse me. I know damn well you didn't just call *my* show and *try* to insult me. You don't fucking know me!" Reese shouted as her blood boiled. "Your dumb ass just started listening to the show, so who the hell are you to pass judgment? Furthermore, no I'm not a lesbian, and I'm not a bitch! I've just had my share of no-good-ass men, so I speak from experience. I'm well aware that men aren't shit. Every last one of them wine and dine you, fuck you good, get you pregnant, marry you, then leave you after ten years of marriage for a young bitch! Thanks for calling. Now, carry your ass back to where the fuck you came from…Marcus!"

Out of the blue, Reese's supervisor Julian appeared with a disapproving stare. Reese furiously ended the call, then threw her headphones down on the table and motioned for Joi to take over. Surprised, Joi watched as Reese quickly exited the studio.

"Dallas, this is your girl Joi and we're discussing being in a relationship with someone who doesn't please you in the bedroom. Do you stay or do you go? Hit me up and tell me your problem."

As Joi took over, Reese proceeded to her office cursing Marcus out under her breath the entire time. Walking into her office, Reese slammed the door then began to pace back and forth. When thoughts about how another man had called her show and tried to disrespect her, the pace increased.

"I wish I knew where he lived. His car would be sitting on fucking bricks if I did."

A few moments later, there was a knock on her door. Sitting down behind her desk, Reese released a harsh exhale, then shifted in her seat. "Come in."

"Rough show tonight I see," Julian said softly, as he placed her weekly fan mail on her desk.

"That guy was a fucking idiot. Talking shit like he knows me. He better not call my show again or he'll really think I'm a bitch."

Julian admired her as she sipped an old cup of sweet tea. "I understand your frustration, but you can't keep going off the deep end like that. Don't forget the callers bring ratings."

"I don't give a shit what they bring. If someone disrespects me, then I'm coming back at 'em. Ain't no man gonna talk shit to me and get away with it."

"Please...just try and calm down," Julian said in a soft tone.

She smiled slightly, glad that Julian didn't ask her to go back on the air. "What you got for me, more hate, I mean fan mail?"

"Yes. You know this is your favorite time of the week. Scanning your mail should bring you some comfort. A lot of the listeners actually love and admire you for your truthfulness. Don't let one asshole caller piss you off." Julian looked at his watch. "Look, it's already 1:30 a.m. Why don't you take the rest of the night off? Joi can take over for you. The show only has half an hour to go. Besides, we can just play a track of you saying general comments to make it seem like you're still on the air." He paused to smile. "The listeners won't know the difference. They can just direct their questions to Joi."

"Why? You scared upper management will get in your ass cause I cursed that guy out on the air," Reese said, frowning at him.

"No...well, yes...I mean, I think you might just need some rest. You look beat."

"I am beat. I haven't been getting much sleep lately."

"Okay, so go home and get a good night's rest. I'll see you tomorrow night."

"Alright, I'm just gonna read a couple of these letters before I go."

"Well, I'll leave you to your mail. Let me know when you leave and I'll walk you out. A beautiful woman like you shouldn't be walking to her car alone."

She ignored him for a moment then uttered, "Alright."

Reese read a few of the letters. As usual, fan mail from her female audience was always filled with love. Her male listeners, of course, were the complete opposite. She never understood why they continued to listen if they hated her so badly. Reese's "Girl Talk" talk radio show had very high ratings. She was famous for having all the hottest gossip on the celebrities in and around Dallas, but most of all people loved the sex talk segment.

While Reese continued to read, she had no idea that Julian was in the doorway staring at her. Julian secretly had a crush on her since she started working at the station four years ago. Glaring at her full lips and beautiful honey coated skin, there wasn't one thing that turned him off. Not even her attitude, that could be nasty at times. But no matter how many times he asked her out, Reese always turned him down. She gave him the, 'because we're co-workers' speech' when the real reason was because he reminded her too much of Eric, and she refused to have a repeat of that pain.

Although Julian's appearance was boring with his Polo shirts and khaki pants, both men had tall statures, perfectly trimmed goatees and Caesar style haircuts. Not to mention, both had complexions the color of Wheat Thins and were even more handsome when they smiled. On the flip side, Reese liked men who were smart and had an edgy side to them, but Julian wasn't that kind of guy. He was born with a silver spoon in his mouth and just to piss his parents off, he took a job they wouldn't approve of. He'd never been in the projects, let alone even seen one.

Julian stood there wanting to tell Reese exactly how he felt about her when she finally looked up.

"What are you doing? I said alright, Julian. You can leave now."

He acknowledged her with a nod. "Oh okay. I'll see you in a few."

As soon as Julian closed the door, Reese opened her desk drawer and pulled out a stainless steel flask filled with Vodka that she kept around whenever she needed to calm her nerves. An enjoyment that started off every now and then, but recently had become an everyday task. Taking a sip, Reese wiped her mouth with the back of her hand, before reading another letter.

She was used to the hate mail. It never stopped coming.

𝓑itter by DANETTE MAJETTE

Men didn't like her raw mouth and direct approach. She wasn't right or wrong about her advice. It was clearly just her opinion, and yet they all seemed to take it personal. But at this point in her life, this is how she felt, so Reese gave them the raw version…uncut and blunt.

Pulling the infamous card from her desk that Eric sent to Melanie that day, Reese took another quick sip from the flask. Keeping the card all this time was a bit extreme. She tried to throw it away several times, but just couldn't seem to let go.

I love you so much Melanie. I can't imagine life without you! Can't wait to make it official.

Love, Eric

Just like all the other times when she read the card, Reese instantly started to get angry thinking that Eric's affair had been going on behind her back without so much as a hint.

"That lying bastard," Reese said after taking two more sips.

Every time Reese thought about Melanie in bed, next to him at night, and Eric pleasing her sexually, it nearly sent her over the edge. "Don't they have enough of our men! I'm so sick of these white bitches," she said out loud.

Reese looked down at the luminous dial on her Chanel watch and saw it was 2:05 a.m. *Damn, I should've just stayed on the air*, Reese thought. Tired and beyond tipsy by this point, she threw away the letters she'd already read and the placed the unopened ones on the floor under her desk. After checking her emails, she called Joi to see if she was ready to go home.

All Reese wanted to do now was go home. Between the drama over Eric's earlier along with the constant drama at work, she was drained. After turning off her computer, she popped a few Altoids in her mouth, grabbed her purse then headed for the door.

With a dozen roses in his hand, Julian met Reese at the elevator. "These are for you."

Reese's eyebrows crinkled. "Where the hell did you get flowers from at this time of night?"

"I can't tell you all my secrets," Julian said with a slight grin. He tried to hand them to her again.

Because she didn't want to give him the wrong idea, Reese

took the roses reluctantly, and said, "Thank you, but I thought we already discussed this. I'm not interested in you Julian."

"Hey. They're just a token of my gratitude for all your hard work. That's all."

Reese paused for a few seconds. "Yeah, whatever you say."

"Anyway, I thought I told you to let me know when you were leaving. You don't look too good. Are you okay?" Julian asked.

"Joi and I are gonna walk out together. Don't worry I'm fine, thanks for the offer though."

"I know you're fine," he replied. "But are you okay to drive home?"

Reese shook her head. "Damn where did you learn that weak ass line from, your father?" She placed her hand on his chest. "Please don't say that shit to anyone else."

Julian almost got a hard on. "Well, let me take you out Friday night." For the past two months, Julian consistently asked Reese out. Each and every time he asked, Reese refused. Tonight was no exception.

"You already know the answer. Why do you keep asking?"

Julian grabbed her hand and pulled her closer to him. "Because I'm hoping one of these days, I'll get lucky and you'll say yes."

Reese laughed. The type of laugh you give when you're feeling awkward. She was relieved when Joi walked up.

"Alright girlie, I'm ready," Joi said.

As the two got on the elevator Julian winked his eye at Reese. *Geezzzz...get a life,* she thought, as she waved.

"Girl, that man is so in love with you. You should see how he stares at you. It's like he's looking into your soul," Joi joked.

"Bitch, shut up!" Reese hit Joi on the arm. "I see you got your party clothes on," she said, referring to the sequin dress Joi was now wearing.

"Yep, I met this guy at the club last week. Dude is fine and he drives a Rolls. Now, if I could just get rid of Lavar's sorry-ass."

"I know that's right. When is he gonna get the message and just pack up his shit and leave?"

"Honey, I have no idea. He gotta know I ain't feeling his ass any more. We don't even sleep in the same room."

Reese's mouth flew open. "Shut up."

"Oh yeah. I make his ass sleep on the couch. I don't even want him to accidentally touch me. Cheating, lying ass bastard. I'm really starting to hate his ass."

"Is he still cheating, or are you talking about when you caught him a few months ago?"

"I haven't caught him lately, but I'm not dumb. Who stays out until six o'clock every morning and always comes in and takes a fucking shower? I mean I know he's out in the street due to his occupation, but come on now."

"I'm not even surprised. I told you to stop messing with him when he hit you a few weeks ago."

Joi lowered her head. "Yeah, I know."

"How are you gonna be on the radio giving women advice about their men when you can't even control your own?" Reese questioned.

All Joi could do was listen.

Despite her lecture, Reese noticed how happy Joi had been lately now that she was out dating other men and partying all the time. She sometimes thought maybe she should take a page from Joi's book and do the same, but she wasn't ready to let another man into her life just yet.

Once the elevator stopped and the doors opened, they exited the building and walked with caution to their cars which were parked right next to each other. Reese looked at her car, then at Joi's new Mercedes CLK before shaking her head.

"I can't believe I went from driving a fucking $75,000 truck to a Nissan Altima." Disgusted, she turned to Joi. "And to think, I sucked Eric's dick every night and he still left me for that bitch! Fuck men," she said, throwing the roses in the trash.

Bitter **by DANETTE MAJETTE**

Chapter 3

Reese yawned and rubbed the grit from her eyes. It was a new morning and she vowed to have a better day. While brushing her teeth and washing her face, she looked in the mirror and noticed tiny lines of fatigue around her eyes. Still tired, she wanted to get right back in bed, but decided to make her daughter breakfast instead. Besides, it was only a matter of time before Sydney would be leaving the nest, so Reese wanted to spend as much time with her as she could. Reese also felt bad about what happened the night before. Having a quiet breakfast together was going to give her the perfect opportunity to discuss how she felt about going off.

When the food was done an hour later Reese yelled for Sydney to come join her. On the menu were scrambled eggs with cheese, pancakes, and turkey bacon...all Sydney's favorites. Reese placed the food on the table and took a seat across from her daughter who was texting as usual.

"So, are you gonna text all through breakfast little girl?"

Sydney placed her phone on the table, "No, I'm not."

Sydney was your typical teenage girl. Not only did they constantly bump heads because Sydney thought she knew everything, but she also drove Reese insane with her constant rebellious behavior. Her early development didn't make matters any better. With 38C breasts along with a Beyonce' waistline and thighs, Sydney looked more like she was twenty-five than seventeen, so horny teenage boys were definitely an issue.

At the same time, Sydney often made Reese very proud. Graduating with honors, Sydney was on her way to Clark Atlanta University, her mother's alma mater on a full academic scholarship. Reese was also skeptical about Sydney going there because she didn't want her daughter to be haunted by her biological father's past. After getting pregnant in her sophomore year, the pressures of having to support a baby got the best of Reese's boyfriend, a huge Clark Atlanta football star. After falling in with the wrong crowd, his hopes for going to the NFL were crushed when he caught a drug charge and ended up going to jail for three years. When he was released, he and Reese talked on the phone a few times, and he promised to come visit his daughter, but never showed up. Reese lost contact with him after that.

Reese looked at her daughter as she placed a piece of bacon in her mouth. "Why are you dressed already?"

"Ma, it's almost twelve o'clock. I can't sit around in my pajamas all day like you do. I don't see how you sleep in every morning."

"Because I don't get off until after two a.m. every night Sydney. Let's switch places since you think this shit is so easy. I'll text all fucking day while you go out and work."

Reese made a decent living working at the radio station, but it was still a struggle taking care of a teenager on her own. To make things worse…she was spoiled. Reese had gone from hi-end boutiques and five star restaurants to shopping at Walmart and disgusting fast food joints. She didn't have the kind of money she used to, but managed to keep up her appearance since she was in the public's eye.

Reese signing a pre-nup meant Eric didn't have to give her spousal support. But his public infidelity kind of played in Reese's favor. He ended up buying her a townhouse, and agreed to give Sydney a monthly allowance until she graduated from college to keep things civil. He also let her keep their Range Rover, even though Reese ended up selling it in order to have a decent savings account.

Reese decided to change the subject. "So, are you gonna

miss me when you go off to school? You'll be leaving at the end of next month."

Sydney played with her long hair that she usually wore in a ponytail. "I'm gonna miss everybody."

"Well, most of your friends are going to Clark Atlanta too so you'll see them."

Sydney took a big gulp of her orange juice. "No, I mean people like Joi, Eric…"

Reese's eyes enlarged. "Eric! Why the hell would you miss his cheating ass?"

"Here we go again! Just when I was starting to enjoy this mother-daughter moment with you," Sydney said sarcastically.

"You better watch your mouth Sydney. I mean, why do you like going over there so much anyway?" Reese looked around the kitchen. "Don't get me wrong, I miss the theatre room and the gym, too, but you act like we live in a damn roach motel."

Sydney played with her eggs that were now cold as ice. "It's not that."

"Then what is it? Why is it that you always take up for him? He's not even your real fucking father."

Sydney couldn't believe her mother would say something like that, especially since Reese knew that was a sensitive subject. Sydney resented her real father. She couldn't understand how he could just turn his back, and had never even made an attempt to be in her life.

Realizing she wasn't in the mood for her mother's normal male bashing session, Sydney was getting ready to head to her room when someone knocked on the door. Wondering who it was, Reese told her daughter to get the door while she continued to eat. Just as she placed some grape jelly on her toast, Reese sat straight up in the chair as soon as she heard Eric's voice.

What the hell is he doing here, she thought after standing up and rushing out the kitchen.

Before she even made it to the front door, Reese caught Eric eyeing her from head to toe. It was hard not to notice her Kim Kardashian type ass hanging out of the polka dot boy shorts she had on.

"You gave all this up, remember?" Reese said.

Eric showed a slight smirk. "What are you talking about?"

"Don't even try that shit. I saw the way you were looking at me. Tired of that ironing board ass, huh?" Reese chuckled.

"Don't flatter yourself. I've never been one who likes old leftovers," Eric replied in an arrogant tone.

Sidney lowered her head to keep from laughing.

"What the fuck do you want? Why are you even here?" Reese questioned.

"I came to see if Sydney wanted to go with Melanie to the spa, my treat of course."

As Sydney's eyes lit up, Reese's seemed to burn a hole through Eric's crisp Hugo Boss shirt. Walking closer to the door, she stuck her head outside and watched as Melanie brushed her long silky hair. Reese was furious.

"Are you serious? How dare you bring that bitch over my fucking house? Get out!" she yelled.

"Look, I know better than to bring her inside. That's why she's in the car," Eric explained.

Reese placed her hands on her hips. "So that's supposed to make me feel better. I don't want her ass anywhere near me."

Sydney couldn't believe the way her mother was acting. Little did Reese know, her actions only made Sydney want to be around Melanie even more. "Once again you're overreacting over something so minor."

Reese looked at her daughter. "What the fuck did just you say?"

Sydney shook her head. "Forget it."

"Yeah...and you can forget about going anywhere with his ass!"

"Maybe this wasn't such a good idea," Eric quickly intervened. He kissed Sydney on the forehead. "I'll call you later."

"No you're not gonna call her later. Sydney is not your daughter, so don't come around my damn house acting like I have to let you see her. Her love and affection aren't for sale."

"I may not be her real father, but I might as well be. I've been taking care of her for seven years. You can't say that about

*B*itter by DANETTE MAJETTE

her real father...now can you," Eric said. He turned around and walked out.

Even though Reese was pissed she hated that fact that Eric was right. He did take good care of Sydney, which is another reason why she hated to let him go. For her Sweet 16, Eric went all out and rented one of the hottest clubs in Texas. He even paid a hefty fee to have Soulja Boy perform. Her party was the talk of Dallas for months. The only thing missing was the infamous car with the big red bow across the hood. Reese said *no* to that. It was something special she wanted to do for her daughter, but hadn't gotten around to it yet.

Reese decided to follow him outside. "Fuck you Eric!" she yelled.

"My God! How long is it going to take for you to get over me?" Eric spat back.

"Muthafucka, I've been over you. You're the one who was just looking at my ass so obviously you can't let go!"

"Whatever," he responded.

Reese walked up to Eric's champagne colored Aston Martin as he got in. "Don't you ever bring that bitch over here again!"

Melanie may've been white, but she was no push over. "You can call me whatever you want, but in a couple of months you'll have to call me, *Mrs*. Eric Kennedy!"

Reese wished she had on more than bedroom shoes as she kicked his driver's side door. She could care less if any of her neighbors witnessed her acting like a complete fool.

"Hey, don't kick my shit. What the hell is wrong with you?" Eric yelled out.

"She's pathetic," Melanie chimed in.

Enraged by Melanie's comment Reese kicked the door once again then tried to run over to the passenger's side. When Eric slowly pulled off, she stopped. Knowing she had to do something, Reese was able to grab one of the windshield wiper blades and pull it off right before his speed increased.

"Good luck in the rain asshole!" she screamed.

Bitter by DANETTE MAJETTE

Chapter 4

Later that day, Reese decided to put some space between herself and Sydney. With a pair Twisted Hearts jean shorts on, and a wife beater, she went down to the basement with her pitcher of tea and took a seat on her chaise. She turned on sixty inch flat screen compliments of Eric and started to flip through the channels when she saw a breaking news bulletin. She turned the volume up.

'*A Dallas woman has been killed in her home. Warning, this next story contains graphic content that might not be suitable for children;* she stuck her head out of the bathroom and concentrated on the television. She knew when they said warning it was going to be very grizzly.

She stood silent and waited for the details. *Shortly after noon today, Vanessa Carr was found dead by her ex-husband, Avery Carr, a member of the Dallas Police Department.*

Hmm...that name sounds so familiar? Reese thought to herself. She usually kept up with current events just in case one of her callers asked her a question about something that happened in the Dallas area, but this time it was different. She'd definitely heard that name before and it was driving her crazy that she couldn't remember from where.

Mrs. Carr was found inside her home where apparently she'd been brutally murdered. A police officer on the scene said she'd been shot multiple times along with a knife inflected wound under her

*B*itter by DANETTE MAJETTE

throat. Members of the community are shocked. Mrs. Carr was said to be very active in a number of charities around the Dallas area.

Damn, someone was mad as hell at her. It was probably the ex-husband, Reese thought as a text from Joi on her Blackberry came through. In a corner of the television a picture of the woman was put up, but Reese was so busy texting Joi back that she missed it.

A spokesperson for the Dallas Police Department said Officer Avery Carr is holding up as best as he can under these circumstances. The couple's two sons who were at summer camp are very distraught over the loss of their mother. This is Ted Ratherford for Channel 5 news.

By the time Reese's attention was back on the story, they were moving on to the weather. She sat on her couch racking her brains. The woman's name was so familiar to her. "Let me think. Vanessa Carr...Vanessa Carr. Oh shit, I think she called into my show a couple of times."

Even though she didn't know that woman personally, she felt bad, especially, for her two children. Reese continued to watch the news. When she heard that it was still a scorching one hundred degrees outside at six o'clock, Reese was determined not to go out until it was time to go to work. July was a brutal month for Texas.

Reese and Joi continued to text back and forth until she finally stopped due to her dying battery. By that time, Reese was ready for a nap so she plugged her phone into the charger then stretched out on her couch. Just as she closed her eyes and began to relax, Sydney walked downstairs.

"Can I spend the night over Nia's house?" It looked as if she dreaded to talk to Reese.

"Not if you're planning on sneaking back over Eric's house." Reese could care less that Nia's house was right across the street.

"Ma, I didn't sneak over there. You told me I could go. I wouldn't lie about something like that."

Reese stared at her daughter. "So, why should I let you go? You haven't had shit to say to me all day, and now that you want something you all up in my damn face."

Sydney wanted to let out a huge sigh, but knew that would make things worse. "Ma I was just giving you time to cool off. You know how you are when Eric pisses you off." When Reese didn't respond, Sydney continued. "So, can I go?"

"Sure, when you apologize."

Sydney rolled her eyes then said with a fake smile, "I'm sorry, mother. Can I go now?"

"That was so insincere, but yes you can go. Just make sure you don't get bold and try to play me again."

When Sydney stomped up the stairs like a little girl throwing a temper tantrum, Reese started to make her stay home. *Four more weeks and I won't have to put up with her nasty-ass attitude any more.* When she heard the front door shut, she grabbed her chenille throw and covered up before laying back down. *Maybe I should give a shout out to all the single mothers on the air tonight because this shit isn't easy.*

Reese's mind kept drifting to her fight with Melanie and Eric from earlier that day. As much as she wanted to, Reese couldn't get Melanie's words out of her mind. Hearing Melanie call herself Mrs. Kennedy hit her like a ton of bricks. At that moment, she made a mental note to go back to her maiden name, Reese Monroe. What hurt her even more was Eric co-signing all the time. It made Reese want to go over to his house and start some shit. Since she couldn't do that she did the next best thing. She took her beef to the airwaves.

"Fuck that single mom shit," Reese said.

Tonight's show was going to be dedicated to women who had a man leave them for a jumpoff.

• •

The ride to work was smooth even though Reese ran several red lights to make it on time. Working at night sucked, but Reese was determined to get her show in syndication so she had to do whatever it took. If she got the job, not only did that mean more money, but more opportunities as well.

Knowing that tardiness was the radio's number one reason for firing disc jockey's, Reese raced into the parking lot and quickly turned off her car. Jumping out, she noticed that Joi was already there.

"Well, at least one of us is on time," she said after activating the alarm, and running into the building.

Normally, she messed with the short, Gary Coleman looking security guard and made small talk about all his kids, but tonight Reese just threw up her hand and headed straight for the elevator. As soon as the door opened on her floor, she ran right into Julian. He was like a hound dog. Every time she turned around, he was there.

Shit, Reese thought. *I know he's gonna have something to say.* "Sorry, I'm late Julian. I…"

"Hi sweetie. It's no problem. I just told the engineer to play a few songs until you got here, so you have time. Besides, Joi is already in there. How was your day?"

Silently in her mind, she was cursing him out. *I'm not your fuckin' sweetie!* She needed Julian to help her get that promotion so now wasn't a good time to offend him.

"It's was good. How 'bout yours?" she said, gritting her teeth.

"I went out on my boat today. Next time, you should come with me. You'll love it."

"Maybe I will. Well, I need to get to work so I'll talk to you later."

"Okay, would you like me to bring you some coffee?"

Oh my God! Leave me alone! "Naw, I'm good," Reese said, walking toward the studio.

Once Reese walked in and got settled in her chair, Joi signaled to the engineer that they were ready. Reese couldn't wait to hear what her listeners had to say about the topic she chose. She knew there would be some good and definitely some bad responses after she let loose, but that was how the game worked. Reese wondered why it was okay for her male counterparts to be confrontational on the waves, but when women did it, they were considered too brash. However, Reese didn't care what anyone said. She was unapologetic to those who misunderstood her. She never claimed to be an expert. She was just a girl from Houston who had a microphone and liked to use it to voice her opinion about her experi-

*B*itter by DANETTE MAJETTE

ences with men.

"What's up, trick?" Joi greeted.

All Reese could do was laugh. "If anybody is a trick it's you, bitch!" Despite graduating with a Journalism degree and her successful radio personality job, Reese grew up in one of Houston's worst housing projects so she was certainly hood at heart. Unlike all her other childhood friends, she just decided not to be a statistic.

When the *on the air* sign flashed. Reese and Joi immediately got into character.

"What's up, Dallas? This is yo' girl, Reese!"

"And this is yo' girl, Joi."

"Welcome to *Girl Talk*," they said in unison.

"Giving it to ya' straight...no chaser," Joi added.

"Okay, so that was Fantasia's song Bittersweet and from what I've heard her relationship with Antwaun Cook was just that," Reese stated.

"It's about to be a little more than that ain't it?" Joi asked.

"Yeah, things are about to get sour cause' his wife is suing her for alienation of affection. And she should! I mean I've totally lost all respect for Fantasia. I wish I could take back my American Idol vote. That bitch don't deserve it. That's right I called her a BITCH!"

Joi laughed, "No, you didn't call her a bitch!"

"Why not, that's what she is? You're gonna tell me that home wrecker didn't know this man was married with children," Reese continued. And does she tell him to get a divorce first then we can talk. No...she breaks up this woman's home. What about his children? His ass got so caught up he forgot how this was going to affect them. But that's typical of men. They're always thinking with the wrong head!"

Joi laughed again. "Oh please! She knew. She's gonna use that 'he told me he wasn't happy and they weren't together when I met him excuse'."

"Yeah, but ain't nobody buying that bullshit!" Reese added.

"You're right because check it out...ain't nobody saying nothing 'bout his T-Mobile working ass. She's taking all the flack. That's why she tried to kill herself. She can't handle all the nega-

*B*itter by **DANETTE MAJETTE**

tive press," Joi chimed in.

"Well, I wish I lived in North Carolina when my ex-husband who was a NBA player cheated on me. They're one of the states that let's spouses sue jumpoffs."

"That's deep!" Joi said.

"Well, Dallas, it's a hot and steamy Friday night and the topic is, Jumpoffs. Hit me up if you got something to say. And don't call talking about dumb shit because I will cut you off."

When she saw the lines lighting up like a Christmas tree she knew she'd struck a cord. That's what her show was all about, getting her ratings up. After calling Fantasia the B word she knew tonight's show was going to be a hit.

"Hello, caller. What's your name and what do you think about all this mess with Fantasia?"

"My name is Meeka and I just think people have no respect for marriage anymore...shame on them. Fantasia is an idiot if that man's wife is able to sue her, and if she wins Fantasia is going to be taking care of her and her kids for a long time."

"Thank you, Meeka. I agree," Reese said. "Caller, what's your name and tell me what you're thinking?"

"My name is Juanita and I think Fantasia is dumb...plain and simple. She's so desperate for ratings and CD sales that she's staging this publicity stunt. I wasn't a fan when she won American Idol and I'm not one now. She needs to focus on her daughter and what singing career she has left. I don't feel sorry for Gabrielle Union either," Juanita included. "She messed up D. Wade's marriage."

"Oh, I almost forgot about that damn jumpoff," Joi chimed in.

"Finally a male caller! What do you have to say about this mess?" She was anxious to hear a male's point of view.

"Who the hell is he again? I don't think about that dude at all, but I do think about you Reese."

"Alright now, playa-playa. What's going through your mind baby when you think of me?"

"I think about how you must get off at night gossiping 'bout other folks and tearing up peoples households with yo' bullshit."

"Excuse me," Reese said with an attitude.

"You heard me!"

Reese tried to respond, but the caller wouldn't let her get a word in. He started ranting and raving like a mad-man. His voice was so distorted they couldn't tell if it was a joke or if it was a legit caller. "You always in somebody's business. Do people know yo' husband left you for a white chick?"

"First of all, we're not talking about me and you shouldn't speak about things you know nothing about!" Reese yelled, trying to cut him off.

"Shut up, bitch!"

Joi was in shock. She knew men got mad when they talked about them, but they'd never had someone go crazy.

"I should come up to that station and strangle yo' ass! Talk about that!" he yelled in a deranged voice. "Just watch your back…"

Reese wanted to keep going off on the man since he had the nerve to disrespect her and the show, but since she was trying to move up in the world, she just simply motioned for the engineer to cut the call. Right before the line was disconnected, the guy said something even more disturbing.

"I'm thinking I'll slash your throat and watch the blood spew from your neck."

Reese sat in amazement while her heart raced. She couldn't believe that the caller had actually threatened her on the air. You could tell by the look on everyone's face that they were trying to gather their thoughts as the engineer decided to play R. Kelly's new song. Meanwhile, Julian came rushing into the studio like he was ready to fight.

"Are you okay?" he asked, nearly out of breath.

Reese was quiet for a second, then she shook her head up and down. "Yeah! I'm just a little stunned. Let's just finish up the show. I'm not gonna let that muthafucka scare me."

"That was crazy," Joi said.

Julian gently placed his hand on Reese's shoulder. "Are you sure? I'm so sorry about that. Trust me. We won't let him through again."

Reese adjusted her body in the chair so Julian's hand could fall. "Yes, I'm fine. Let's go."

●●●●●●●●●●●●●●●●●●●●●●

As they wrapped up for the night a few hours later, Julian came back in the studio still fired up. Furious, he started pacing the floor and mumbling under his breath.

Reese couldn't believe how he was acting. "Julian, calm down. It's over! Plus, it's not like this should be a big surprise to us. We all know that they're people out there who hate us. Look at all that crazy mail we get."

"Yeah, but we've never been threatened before. He was very disrespectful to you and I don't like that. No one's going to talk to you like that again!" he responded.

"What the hell do you mean by *we* were threatened? He said he wanted to strangle me, not you," Reese said jokingly. She needed to do something to lighten up the mood because Julian's behavior was starting to become a concern.

"It's not just that. I didn't tell you about the letter that came to the station begging us to fire you. Someone is claiming that their girlfriend, Vanessa Carr was killed and it was your fault."

Instantly, Reese remembered the news report where the name was mentioned. "Me?" she questioned, holding her hand over her chest." Her eyes showed that she was puzzled.

"Yes, you. We ran the tapes back and realized, Vanessa Carr called into the show a few times. You did give her advice about her ex-husband one night, but her ex-husband didn't kill her. The police say he found her dead and is still distraught to this day. So, none of it makes sense."

"That's crazy. I don't remember my advice, but I knew her name sounded familiar."

"Hey, why don't you let me take you home? You can just leave your car here for the night," Julian suggested.

Joi couldn't help but smile as she took her headphones off.

"Look, stop acting so crazy. I'm driving myself home." Ju-

𝓑itter by DANETTE MAJETTE

lian gave Reese a disapproving look. "Don't worry, I'll be fine."

As Julian kept trying to get Reese to leave her car and ride with him, she continued to ignore him. She was used to his unwanted gifts and sexual comments, but this time his obsessed demeanor was kind of alarming.

"Oh, that' so sweet how you want to protect her," Joi teased.

Reese gave her co-host an evil glare. "Joi, are you ready to go?" she asked.

Joi knew exactly what Reese meant. "Yep!" She stood up and threw her Valentino handbag over her shoulder.

"Have a good weekend!" Julian blurted out.

On Joi's heels, Reese quickly grabbed her bag as well. She didn't want to be in Julian's presence any longer then she had to be. Once they were on the elevator, Reese asked, "What the hell's wrong with him?"

"I have no idea. Damn, imagine if you were to give him some," Joi said, laughing her ass off. "That nigga was acting like you were his woman."

"Joi, this is serious. This is getting out of hand. I mean I tried to overlook some of the things he's been doing, but tonight was weird.

"I couldn't wait to get out of there so I could fuck with you. It's kinda' sweet though."

Reese rolled her eyes as hard as she could. "Shut the hell up. I'm so glad I don't have to deal with him until Monday."

"On another note, what do you think about that crazy-ass caller?"

Reese paused for a few seconds. "For a dude to be that mad at someone he doesn't even know all I can say is, he desperately needs some pussy." Reese wanted to laugh, but deep inside she felt uneasy. "Girllll, people crazy," she uttered.

When the elevator doors opened, the women stepped off and looked around before they got into their cars. Once they said their good-byes, Reese was about to pull off when she noticed a piece of paper on her windshield. She got out of her car, and grabbed it. She was flabbergasted by the contents.

ℬitter by DANETTE MAJETTE

Bitch, you betta watch yo' back!

Everything seemed to move in slow motion as she looked around to see if anyone was watching her. Quickly, Reese jumped inside and speedily slammed her gear in drive before speeding off the parking lot. She knew a lot of people hated her, but this shit was starting to get out of hand.

As soon she pulled onto Preston Road, Reese turned on her radio to listen to the show that came on after hers. The DJ was only in his mid-twenties and played mostly southern rap songs and unsigned artists.

He's so corny, she thought to herself. Out of all the shows on her satellite station, Reese knew hers was the best and had the most people tuning in.

"There's no way I shouldn't get that syndication," she mumbled to herself.

Reese drove about a mile when she noticed a car following closely behind her.

"Why the hell do they have their high beams on?" she asked herself.

At first she thought it was someone trying to pass her until the lights started flashing on and off. It was almost as if someone was trying to get her attention.

"I know damn well that ain't Julian following me! If it is, he's gone too damn far now!"

Reese tried to get a good look at the car in her rear view mirror, but couldn't seem to make it out. At that point, she tried to switch lanes, hoping that would work, but the other car did the exact same thing. Whoever it was seemed to follow her every move. Suddenly, Reese hit the gas, gaining a few feet in between her and the other car and was finally able to make out the color and make of the vehicle. It was a white Ford Explorer. Even though the cars were the same color, Reese knew Julian drove a Chrysler 300, so it wasn't him.

What if it's the caller who threatened me earlier, Reese suddenly thought. Trying to get away, she made a quick right hoping that would alleviate her assumptions, but when the Explorer did the same thing Reese was convinced she was definitely being followed. She even slowed down so she could see who was driving, but her view was obstructed from the bright lights.

"What the fuck?" Reese said, taking quick glances in her rear view mirror and trying to keep her eyes on the road.

With her heart pumping fast, she tried to lose the car by pulling in front of other cars at just the right time so the Explorer couldn't get behind her. After trying that a couple of times, Reese was ready to give up. Either way she was going to die, if not from the person in the car, then in an accident. She made one last ditch effort to lose the Ford by making a right turn from a left lane. When she did, someone in a Honda Accord started honking their horn. She immediately looked in her side view to see if the Ford was still behind her, but the driver finally turned off.

"Damn, I must really be tripping," she said with a nervous laugh.

Reese was so relieved when she pulled into her garage a few minutes later. Despite the Explorer turning off, she still ran inside the house like someone was chasing her. After turning the alarm back on, Reese dropped her bag by the door and headed straight to her bar to pour herself a shot of tequila. But she didn't stop there. She ended up taking two more shots before sitting down at the kitchen table. As Reese reflected back on the night's events, her heart almost stopped when she turned around and Sydney was standing right behind her.

"Shit! You scared me!"

"My bad," Sydney said casually

"Why are you here? I thought you were staying over Nia's?"

Sydney sat down next to her mother wearing her favorite Victoria Secret Pink pajamas. "I changed my mind." Reese stood up and walked back over to the bottle of Patron. After watching her mother drink another shot, Sydney asked, "Guess who asked about you today?"

"Who?" Reese asked unenthused.

"Mr. Nichols."

"Child please! Ain't nobody checking for Nia's father. Every since her mother died last year, I see him he's peeking out the damn window at me." Reese replied with an attitude. "That spells pervert."

"Ma, he's a very nice man. He always asks about you. Why do you always act like you're in mourning?"

Reese was really about to let her daughter have it after that comment. "I'm not mourning as you so call put it. I'm just not gonna put up with no more no-good-ass niggas."

"I see your point, but not all men are dogs."

"Well, ninety-nine point nine percent of them are," she countered, sitting back down. "Then you got these sideline hoes ready to pounce on any dude who looks like he's holding. Just like that tramp Eric left me for."

Sydney sighed, "Ma, she's not a bad person."

"Don't plead that chick's case to me, okay. She knew he was married when she met him, but the bitch just said oh well."

Sydney tried her luck when she said, "Umm…Ma her name is Melanie."

"I don't give a fuck what her name is? She's gonna leave his ass as soon as the next nigga comes along with more money than he got. Did she forget that he doesn't play in the league anymore? He's a damn sports commentator now!"

"I don't think so. She really loves him. You should see how she worships the ground he walks on."

"She's the type of girl who'll charge it to the highest bidder. That's Eric right now."

"It's not always about money you know."

Reese was starting to get very irritated. When she jumped up suddenly, Sydney thought she was about to hit her. Instead Reese poured herself one more shot.

"Judgment day is coming real soon, baby. Now, take your ass to bed," Reese said, to her daughter before throwing back the alcohol like a pro.

Chapter 5

The next day, Reese and Joi met at the Galleria Mall to do a little Saturday afternoon shopping. Of course Reese's shopping these days were nothing compared to when she was married to Eric. Instead of never looking at a price tag she now shopped on the sale and clearance racks. Having a budget was the worst, but Reese was determined to stay fashionable.

"Hey, Joi," Reese said looking down. "Now how the hell are you supposed to walk around the mall with four inch stilettos on?"

"Oh, it's easy. Besides these are the only shoes that match this Alexander McQueen tank top."

"I'll give your crazy ass about an hour before you start complaining about your feet," Reese said, shaking her head.

"Whatever. Let's go."

As soon as she walked past Reese in her tight True Religion jeans, Reese shook her head again. Wherever they went…Joi always had to be dolled up. A chocolate bombshell who stood at 5'7, Joi loved fake eyelashes, and always wore nude Mac lip gloss. To add to her goddess appearance, she always kept a fresh weave and her acrylic nails were done every week. Luckily Joi's boyfriend, Lavar was one of Dallas' biggest drug dealers, otherwise Reese knew her friend couldn't afford all her fetishes along with the luxury, high-rise condo.

"Girl, I was so tired I forgot to call you when I got in the house last night," Reese said, as they walked past the Gap store.

"Please don't tell me something else happened. I mean we already had a crazy night at work."

"Well, that was nothing compared to when I left."

"Don't tell me Eric came over starting shit again."

"I ain't in jail am I?" Reese stated with a serious stare.

Joi's giggled at Reese's comment before being told how Reese thought she was being followed after leaving the station. Joi was completely shocked. "What?"

"Yeah…but it turns out I was tripping girl. I think that crazy caller just had my nerves all fucked up."

"You sure it wasn't Julian making sure his boo got home safe," Joi sang.

"I'm not his damn boo! I still can't believe how that fool was acting last night. The only reason I even talk to Julian is because I need him to help me get this job."

Julian was the golfing buddy and right hand man of a top executive over at Radio One. All she had to do was keep Julian happy and she was sure to get the job.

"You never know, you might end up liking him. You could use a man in your life."

"What, so I can end up like you?" Reese asked. "If that's the case, I'll pass." When Joi looked at her friend and frowned, Reese instantly felt bad. "I'm sorry that was inconsiderate of me."

Joi's whole demeanor changed. "Hey, it is what it is."

It was well known to everyone at the station and around Dallas that Lavar had been caught cheating on her with several women and had recently fathered two kids. If the child support papers hadn't come to Joi's house, she would've never known about the newest baby. Joi even got into a fight with one of his baby mama's for coming to her house unannounced, and ended up getting arrested. Even though the charges were later dropped, Joi almost lost her job over the negative publicity it brought to the station.

Every time Reese tried to talk to her about it, Joi would change the subject. Joi knew what she was getting into when she met him, but his money was just too attractive to avoid. Now that the whole city knew he was a loser, she chose to ignore it rather than face the issues head on.

"Well, I don't have the time or the energy to deal with a man right now," Reese reiterated.

"You might want to rethink that. The nights are about to start getting cooler when September hits," Joi finally commented.

"That's what comforters are for."

Joi laughed. "You're right, but it's nothing like waking up next to a soldier saluting you," she said, looking at a pair of sandals inside the Nine West window display.

Reese displayed a wide grin. "Now, you got a point."

They made a quick pit spot inside of Saks Fifth Avenue to see what they had. Weekly shopping sprees were nothing new to them. They'd been doing this ritual since meeting back in college. By the time they graduated, both women had gotten internships at the same radio station in Florida. They worked there together for years until Reese was offered the job with Direct Satellite station. When she saw how pressed they were to have her, Reese told them the only way she would take the job was if they hired Joi as her co-host. Luckily, they agreed.

After leaving Saks and making their way through the mall, several men almost broke their necks trying to look at Reese. However, she wasn't the least bit flattered. She was used to the attention. After all, with breasts as huge as hers, men couldn't help but stare. One guy was so mesmerized he bumped right into his wife who walked a few steps ahead of him. When she saw his attention was elsewhere she smacked him in the back of the head.

"If your ass don't wanna get put out, you better control those eyes!" the woman yelled.

Reese couldn't help but laugh. "See, that's why I'm staying single."

When the two of them got to Neiman Marcus a few moments later, they almost passed out after seeing the new fall handbags.

"Girl, I need to call Lavar and tell him to come in here and get me this bag," Joi said, running her hand across the new Dolce & Gabbana leopard print tote.

"Ahhh... I remember the days when I could come in here and get whatever I wanted. Now look at me. Most times, I have to window shop. Ain't that a bitch," Reese sulked.

"Girl, don't even worry about it. I'ma hook you up with one of Lavar's friends. They all got paper...and I mean big paper."

"No thanks. More money more problems," Reese said sternly.

"You ain't got to get married. Just have a little fun and get what you can out of them."

"Listen to me. I don't want a man and I damn sure don't need one. As soon as they pay a few bills they start talking shit and throwing it up in your face. I don't know if you've noticed, but I don't need anyone to pull me up by my boot strings. I'm already the shit!"

"I heard that," Joi said, giving Reese a high five.

"Besides, why hook me up with one of Lavar's friends when you're messing around on your man anyway?"

Joi let out a slight grin. "I know right. That would be dumb."

"Why are you still with him if you're not happy?"

"Because of his money," Joi blurted out. "After all the shit that nigga has put me through, I'ma milk his ass for everything I can get. Fuck him."

"Just be careful," Reese said, staring at her friend. "If you're not happy, it's no sense of playing the same games he does. That's how people get hurt."

"Don't worry. I plan on getting rid of Lavar before he finds out he's sharing this pussy."

Reese and Joi browsed a little in the shoe department before deciding to go to the women's clothing section. While walking past the men's sportswear department, Reese bumped right into the finest man she'd ever laid eyes on.

"Oh my God! I'm so sorry," she said mesmerized.

"Are you okay?" the gentleman said, licking his lips. Although she was looking right at him she didn't hear a word he said. "Are you okay?" he asked again.

When Joi nudged Reese with her elbow, they looked at

Bitter by DANETTE MAJETTE

each other and started giggling like two teenagers in high school.

Reese looked at the man and tried to act cool. "Umm...yes I'm fine."

As the man introduced himself, Reese was drawn to his physically fit body and gorgeous big brown eyes. Everything about him reminded her of Idris Elba. He literally took her breath away for a moment.

"Hi, my name is Xavier." His smooth skin, six foot plus height, and rock hard physique made her knees weak.

"Hi, I'm Joi and this woman here who seems to have lost her voice is my best friend Reese."

"Hello Joi." Xavier shook her hand, then directed his attention to Reese. He took her hand, "You're breathtaking," he said, with an intense look in his eyes.

His grip was firm. Too firm for Reese. At that moment she felt her pussy squirm in her Juicy Couture sailor shorts. She felt embarrassed that she was actually so turned on.

"Thank you for the compliment and I'm sorry again. I wasn't watching where I was going." She studied his mannerisms and attire closely.

"Well, I can't accept your apology."

"Excuse me," Reese said, ready to go off.

Xavier crossed his arm over his chest, "Let me put it this way. The only way I will accept your apology is if you go out with me."

He reached in his pocket and pulled out his business card and handed it to her. Joi looked at her friend who stood there with a blank look on her face, then took the card from Xavier.

"Ummm... so Mr. Miller you're an investor. Isn't that a risky business to be in with the economy the way it is?" Joi asked.

Reese was so embarrassed she put her hands over her face.

"It's okay," Xavier said, pulling Reese's hands down. "It's actually a good question." He looked at Joi. "It is a risky business but because most of my clients are wealthy businessmen I've been able to do very well. If they lose tens of thousands of dollars it doesn't affect them as much as say someone like you or I."

"That sounds very interesting. Maybe you two can talk

𝓑itter by DANETTE MAJETTE

about it a little more. Say over dinner," Joi said.

"Joi!" Reese yelled.

Joi ignored her. "I'll make sure she calls you."

Reese pasted a smile on her face, then turned to Joi. "I can speak for myself." She turned back to Xavier. "Thank you, but no thanks," she said before walking away.

"Don't worry. She'll call you," Joi whispered, giving him the thumbs up. "Hey Reese, hold up!"

As they walked away, Xavier took a quick look at Reese's curves. *Damn,* he thought. *Nice body!*

When Joi caught up with Reese, she immediately starting teasing her. "Damn, ole' boy had you speechless, huh?"

"No, he didn't. He just startled me when I bumped into him. That's all!"

"Stop lying. That man had them panties nice and wet."

Reese gave her a disapproving frown. "You're so nasty."

Joi laughed. "No, you're the nasty one. By the way here's his card." When Reese wouldn't take it, Joi stuck the card in her purse. "I can't wait to tell your boo Julian that you got yourself a new man. He ain't gonna like that shit at all."

"Bitch, why do you keep joking like that? Julian is not my boo!" Reese stopped walking to look at a bag in the window of the Micheal Kors store that matched her shoes. "Seriously, I'm not feeling him like that." She continued walking. "We'll never be more than friends. I just can't see myself going there with him."

"Well, apparently he can because he's definitely in love with you."

It really didn't matter to Reese how Julian felt. All she was focused on was getting her show syndicated and joining the Radio One family. If she had to use Julian to do that, then that's what she was going to do.

"Did you notice that guy wasn't wearing a wedding band?" Joi asked.

"That don't mean shit! He could've taken it off."

"I don't think so. I would've seen a tan line."

"Why is it so important to you that I find a man?" Reese questioned.

Joi grabbed Reese by the arm and led her to a bench in the middle of the mall.

"Look, ever since you and Eric got divorced it's like you've built up this wall. I know you and you're still not over him yet. He's probably the first thing you think about when you wake up and the last thing you think about when you go to bed." Suddenly, a few tears fell from Reese's eyes. "It's time for you to open up your heart again."

Wiping her face, Reese looked her friend in the eye and told her that she was right.

"Give Mr. Hottie a call tonight."

"Okay," Reese said, hugging Joi.

They made a few more purchases from Juicy Couture, Betsey Johnson, Aldo and BCBG. The more they shopped, the more Reese thought about her mystery man. Sure she knew his name, but that was about all she knew about him. He was too fine not to have some bullshit up his sleeve. *All men do*, Reese thought.

The ringing of her phone interrupted her thinking. However, by the time she pulled the phone out, she missed the call. "Damn, my battery is going dead again."

"Your battery is always dead. I don't think I've ever met someone who talks on the phone as much as you do."

"I know. I need to buy an extra battery."

"Yeah, that's a good idea. Now, back to what I was saying about Julian…"

Joi started in again about how cute she and Julian would be together, but Reese ignored her antics. She'd become immune to Joi's teasing. She hated it most times, but Joi's personality was infectious. You couldn't stay mad at her for long. She was just that much fun to be around.

"Where to next?" Reese asked.

"I don't know about you, but I gotta go home and play step-mommy to these damn kids that ain't mine."

Shaking her head, Reese dug around in her purse to find her keys. "Alright. I was hoping we could go to P.F. Chang's and eat."

"I'm sorry, sweetie."

"It's cool. We can do that next time," Reese replied with

disappointment in her voice.

As they both walked back toward their cars Reese noticed a soda machine. "Let me just get something cold to drink."

Joi knew exactly what Reese was up to. "Damn, you can't even wait until you get home," she said, disappointed in her friend.

"I just need something to take the edge off," Reese replied, putting a dollar into the machine.

Seconds later, she grabbed her cold can of Coke from the bottom and quickly blew dust off the top. Joi rolled her eyes. She'd watched Reese slowly become a functional alcoholic to ease the pain of losing Eric. When she went from having one drink to two or three in order to make it through the day, Joi became concerned, especially during one of Reese's severe mood swings. Joi desperately wanted to say something to Reese about her drinking, but didn't want her to take it the wrong way. In retrospect, her remaining silent was enabling her.

Once the girls reached the parking lot, they hugged one another and said goodbye.

"Okay, call me tonight. No, scratch that…call that big, black handsome man you met today. You don't have to marry him just get you some dick. You know you want some."

"You're sick! You know that," Reese said, laughing.

Joi could always make her girl laugh, which was one of the reasons they'd remained friends all these years. She always had a way of making things better when Reese was feeling down. They were more like sisters than friends. Even nights when Reese used to cry herself to sleep, Joi never left her side. A true friend is what Reese defined her as.

After Joi walked away, Reese dug around in her purse to retrieve her keys. Once she found them she unlocked the doors and placed her purse and bags inside. She then opened her can of Coke and poured most of it out. Sitting in her car, Reese dug under her seat for the bottle of Vodka she kept in her car.

Opening the bottle, she poured what was left into the Coke can. That way she could drink on the way home without any problems. Besides, drinking soda wasn't illegal the last time she checked.

Bitter by DANETTE MAJETTE

Debating whether or not she should call Xavier, Reese sat in her car for a few more minutes. *He was fine. Maybe Sydney and Joi are right. Maybe it's time for me to get my feet wet again.* She pulled Xavier's card, plugged her phone into the car charger and started to dial. There was something about the attractive man that made her want to get to know him. However, when Reese got to the last number, she decided against it.

He might be a cheater too and that's the last thing I need in my life. She put the card back in her purse before she started her car. While her car cooled off she stuck her earpiece in her ear then pulled out of the parking lot.

On the way home, Reese sipped on her drink and listened to an oldie but goodie station. She loved old school Rap, R&B, Soul, and Jazz music. It always took her back to the days when people were carefree. Music meant something back then. The artists made music that filled your soul unlike the music today.

About three blocks from her home, Reese was starting to get a buzz and wanted to get home quickly but speeding wasn't an option. She couldn't risk getting pulled over since she was drinking. As she came up on a stop sign, she made a complete stop looked both ways then proceeded to go slowly. However, Reese had to press on her brakes quickly when a little girl on her bike suddenly darted out in front of her. Reese's heart dropped when she felt a little bump.

"Where the hell did she come from?" she yelled. She sat there for a minute in shock as her heart pounded

Oh God, did I hit her? She sat there for just a moment. Holding her chest, Reese took a deep breath trying to calm down. Moments later, she finally jumped out of her car to see if the little girl was okay.

"Sweetie! I'm so sorry," Reese said to the girl who appeared to be about eight years old and of some type of Spanish decent.

After quickly examining her body, Reese realized that the girl was okay. Only a few scrapes to her elbows and knees. She picked up the girl's bike and sat it on the curb. The front wheel of the bike was a little dent but there was no major damage.

*B*itter by **DANETTE MAJETTE**

"I'm okay," the little girl said.

By this time there was a small crowd forming. This made Reese nervous because she knew that it was only a matter of time before the police would be on the scene. Reese knew she needed to get out of there before someone realized she'd been drinking and driving. This would kill any chances of her show getting picked up and she wasn't having that.

"Where is your mother?" Reese asked. She looked around to see if anyone was with the girl.

"She's at home."

Reese was vexed. She couldn't believe the young girl was wondering the streets alone. But she was also glad that the girl's mother wasn't about to appear from the crowd and go off. Any drama would've prolonged her departure. "Hey ain't that the lady from the radio?" one of the spectators said to a friend.

"Yeah, I think so," the lady said, shooting a video of the incident.

After telling the girl to go home, Reese quickly headed to her car.

"You just gonna leave her like that?" one lady yelled.

"Damn! She said she was alright. What else do you want me to do?" Reese said with an attitude.

Not caring what the spectators thought of her, she jumped in her car and drove off. You would've thought the entire incident had taught her a lesson, but instead it caused Reese to drink even more. Gripping the steering wheel with one hand, she picked up the can with the other and took a huge gulp.

Reese was almost home when her cell rang again. She saw it was from an unknown number so she decided not to answer. But something told her to answer.

"Hello!"

"Ma!" Sydney yelled into the phone.

"What's wrong?" Reese asked hysterically.

When Sydney told her that she was at the police station and why she was there, Reese thought she was hearing things. She threw the phone down and hit the pedal heading to the Highland Park Police Station.

Chapter 6

A week passed and life hadn't gotten any better for Reese. Between work and faxing documents to Clark Atlanta University for Sydney, she'd had several hectic days. To make matters worse, she was dealing with the effects of Sydney getting arrested. After being released on her own recognizance, Sydney was released to deal with her mother's wrath. Reese was livid with Sydney. She along with several other kids from her high school had been arrested at a friend's pool party after drinking massive amounts of alcohol, and acting disorderly in the neighborhood. Her arrest not only put her mother's reputation on the line, but she was now at risk of losing her scholarship to Clark Atlanta if she were convicted.

Reese walked into the Convention Center thinking about how crazy her life seemed to be getting. The thought of having to spend the whole day standing next to Julian at a back to school event wasn't her idea of fun for the day. *Back to the Basics*, was an event the station did every year for underprivileged kids. The station along with other sponsors would hand out school supplies while the kids got to meet celebrities, athletes, and several radio personalities. They also got to eat and drink for free all day. It was for a good cause but Reese could think of better things to do on a Saturday like going shopping or going out to eat at one of her fa-

ℬitter by DANETTE MAJETTE

vorite restaurants.

The Dallas Convention Center was buzzing with children and their parents from all over the city. When Reese walked up to the station's booth, she was speechless. Julian had really out done himself. There was a huge backdrop with a picture of Reese and Joi along with a title that read, '*The Bad Girls of Talk Radio.*' Everyone who walked by couldn't help but stop and look at it. It was big, colorful, and the girls' pictures were flawless.

"It's about time you got here," Joi said, hugging Reese.

"I know. I'm sorry. I couldn't find a parking spot. I had to park in this garage down the street." When Reese looked over at Julian, she noticed a man in a security uniform standing beside him. "Why is there a security officer here?"

Julian looked around the booth. "Hey, there are a lot of people who like you and there's a lot who don't like you. And after the other night I just wanted to make sure you're safe."

Joi chuckled. "Anything for you," she whispered in Reese's ear.

Reese frowned and pushed her away. "So, what do you need me to do?"

Julian walked over to a table and pulled out a chair. "Just sit here and look pretty. You too, Joi."

"I don't want that half ass invitation," Joi said, rolling her eyes as she took a seat next to Reese.

Reese looked at her friend who could've easily been mistaken for the actress and former Miss USA, Kenya Moore. "Don't hate because I'm cuter," she joked.

Reese and Joi were laughing and talking while they signed autographs for an hour straight and took pictures. Tired, the girls were about to take a breather when a woman came up and asked for Reese's autograph.

"I just love your show. I'm your biggest fan."

"Here we go with the bullshit again. I can't tell you how many times we've heard that shit today," Reese said, sucking her teeth.

Joi had to turn her head. She couldn't believe Reese went on the lady like that. After Reese signed the woman's picture, Joi said, "Be nice. It's for the kiddies."

"Girl, fuck these people. Half of them hate us anyway."

"True, but some of them love us and we need to keep them happy if we want to get ahead in this business."

"Girl, whatever! Save that Oprah shit," she said, pushing Joi away from her.

For the next two hours, the girls signed autographs and took pictures with their fans while the security officer stood close by. Reese couldn't wait for the event to be over but she made the best of it. She was in the middle of taking a picture with a woman who said listening to her gave her the strength to leave an abusive relationship when she looked up and saw a familiar face. Once the picture was taken and the woman left, the man walked up and said hello.

"What are you doing here?" Reese asked, obviously confused. When Xavier walked up to her, the guard extended his arm. "It's okay, I know him," Reese stated.

"Wow, I had no idea you rolled with security. Why wasn't he at the mall that day?" Xavier asked.

"He comes with the job."

Xavier nodded his head. "Oh, okay. Well, I heard about the event on the radio so I decided to come down and check it out. I had no idea that you worked for the station until I spotted you a few minutes ago," he said, keeping his eyes on the burly guard.

Seeing him put a huge smile on Reese's face.

"My, my, my...what do we have here?" Joi said, walking up.

Julian was right on Joi's heels. When she turned around and saw the look on Julian's face she couldn't help but laugh. Julian was red with jealousy written all over his face.

"Reese, why don't you take a break? There's a Starbucks downstairs," Joi informed.

"What if someone wants to get her autograph or take a picture with her?" Julian asked.

"Well...they'll just have to come back now won't they," Joi replied, with her hands on her hips. "Go, Reese. Julian and I will be fine." Joi gave him a deadly stare. "Won't we, Julian?"

Julian didn't answer. He was too focused on his competition.

Reese told Joi thanks, then reached under the table and grabbed her purse.

"Okay, I'll be back in a few." The security officer followed.

"You can tell him to stay here. I'll protect you," Xavier said.

When Reese told the officer she was in good hands, he looked over at Julian who had hired him. Julian waved him off.

"Yeah, let her go."

"Hey, you kids have fun now! Oh yeah, and it's nice to see you again, Xavier. Take care of my friend!" Joi yelled out.

"I will." Xavier smiled, showing his perfectly aligned white teeth.

As soon as Xavier and Reese were out of sight, Julian instantly started grilling Joi.

"So, who was he? Is she seeing him?"

"Maybe," Joi said in a playful tone.

"Where did she meet him?" Julian asked in a matter or fact way.

"Hey, when I said maybe, it wasn't an invitation for you to keep hounding me."

"I'm just trying to look out for her. You of all people should know how devastated she was after the divorce," Julian said, trying to play on Joi's intelligence.

"You're right. I do know. I also know it's time for her to move on from that phase of her life. She says she doesn't want a man in her life, but I know her. She's lonely. She's a good person and she deserves to have someone special in her life."

"I understand that, but what do you know about this guy," Julian said, pleading his case.

"Not much, but I do know he's fine as hell." Joi snickered. She turned her chair around and looked Julian straight in the eyes. "This has nothing to do with you wanting to protect Reese from that guy. It's about you being jealous that she has eyes for someone and it ain't you, boo!"

𝓑itter by DANETTE MAJETTE

Julian laughed. "That's ridiculous!"

"Oh so you're trying to deny the fact that you fiend like a crack head for her," Joi said, moving her head around like a true sister.

Julian didn't respond. But the redness across his face said it all. He got so pissed, he just got up and walked off.

Bitter by DANETTE MAJETTE

Chapter 7

Her drink choice would've been something a little stronger, but Reese settled for a Frappuccino instead. Xavier decided on black coffee. Taking a seat at a table in the corner, it didn't take them long before they started to get to know one another. It was so awkward having to go through the basic dating questions like, what's your favorite color, what do you like to do in your spare time, and what are you looking for in a mate. Reese wasn't interested in any of the answers anyway. Instead, she got straight to the point.

"So, are you married or have you ever been married? Any kids?"

"Whoa, one question at a time beautiful," Xavier replied with a grin. "No, I've never been married and no kids."

No wife and no kids...now that's rare, Reese thought. "Are you gay?"

Xavier continued to smile. "Absolutely not."

So, no wife, kids and he's not gay. There's gotta be something wrong with this dude then. "Where are you from?" Reese asked.

She knew he couldn't be from Dallas because she knew damn near everyone who lived there, especially fine black men.

Xavier told her he was from a town outside of Dallas called Grand Prairie. He then went into a detailed description about his

*B*itter by DANETTE MAJETTE

job. After that, he quizzed Reese. She however was a little more evasive with her answers. She didn't want to give him too much too soon.

The questioning continued for thirty minutes before Reese cut the conversation short so she could get back to work. When Xavier stood up and helped Reese out of her chair, she wondered if this perfect man could be real. He had the looks, the body, and the intellect. But was he too good to be true. The only way she was going to find that out was to see him again. After walking her back to the booth, Xavier gave her a kiss on the cheek.

"I'll talk to you soon my love."

Suddenly, several butterflies in Reese's stomach started to float around.

"Okay, I'll call you," she said, watching his firm physique walk away.

When Reese walked over to Joi and Julian she had the biggest smile on her face. Could Xavier be just what she needed?

"I thought you didn't like men anymore," Julian said with an obvious attitude.

Looking at him with contempt, Reese wanted to smack Julian in the face for trying to be a smart ass, but couldn't. Then again she wasn't too worried about getting fired because the station wouldn't last a day without her show. Still needing him to climb up that corporate ladder, she settled for telling him off instead.

"Mind your damn business and stay out of mine please!" she snapped at him then walked away.

Joi turned to Julian and said, "Ha! I guess she told you."

You could see smoke coming from Julian's ears. This was the first time Reese had ever talked to him like that and he didn't like it. He was just trying to be a good friend, he wanted to say. Instead he watched her backside.

Hours passed and as the event started to wind down, Julian continued to stand in the corner acting like a woman on her period. But knowing the girls were tired, he eventually got himself together and told Reese and Joi they could leave. His gesture almost made Reese sorry for going off on him, but her private life wasn't his concern.

Once they gathered their belongings, Reese and Joi didn't waste any time heading out of the Convention Center. When they first arrived it was bright and sunny outside, but now it was dark and gloomy.

"What time is it?" Reese asked.

Joi looked at her Gucci watch.

"It's a little after nine."

"Damn, I didn't think we'd be here this long."

"I know. My whole day is gone now," Joi replied. "I'm parked right out front. I'll drive you to your car. I remember you said it was parked down the street."

"You don't have to do that. All I have to do is go out the B exit and the garage is right there."

"Are you sure?" Joi inquired.

"Yes, plus I could use the exercise."

After convincing her friend that she would be okay, Reese gave Joi a hug before walking in another direction of the Convention Center. Once Reese was out of the building, she walked east toward the parking garage. After walking a block or so, she strolled through the gate where the attendant was stationed and took the elevator up to P2. Reese was so tired she could barely stand.

I can't wait to get out of my clothes and get in the bed. But first I need a night cap, she thought to herself then tapped the elevator button.

When the doors opened, Reese stepped on. However when she got off on P2, she seemed a bit confused. Reese knew for sure her car was on that level because she remembered the blue colored columns. She looked around. There was no one in sight and it was dark as hell. *Maybe it was P3*, she thought.

Pushing the button to get back on the elevator, Reese waited for almost a minute before realizing that it was taking too long to come. Moments later, she decided to take to the stairs. As soon as she opened the door, she heard a door from the lower level open as well, but shook it off as merely a coincidence. Starting up the stairs, Reese was just about to think about Xavier when she realized the footsteps were beginning to get closer. The more she sped up, the footsteps seemed to do the same.

An eerie feeling came over her as she held her purse closer to her side. When the words P3 painted in red appeared before her, she couldn't be happier. However, as soon as Reese grabbed the knob and flung the door open, she could hear someone breathing hard like they'd been running.

Damn, I should've let Joi drop me off, she started thinking.

At that point, Reese ran to her car like her life depended on it. She never realized she was running in the wrong direction until she noticed several private parking signs that weren't there earlier.

"Shit!" she yelled.

Her heart raced, but she kept moving. She quickly headed back in the opposite direction. That's when she caught a glimpse of a black shadow running up the stairs. From behind, she could hear the door open.

"Hey! Hey!" the man yelled out. "Come here!"

Reese started to panic. She was so terrified she couldn't get the words, "help me," out of her mouth. From a short distance, she could see her car. She kept running, taking quick peeks behind her.

"Lady, wait a minute!"

Reese kept going. She couldn't even comprehend what the guy was saying, nor did she care to know. All she knew is that he was after her, so it would've been a dumb-ass move to stop.

With her car in sight, Reese started to see safety even though he was on her heels. All she needed to do was get inside her car, but he was too close. That's when she realized something very important. Determined to go out with a fight, Reese stopped, turned around and kneed the guy right in the groin.

"Ahhhh!" he screeched in pain. Reese started to give him a hard kick to make sure he was down for good when he held something up to her. "I was just trying to give you your keys. You left them at the booth," he said, barely audible.

"What the fuck?" she said, snatching her keys from the guys hand. "Why didn't you just say that dumbass?"

"I tried to. Didn't you hear me calling out to you?"

"I did but I didn't understand what you were saying," Reese replied. She helped the guy to his feet. "You need to learn to

𝓑itter by DANETTE MAJETTE

speak English a little better."

The guy pulled away from her. "Yeah...yeah!" he said just wanting to get away from her. He wobbled back to the elevator and waited for it to come up so he could go back to his station.

As soon as Reese sat down in her car, she opened her glove compartment and pulled out a plastic bottle that was a mixture of Hennessey and Coke then took a couple of sips. The taste was nowhere near as pleasant as her Vodka, but since she was fresh out of her beverage of choice, this would have to do.

After thinking about it, she couldn't help but laugh at herself. The entire time, it never dawned on Reese that the man chasing her was the parking attendant.

"I wonder if he's gonna charge me extra for dropping him," she joked.

She turned the key in the ignition and pulled out toward the exit sign. When Reese got close to the booth, uncontrollable laughter came over her as she handed the guy her ticket. He was without a doubt cursing her out in his native language to his partner the minute she pulled up.

"Twelve dollars!" he yelled with an attitude.

"Muthafucka! Who you yelling at?" They eyed each other for a second before she handed him a twenty. "Don't get your ass kicked out here."

He stuck his hand out of the booth and took the money from Reese. After giving her the change he slammed the window shut.

"Fuck you too! You need to take your ass back where you came from cause we don't play that shit here!" she yelled, then pulled out slowly.

As Reese drove toward Interstate 45, she envisioned herself laying across the bed once her exhaustion kicked into overdrive. The usually twenty minute drive to her house was going to turn into forty due to all the traffic and closed streets for the event. Any other time Reese would've been pissed, but as long as she had Mr. Hennessey as her company, she would be fine.

*B*itter by DANETTE MAJETTE

Chapter 8

Sitting in the living room of her parent's house, Joi waited for Lavar to call so they could switch cars. He'd taken hers early that morning for whatever reason, and had yet to bring it back. Even though, she loved driving his Bentley, Joi didn't care for the unwanted attention the car often got. With dark tinted windows and twenty-three hundred Asanti rims, it was hard not to get noticed.

Seeing her mother in the kitchen cooking and her dad watching television in his favorite chair brought back memories of when she lived at home. It was like old times, but things just weren't the same anymore. Life seemed so much easier back then when she was happy and full of life. Of course, all that changed the day she met Lavar. When they first met he was her knight and shining armor. Along with a fresh batch of long stem roses delivered every day, he also took her on expensive shopping sprees and they would often vacation at lavish resorts.

Although his notorious reputation preceded him, Joi still decided to explore a relationship. She wanted to judge him for herself and not because of all the hearsay. But it didn't take long for her to see that everything said about her new man was true. He ended up being a compulsive liar, a cheater, and most of all…a very volatile man. Joi knew it was best to end the relationship as soon as possible, especially before Lavar found out that she was seeing other men. But every time she thought about her bills, her

Bitter by DANETTE MAJETTE

mind quickly convinced her otherwise.

Joi's stroll down memory lane was cut short when her cell phone rang. Annoyed, she let out a long sigh, before walking into another room.

"What?" she answered aggravated.

"Why you gotta answer yo' phone like dat?"

"Excuse me. I can answer my phone any way I want."

"Where you at?" Lavar questioned in a possessive tone.

Joi could tell Lavar was up to no good because he always called to pinpoint her location.

"I'm over my parent's house," Joi responded with one eyebrow raised. "Where you at?"

"Oh, I'm on my way to Mesquite. Gotta see one of my boys out there," Lavar said. "I don't have time to bring you yo' car, so just keep mine."

"Really?" Joi said, knowing he was lying.

"Man, why we gotta go thru dis everytime I call."

"Because you're a damn liar! Don't you get it…I know your whole routine by now. When I call you back in about an hour your phone will be turned off. And if you do happen to answer it, you'll tell me you got some business to take care of so you're turning your phone off. When in actuality you're probably gonna be somewhere fucking somebody. The gig is up muthafucka. I know your ass like a book."

"You gon' stop…"

That's as far as Lavar got before he heard the phone disconnect. Any other day he would've tried to call back, but Joi was right. He was definitely up to no good so he just let it be.

When Joi walked back into the living room her father could tell she was upset. "You could always come back home," he said, pulling his handkerchief out of his pocket.

She smiled.

"I know you would love that, wouldn't you."

"Sure would."

Mr. Franklin coughed slightly into his handkerchief.

"Daddy, you still have that cold?"

"Yeah."

Joi shook her head at him.

"Why don't you go to the doctor?"

"I ain't going to see nobody's doctor. They make it worse. You go in there for one thing and they give you medication that causes another problem. No thanks!"

Mrs. Franklin stuck her head out of the kitchen and said, "I've been trying to get him to go for three days, but he's so damn stubborn. Maybe you can talk some sense into him."

"Don't even waste your breath," he said, cutting his eyes at his wife.

For as long as Joi could remember, her father hated doctors. He wouldn't even take a simple physical until her mother threatened to throw away his chair. Sometimes that wouldn't even work.

When her mother joined them in the living room, she walked straight to the couch and sat down.

"So, how is Lavar?"

"He's alright," Joi answered not giving her mother eye contact.

When her father mumbled something under his breath, Joi knew it was time to leave. Even though her father didn't approve of her relationship, he allowed her to make her own mistakes.

"Well, I better get going," Joi said, grabbing her purse and phone.

"You're not gonna stay for dinner?" her mother asked.

"No. I already ate. But I'll come by next Sunday for dinner." Joi got up and hugged her father who was stuck to his chair like glue. "If you need anything Daddy, you better call me."

"I sure will," her father replied, knowing he wouldn't. As a prideful man, he was never big on handouts.

"Okay baby. You be safe," her mother said, walking her to the door.

She hugged her mother tightly.

"I will," Joi responded then walked out.

Cranking Nicki Minaj, Joi had just hopped on the Dallas Tollway when she spotted Lavar cruising by on the opposite side of the street. Joi immediately noticed that he wasn't alone. In fact, there was a woman driving as Lavar sat in the passenger seat talking on the phone.

"Hold up. I know that lying bastard don't have a bitch driving my car!" Joi yelled, as she made an illegal u-turn almost causing an accident.

After catching up to them, she followed closely, but still left some room so Lavar wouldn't notice that he was being followed. After about fifteen minutes of tailing them, her Mercedes pulled up to a Fairfield Inn on Market Center Boulevard. Watching her live-in boyfriend jump out of her car and walk inside the lobby, Joi's insides began to boil, especially when she noticed the stripper-looking girl touching up her lip gloss in the rearview mirror. Fuming, Joi sat in Lavar's car and waited for him to come back out. There was no need to confront the girl alone. She needed both of them to be present for the show she was about to put on.

As soon as Lavar walked back through the sliding doors, Joi drove up so fast all four tires instantly screeched.

"Muthafucka, you must be out of your mind letting this bitch drive my car. I thought your ass had to drive to Mesquite today!" she jumped out of the car like a cop during a sting operation.

Lavar was so surprised he started stuttering. "I...I said I was on my way there."

Joi walked over to her car and opened the driver's side door. "Who the fuck is this?" She pointed to the female.

"Look, Joi it ain't what you think. I need her to do somethin' fo' me," Lavar tried to explain.

"You need her to do what? Suck your nasty-ass dick? Did you forget that you're at a fucking hotel?" At that point, Lavar ran around the car and tried to pull Joi away, but she snatched her arm back. "Get the hell off of me!"

"Lavar, who is dis bitch?" the girl finally spoke.

"What did she just call me?" Joi asked no one in particular before taking off her heels.

Seconds later, she reached inside the car and grabbed a hold of the girl's twenty-inch blonde weave. She even managed to get a few quick jabs in before Lavar pulled her away. When an elderly security officer came outside a few seconds later and heard Joi

*B*itter by DANETTE MAJETTE

yelling, he high-tailed it back inside and called the police.

Needing to leave before the police arrived; Lavar picked Joi up around the waist and took her a few feet away from the car. While he was trying to calm Joi down, the girl picked up her hair off the ground.

"Let dat bitch go!" the girl yelled.

Her face was turning red with each passing second.

"Yeah, let me go!" Joi reiterated.

"Look, just calm down so I can explain," Lavar pleaded.

"Fuck you and your explanation. I can't believe you, Lavar. You let that bitch drive my car. Look at her! You can't tell me she's not a stripper or a prostitute!" Joi eyed the girl who reminded her of Ronnie from *The Player's Club*. Full lips and all. "Your ass better not ever touch me again!" Joi yelled, as she put her heels back on. "It's okay though. Because, I'm about to show your ass how it's done."

Lavar's walnut colored face suddenly frowned. "Whatchu mean by dat?"

Joi walked over to Lavar's Bentley to retrieve her purse.

"Tell your *girl* to get the fuck out my car first, then I'll let you know."

"Yo' get out!" Lavar yelled. When the girl sucked her teeth, Lavar got even more hyped. "Did you hear what I just said? Get the fuck out her shit!"

As soon as the blonde-headed girl followed his orders, Joi didn't waste much time jumping into the driver's seat.

"So, what does dat mean?" Lavar asked again.

"That means I'm going to find me somebody to fuck," Joi boldly stated.

"Oh yeah! You try dat shit if you want to. I'll kill you and dat nigga!"

Lavar's deep baritone voice yelled as Joi threw the girl's ghetto Baby Phat purse out of the car window. He didn't get a chance to say anything else, before Joi sped off.

His plans had been ruined, but Joi's however were just getting started.

Bitter by DANETTE MAJETTE

Chapter 9

Her eyes were bloodshot red by the time she got to Reese's house. Ringing the doorbell twice, all Joi could think about was how Lavar had played her for a two dollar whore. Sure, she knew he'd never been faithful, but Joi never thought Lavar would stick his dick into someone who looked like she hadn't taken a bath in days.

"What the hell happened? I didn't understand a word you said over the phone. You were screaming so loud," Reese said as soon as she opened the door.

"I caught that nigga! That's what happened. I ran up on Lavar with some dirty-ass girl at a hotel. And to top it off, he had the bitch driving him around in my ride!"

Reese's eyes enlarged. "What? Are you serious?"

"Yes. They were about to get it in honey, but I axed that shit! I pulled that bitches weave out and everything…even got in a few punches."

"Now, you know you're too old to be fighting," Reese said sounding like an old woman.

"Oh, that wasn't a fight. I just whipped her ass," Joi said, taking a seat on the couch. "I don't even know why I'm acting so surprised. This is his M.O."

Although Joi shared everything with Reese about Lavar, there were still some emotional issues and secrets she managed to

Bitter by DANETTE MAJETTE

keep to herself about him.

"Damn, I would've loved to see his face," Reese said.

"That shit was priceless! I guess I should've listened to you and everyone else who told me to leave his ass alone. I went against everyone's advice and now I'm living with the consequence."

A single tear ran down her face.

"Don't beat yourself up about it," Reese said, wrapping her arms around Joi's shoulder. "Remember what you told me when I found out Eric was having an affair with Melanie? He's not worthy of your tears."

"Oh God, did I sound that whack?"

"Yes, you did, but it was so true."

"You know what…you're right. I don't know why I stayed with Lavar this long. He's cheated on me so many times I've lost track. I'm tired of getting hurt over and over again. Honestly, I'm through with this love shit."

Joi was so grateful to have Reese as a friend. If anyone knew what she was going through it was Reese. At that moment, Joi decided she was going to start living for herself and not a man.

A few minutes later, Reese heard loud music outside of her home. Rising from the couch, she went to the window, and watched as Lavar walked across her yard.

"Shit, it's Lavar," Reese shrieked.

Knowing how Lavar's temper could get, Joi quickly became concerned.

"You gotta get rid of him. He's probably pissed at what I said to him back at the hotel."

"Don't worry, I got it." Reese said. As soon as she opened the door, Reese made sure to close it behind her. "Damn, I told my garbage man about leaving trash behind," she said with one hand on one hip.

Lavar smiled. "You wish you had a man like me, don't you? You probably wish you had a man period…huh?"

"Don't fucking flatter yourself, loser. I don't know why Joi puts up with your trifling ass."

"What chu say?" Lavar asked with fire in his eyes.

"You heard me. You have no education, no manners, and most of all, no morals."

"Where Joi at?" he yelled, annoyed at this point.

"Stop yelling like you in the hood. She's not here!"

Lavar looked at Joi's car then looked back at Reese.

"What…her car drove ova here by itself?"

Reese shrugged her shoulders. "Maybe."

They went back and forth for a few more minutes before Lavar took it to another level. He didn't have time to play games, and wanted it to be known.

"Bitch, I already don't like yo' phony ass, so don't test me. I would hate for yo' brakes or somethin' to go out while you drivin' that…what do you drive again…oh dat's right a Nissan," he said cracking up. "You drivin' dat shit while dat white bitch sportin' a new S550. Damn."

Reese's nose flared. "Lavar, get the fuck away from my house."

He abruptly stopped laughing and got up close to her face.

"I'm not goin' anywhere until you tell me where Joi is."

"You don't scare me."

"Well, I should scare you. I kill bitches like you jus fo' fun."

Suddenly, Joi came to the door and looked up at his massive 6'4 two hundred and sixty pound frame.

"Did you just threaten my friend?"

When Lavar looked at his girlfriend, he felt bad about his disloyalty. Joi was a beautiful woman, who didn't deserve to be disrespected, so he needed to make things right.

"Let's go home and talk," Lavar suggested.

"Answer my question. Did you just threaten her?" Joi asked again.

"Yes." Lavar didn't feel the need to deny anything. He hated Reese and didn't have any qualms about letting her know how he felt.

When Joi told Lavar she wasn't going anywhere with him, he grabbed her by the arm and pulled her outside.

"We need to talk. It wasn't what you think," he roared between gritted teeth. "I needed that broad to bring somethin' back fo' me. I told you bout' it last week." He wrapped her arm around his waist to make sure she felt the gun that was tucked away in his jeans. "You remember?" he whispered in her ear.

"Yeah, I remember. But you still lied about where you were and you let that filthy bitch floss in my shit like she pays the fucking note!"

"How many times have I told you I can't be talkin' stupid over the phone?" Lavar questioned. "You want the Feds to know my every damn move?"

Joi stared at Lavar for a few minutes as he tried his best to display a sign of remorse. Even though she knew he was lying, she decided to go with him anyway.

"Let me get my purse," Joi said then turned around.

Reese wanted to flip out.

"Are you serious? You actually believe him?" she asked as Joi ignored her and walked back into the house.

"Next time, stay in your lane," Lavar advised.

Reese wanted to slap the smug look off of his face as she watched him stroll back toward his own car as if he'd won the battle.

"I'll call you later," Joi said to Reese when she came back outside. "And don't worry... I got this."

She didn't even give her friend a chance to respond before jumping into her car and pulling off.

Joi definitely had something in mind for the habitual liar. She was making sure her paper was stacked before she left. So while he was out running around fucking everything with two legs, she was taking his money and stashing it away for herself.

Reese still couldn't believe Joi was actually going to leave with him, but she also knew her friend. The sneaky look on her face meant she had something in store for him. She would bet top dollar on that.

After Joi left, Reese took a hot shower and positioned herself in front of the television to watch "The Wendy Williams Show." She had missed the last episode but recorded it on her DVR. She never missed a show because Wendy kind of reminded

Bitter by DANETTE MAJETTE

Reese of herself. Everyone loved to hate her because they told the truth when people didn't want to hear it. The show had gone to a commercial break when Reese's phone rang. When she picked it up and saw Eric's name on the screen, she wanted to sling it across the room. The mere mention of his name irritated her these days so she definitely didn't want to talk to him.

"What?" Reese screamed into the phone.

"Do you have to answer your phone like that? And you're supposed to be a professional business woman. That's a joke."

"Fuck you! If you don't like the way I answered my phone then don't call me no more!"

"Trust me, I won't. I just called to tell you that I convinced the District Attorney to drop the possession and consumption of alcohol charges against Sydney."

"What did you do? Pay him off."

"No! He happens to be an old golf buddy of mine."

"Yeah. Whatever!"

"Oh yeah, before I forget. Do you think Melanie and I can go with you to take Sydney to college?"

Reese lost it. "Muthafucka, you must've bumped your damn head!"

Click.

Bitter by DANETTE MAJETTE

Chapter 10

Fortunately for Reese, the next day turned out to be a better one. With one knock at the door and a bottle of Kendall Jackson in hand, her neighbor and Nia's father, was able to put a smile on her face. With a small, clever introduction, Wayne weaseled his way inside and made small talk with Reese for what seemed like hours. His warm spirit and strong cologne had Reese on cloud nine. He wasn't the most handsome guy she'd met, but his sex appeal was powerful. She laughed infectiously as if she were really happy in life.

Wayne told her all about why he'd moved to Dallas and how he'd been watching her for a while, but was afraid to say anything to her. Reese thought it was cute, but wasn't even considering dating her neighbor. Contrary, the wine had her feeling like fucking him was now an option. The fact that she hadn't had any dick lately, combined with the effects from the second bottle of wine that she'd pulled from her stash, meant trouble. By the time the second hour rolled around, they found themselves giggling and laughing like old friends. Tipsy and horny, things began to heat up; especially when Wayne got out of his seat and kissed Reese dead on the lips without warning.

"Whoaaa," Reese reacted.

"I'm not moving too fast am I?" he asked in a seductive tone.

𝓑itter by DANETTE MAJETTE

She paused momentarily. "No, you're okay," she said, ready to attack back.

They looked into each other's eyes and stayed quiet for a while, all along while Reese questioned herself. Should I? Shouldn't I?

Wayne started rubbing her in all of the right ways. By this time, she was eager for him to get inside her so she raised her arms, removed her t-shirt and tossed it on the floor.

His eyes widened when he saw how her big breasts flowed out of her bra. Wayne knew not to keep a desperate woman waiting. He placed both hands beneath her breasts and started to caress them.

"You're so beautiful. You know that?" he said.

"Actually I do," Reese said in a conceited tone. Wayne smiled. "Suck'em," she begged.

Wayne was shocked at her boldness, but obliged, making sure to suck each nipple perfectly.

"Ummm...that feels good," she said moaning.

"You glad I came over?"

Reese didn't answer. Her eyes were closed as she enjoyed the pleasurable feeling.

"Tell me what you want?" Wayne urged.

Again, Reese said nothing.

She simply leaned back on the couch and unbuttoned her jeans slowly, while Wayne ripped his off, showcasing how built he was. Quickly, her butt cheeks rose from the couch so he could remove her pants along with her thongs.

"Your body is amazing, Reese," he told her in between licking his lips.

Reese smiled, then opened her legs widely so Wayne could get a good look at her pussy. His eyes bulged and his cock pointed straight to the ceiling. Reese watched and smiled as she hoped Wayne would give her the fuck of her life.

Quickly, he slid off the couch and knelt on the floor in front of her, devouring her tits in rotation. He sucked on one and caressed the other with his hand kneading her nipples. His hands felt so good on her body, Reese wanted to scream. Instead, she moaned.

"Yes, Wayne. Yes."

Instantly, Wayne inserted one finger inside then held it up to her face so she could lick her own nectar. With hard nipples and a wet pussy, she ordered him to sit down on the couch because it was her turn to taste him.

Without delay, she grabbed his dick and inserted it in her mouth. His bulge began to grow larger with each lick.

"How does that feel?" she asked in between slurps.

"Yes, baby. It feels real good."

"Does it?"

"Y-e-s-s-s-s-s-s."

She slurped again. Then more and more.

Wayne grabbed the back of her head and began to fuck her face ferociously. He was enjoying himself so much he started talking dirty to her. "Suck this dick, baby, and Daddy will fuck you good."

That thought had Reese going wild. After circling the tip of his head with her tongue he couldn't take it any longer. He was about to explode so he pulled her up. After laying her on her back gently on her living room floor, he licked the inside of her thighs. He softly kissed her lips then sucked gently on her ear lobes. He then put on a condom he had retrieved from his wallet and spread her legs.

He lined his dick up with her pussy, rubbing it up and down almost putting it inside but not quite. "You want this," he teased.

"C'mon, Wayne. Fuck me," she begged.

After teasing her, he leaned forward to fully engage his swollen dick inside her. Thrust after thrust, he went to work, making sure to please her fully. Reese felt like she'd finally been awarded some good dick. She wrapped her legs around him and met his thrusts, wondering how many orgasms he would give her.

Reese met each of his thrusts with one of her own and her soft moans turned into very loud groans. She couldn't believe she was having sex with a stranger and loving it.

"Damn," she exclaimed.

"Ooooh…shit," he coaxed.

"Yes fuck me….fuck me!"

He did just what she asked. As he pushed deeper, Reese yelled in pleasure.

When she started cumming, he could feel her pussy contracting and pulsating. Within minutes, he was shooting his cum into the condom. Reese shouted at the top of her lungs. "Yes! Yes! Yes!"

She wasn't finished though. She needed to see what else, Mr. Muscle-Bound Wayne was working with. She got on her knees and ordered him back inside so she could feel him from behind.

"Oh my God Wayne, your dick feels so good!"

With one hand, he pulled her towards him as he dug deeper. With the other, he smacked her on the ass. As he held on to her hips he noticed what a nice ass she had. Turned on, he started thrusting into her pussy as he pulled her ass toward him.

Reese started yelling, "God, you feel soooooo good."

He could feel his dick pumping against her walls. This time it only took him minutes before he came again while she had orgasm after orgasm. Tired, they plopped on the floor.

"Damn, that was good," he said, trying to catch his breath.

"Yes, it was," Reese agreed. She looked at him. "I can't believe we just did that."

"You regret it," he asked, as he kept rubbing her breasts.

"No, I don't.

"So."

"So…you're Nia's father. Not to mention, my neighbor. That's weird."

"Not for me. That means you're only five steps away from good loving."

Reese laughed. "What I mean is, I barely even know you."

"So, why are you naked in front of me," he teased.

Reese hopped up, ready to take off until Wayne grabbed her arm. She turned around and saw that his dick was full again.

"Oh honey, I can't go anymore," she said.

She reached for the bottle of water on the stand nearby and took a sip. Wayne took the bottle out of her hand and sat it down. Without warning he picked her naked body up and sat her on the

*B*itter by DANETTE MAJETTE

counter.

"I told you, I can't go again."

"You don't have to do anything," he said.

With his tongue, he started to kiss her stomach. Licking her outer parts in a slow motion made her moan in pleasure. Reese directed his face to her clitoris which had become big by now. He began to bite her clitoris while teasing her ass with his thumb which made her moan even louder. The way she was squirming and breathing he could tell he was doing a good job. After about fifteen minutes of licking, sucking and biting she reached another orgasm.

She sat on the counter until she got her breath then slid off.

"Okay Wayne, this is crazy. I can't remember the last time I had that many orgasms," she said, running her hands up and down his chest. She wondered if he used to please his wife the same way.

"I aim to please, baby."

When he called her baby, and gave her a possessive look, she started to feel a little uncomfortable. She excused herself and went into the bathroom to wipe the juices off her legs. Looking in the mirror, she wondered if this was his plan all along. She had seen him watching her come in and out of her house for the last few days, but she never gave him the time of day.

This ain't gonna happen no more. I had a good time and it's what I needed, but I have to shut this shit down.

By the time Reese returned from the restroom, Wayne was dressed and had made himself comfortable back on the couch. "What's to eat around here?"

She looked at him. *I hope he doesn't think this meant anything.* "Nothing," she finally responded. "What had you planned on eating before you came over here?"

"Should I take that as a good comment or bad?"

She shrugged her shoulders, as Wayne picked up a photo of Sydney that was on the coffee table.

"You have a wonderful daughter. She's always so friendly when she comes over. I guess she gets that's from you."

So not true, Reese thought to herself. But then she could see how he would think that. After all, she had just had sex with

*B*itter by DANETTE MAJETTE

him after only knowing him for thirty minutes. She couldn't believe him coming over with a bottle of wine would lead to sex. She wondered if he used the fact that the mail man had delivered some of her mail to his house as an excuse to come over and meet her. She knew from Sydney that he had been asking about her. But she wasn't interested even though he was a nice man with the body of a god.

"So, are you friends with anyone else in the neighborhood?" Reese asked.

"Yep. But I'd much rather be friends with you, especially the way you welcomed me," he said laughing.

Reese didn't find the shit funny so she just gave him a fake smile and said, "Is that so?"

"So, are you seeing anyone?" he asked.

Where the hell did that come from, she thought. "No…I'm not. You?"

"Naw. I haven't really met anyone I'm interested in. That's until today, of course."

"Well, I'm single because I don't want to be in a relationship at this point in my life."

"Why is that?"

"I just like being single," she said, hoping he would get the message.

"I heard that."

After twenty minutes of answering his questions with yes and no answers, Reese was ready for him to leave.

"Hey, I think you should go now. I don't want my daughter to come home and find you here."

Wayne felt it was time to make his move so he asked, "You think after I shower I could come back over later and maybe watch a movie or something with you."

Hell no! You need to take your ass home. She thought as she looked at him.

"No. I don't think so," she said, as she slipped her clothes back on. "I hope you understand this was just a one-time thing."

He shook his head and said, "Wow! Okay, that's cool. I understand."

He had no choice but to understand. Reese's expression showed that she meant it.

"No morning kisses either?" He laughed at his comment.

"Nope. Just hello and goodbye." Reese felt it was only right that she smiled after making the statement.

Disappointed and pissed, he felt like a woman instead of a man after being shot down. He got up and walked out of the door, without even a goodbye. Reese followed him without saying another word.

"Yes, get the fuck outta here!" she whispered, exhausted from the fabulous fuck he'd given her.

Bitter by DANETTE MAJETTE

Chapter 11

That following Saturday night, Joi had somehow convinced Reese into going out with her. She thought her girl was lonely and needed to get out of the house.

"Hey girl. I'm almost there," Joi informed.

Hesitant about going, Reese told Joi she really didn't feel like being up in somebody's club. Unfortunately, Joi wasn't taking no for an answer.

"Bitch, I will be there in ten minutes so have your ass ready."

Pissed, Reese's cell phone went flying across her bed as she paced the floor a bit. The club scene wasn't her thing. Besides smelling like smoke, the guys were so corny and way out of her league. One thought was to call Wayne back over and fuck his brains out again. Then she thought about it...he seemed too clingy so she didn't want to chance a second rendezvous with him.

She kept looking at the BCBG one shoulder dress she was wearing. *I wonder if this is okay,* Reese thought as she checked herself out in her full length mirror. She hadn't been to a club in ages and didn't want to be dressed like a video chick, but also didn't want to be overdressed either. She started to go to Sydney's room to ask her advice about her outfit, but then she remembered she was sleeping over at a friend's house for the night. *Oh well!*

Reese had just finished applying her mascara, when she

Bitter by DANETTE MAJETTE

heard someone leaning on the horn. Running to the window, all Reese could do was shake her head after pulling the curtains back, and watching Joi get out of her car. She even had the nerve to be yelling Reese's name like she was in the projects.

"Oh Lord, I should've known it was her ass."

Reese ran down the stairs and opened the door before Joi could ring the doorbell.

"Let's go, whore!" Joi yelled.

It was a good thing Joi often used the word 'whore' and 'bitch' as terms of endearment. Otherwise Reese would've had a big problem with her choices. She actually remembered the first time Joi called her a whore. Reese thought she'd lost her mind, especially when Joi changed men like she changed her shoes. They almost came to blows that day. She explained to Reese that was just something she called all of her girlfriends and didn't mean it in a negative way. They laugh about that day all the time now.

With her clutch tightly under her arm, Reese locked the door behind them and set her alarm.

Joi had Reese in stitches all the way to the Beamer Dallas nightclub. They pulled up in front and one of the security men jumped in Joi's Mercedes as they got out. He drove around towards the back of the club. As soon as Joi walked up, security started moving folks out of her way like she was a celebrity. In essence, she and Reese were local celebrities, especially since they were on the radio. It was free publicity for the club if they had a good time, so the club always laid out the red carpet for her. They were ready to get their party on.

Sitting in 'The Velvet Room' was Joi's Spanish friend, Angelo. The Velvet Room was a VIP section of the club that was decorated with red velvet drapes, chairs and couches. As soon as he saw Joi walk in, Angelo immediately sat his drink down and got up to greet her.

"Hi, Papi. This is my friend, Reese," Joi greeted in a bubbly manner.

Reese hadn't seen Joi this happy in a while.

"Hola Senorita Reese" he spoke before introducing his brothers Ricardo and Marcos.

"Toma asiento," Angelo said, pointing to the love seat behind them.

After everyone sat down, Ricardo didn't waste any time pouring each of the girls a glass of champagne, then handed the flutes to them.

"Gracias," Reese said, admiring his physique. *He's pretty hot,* she thought.

Standing at 5'10, Ricardo's toned body didn't weigh any more than one hundred eighty pounds. Along with being impeccably dressed, he appeared to be in his late thirties and smelled just like he'd stepped right out of a cologne ad. All three of the brothers looked alike and Reese could easily see why Joi would be attracted to Angelo. He was polite, respectful, and fond of her. Everything Lavar wasn't.

Suddenly, Joi looked over at Reese and shook her head in Ricardo's direction. But Reese shook her head no and rolled her eyes. *I should'a known her ass had an ulterior motive for getting me out,* she thought.

Checking out the competition, Reese looked around at the women in the club before getting mad as hell that she'd wasted a four hundred dollar dress. Even though it wasn't new, Reese knew she could've worn her sweats and still looked better than most of them. Then there was the music. Reese was sure anyone could make a record these days. Got a problem with your baby mama and all you had to do was write a song and it would be a top ten on the Billboard chart.

"So, Reese what do chu do for a living?" Ricardo asked in his thick Spanish accent.

"I'm a radio talk show host."

"Oh, I see." He refilled her glass and whispered in her ear. "Chu are such a beautiful woman."

She smiled. "Thank you."

The club started going nuts when the DJ played Frankie Beverly and Maze's song *Before I Let Go*. By this time, Reese had another glass of champagne and was finally loosening up. Joi hopped up and grabbed Reese by the hand. The girls started dancing and having fun like they used to in college. Angelo rose from the sofa and joined them as Ricardo and Marcos looked on. The music kept getting better and better so the girls kept grooving. The DJ played oldies like The Fatback Band's, *I Found Loving* and Cameo's *Candy*.

Ricardo got up and yelled to Angelo that he and Marcos were going outside. Angelo was having so much fun he just brushed them off.

"Okay...okay...go...go," he said, not missing a beat.

Reese watched as they walked towards the front door. Beamers was a smoke free club so they had to go outside to smoke. Of course that didn't stop people from smoking but I guess they wanted to smoke something other than cigarettes.

The place was hopping and the girls were having fun. That's until Joi looked over at Reese who had stopped dancing and saw a blank expression on her face. She turned around and saw Lavar standing behind her looking like a crazed animal.

"What da fuck you doin'?" he said, grabbing her from behind.

"What does it look like I'm doing? I'm dancing and having fun."

She turned her attention back to Angelo and Reese. Embarrassed by the way she was grinding on Angelo, Lavar grabbed her arm.

"You must be out yo' damn mind sittin' here doin' dis shit right in front of me."

"Oh you can do it, but I can't. What part of the game is that?"

Reese walked over and asked Joi if she was okay which sent Lavar through the roof.

"Bitch, why don't you mind yo' own bizness?"

"Who the fuck you calling a bitch?" Reese yelled over the music.

Joi pushed her back. "Don't be talking to my girl like that!"

"Fuck you and yo' girl!"

Angelo walking over to check on Joi didn't help matters. Lavar started in on him.

"Nigga, you can sit yo' pretty ass down. Dis my woman!"

*B*itter by DANETTE MAJETTE

"She's not a piece of property. She is a woman. Her own woman," Angelo stressed.

Joi smiled at Angelo when she heard him say that about her.

"Oh, so dis who you wanna be with?" Lavar asked, looking at Joi with such intensity that she knew he had finally got a dose of his own medicine.

"Homes, it looks to me like she don't wanna be bothered with you!" he said, lifting his shirt sleeve to display his gang tattoo that read 'Untouchable'.

"Is dat suppose to mean sumthin' to me?"

"It should homie!" Angelo said, eyeing Lavar up and down.

Not wanting things to get out of hand Joi told Lavar, "Why don't you just go be with your groupies?" She grabbed Angelo by the arm and led him back to the sofa behind them.

Reese laughed at Lavar, then followed Joi. As they sat on the couch drinking and having fun, Reese had an uneasy feeling about Lavar just letting Joi clown him like that. He was too calm when he finally left. Within minutes, the girls were back to drinking and having fun again. After going through another bottle of champagne, Angelo excused himself.

"I have to go to the men's room. I shall return briefly my beauty," he said, gently kissing Joi on the cheek.

He stepped down from the VIP booth and made his way through the packed bodies on the dance floor.

The girls kept drinking and dancing.

"See girl, I told you we were going to have fun," Joi remarked.

"I can't remember the last time we had fun like this," Reese commented back. "It was especially fun to see Lavar leave with his tail between his legs for once."

"He's probably in a corner somewhere with some hoochie," she said laughing. "I don't even care tonight!"

Little did they know, inside the bathroom things weren't so good. As soon as Angelo zipped his pants up he felt a sharp, stabbing pain in his back. The pain was too immense to bear. He struggled for moments trying to catch eyes with the two guys he'd seen

Bitter by DANETTE MAJETTE

inside the bathroom. Suddenly, someone grabbed him from behind. Before he knew it, his head was smashed against the wall and he was stabbed again. This time his chest. And again. And again.

Finally, his limp body fell to the ground causing a loud thump.

"That's what you asked fo muthufucka!" a voice sounded.

Angelo bled profusely and could barely breathe because of all of the stab wounds to his back, chest and neck.

Looking at the guys in the bathroom, Lavar suddenly pulled out his gun.

"Y'all see what happened?"

All the guys shook their heads' no.

Lavar washed his hands and walked out just as calmly as he walked in. He quickly turned around and grabbed a paper towel and dabbed Angelo's back with it. The guys were stunned. They didn't understand the purpose of the bloody paper towels. But knew they didn't want to be witnesses and die themselves later.

Standing by the men's room door was LaQuita, a hostess Lavar used to sleep with. Only five feet one, with short, spiky hair, wearing black booty shorts and black platform shoes, LaQuita was the kind of girl that was down with anything. She took the bloody paper towel over to Joi.

"I think yo' man needs some help in da bathroom."

Joi was confused. "What the hell are you talking about?" she yelled, refusing to take the bloody paper towel.

By this time, people were aware there was a dead body on the bathroom floor. People starting running and screaming as security evacuated the club.

As the party goers ran out of the club Ricardo and Marcos tried to ask some of the people who were running out what happened. They all said the same thing that some guy was dead in the bathroom.

"Damn, what a way to go?" Marcos said.

They kept smoking until they saw Joi and Reese run through the door.

"Hey, where's Angelo?" Ricardo asked, grabbing Joi by the arm.

"They said someone stabbed him in the bathroom, but they wouldn't let me go in there. I was coming to get you so you could try to get in there and see what's going on?"

Ricardo and Marcos took off throwing people out of their way. They broke down when they got to the bathroom door. Seeing their beloved brother lying on the floor... dead, sent Ricardo and Marcos into a rage. They asked security if they knew what happened but of course no one was going to say a word even if they did know because they didn't want to end up dead next.

The police arrived within minutes and quickly sealed off the bathroom. Ricardo and Marcos were devastated. They vowed to find his killer by any means necessary.

When the valet brought Joi's car up to the front, he handed her the keys and she and Reese jumped in. With the car in gear, she waited until there were no cars coming before she peeled out of the parking lot. Joi felt bad about just leaving Angelo like that but she didn't want to be involved. Especially since she had a good idea about who killed him.

"I can't believe someone would just kill him like that," Reese said. She turned her head to Joi. "You don't think Lavar did it, do you?"

"I can't say for sure but my gut says, yes."

Reese gasped. "Joi, you need to leave that fool. He's getting way too dangerous."

"I know! I just need a little more time."

They were a quarter of a mile from the club when they saw several police cars headed that way. Then suddenly, the sound of gunshots.

"Oh, my God! See, this is why I should've stayed my ass home," Reese shouted.

"Look, I got some money stacked. I just need to get my own place." She paused. "That's not really the problem though," Joi said out of the blue.

"Why you say that?"

She looked over at Reese.

"Do you really think he's gonna let me leave just like that?"

"You have a point, but you have to do something. His shit

is getting too crazy."

When Joi pulled in front of Reese's house, she apologized to her.

"Why are you apologizing? You didn't do anything wrong."

"I know but what if he died because of me?"

"Well we still don't know for sure that it was Lavar."

Joi didn't have to wonder or second guess. She knew Lavar had killed Angelo. And he would kill her too if she left.

●●●●●●●●●●●●●●●●●●●●●●

Walking into her condo, Joi's first thought was to pack her shit and get the hell out of dodge. Lavar was so out of control and his behavior was sure to bring her down. She had a good job and was respected in Dallas, but all of that was in jeopardy if she continued to be with a man who was his own worst enemy.

Joi was in the middle of brushing her teeth when she heard the door open. As usual when he would do crazy shit, he just walked in and acted like nothing was wrong.

"Did you kill that man?" she yelled.

"What?"

"You heard me."

Lavar stood there with a smirk on his face. "I guess he wasn't as untouchable as he thought. Huh?"

A sharp pain sprinted across Joi's heart. "I can't believe you would do something like that! Do you know the Untouchables are a treacherous gang?"

"Fuck them Mexican muthufuckas! Their gang don't touch my niggas!"

"What if they retaliate, Lavar? Have you thought about that, Mr. I'm So Smart?"

Lavar grabbed a bag of chips and a beer out of the refrigerator and walked into the living room nonchalantly. With the remote in his hand, he turned on the television and waited to see his handy work make the early morning news.

Joi was so over his ass. She knew it was only a matter of time before either she or Lavar ended up dead.

Chapter 12

It was the 1st week of August and not only was the heat in Dallas hot, but so was Reese's coochie. After two weeks of ignoring Xavier's calls, she finally decided to call him back. It was either that, or call Wayne back over.

She was highly attracted to Xavier but she'd learned from previous experiences that someone could be handsome, look like an upstanding guy, and be a cheater at the same time. Then she thought about what Joi said about her just getting some. Sure her friend, *Buddy* was taking care of her needs and the fuck fest with Wayne had served its purpose, but it would be nice to be held by someone that she really wanted. She pulled his business card out of her wallet. *Why can't I get you off my mind Mr. Xavier Miller?* She picked up her cell phone and dialed his number. After ringing four times, Reese was ready to hang up.

"Hello," he said, in a sexy tone.

"Umm. Hi. This is Reese."

"Wow, you must've been reading my mind."

"Why you say that?"

"Because, I was just thinking about you."

"I was thinking about you too that's why I called. I was wondering if you would like to go out."

Reese's hands were sweating. This was a big step for her and she was nervous about it. She had been single so long she wasn't sure if she even wanted to go out with him. Of course when he said yes, it was too late to back out.

"How about tonight?" Xavier asked.

"Okay."

"How does eight sound?"

"That's fine. I'll text you my address," Reese responded with a smile.

"Alright, see you then."

As soon as Reese hung up, her heart started pumping very fast. She had no idea what she was going to wear so she rushed up to her room to find the perfect outfit for her date. She wanted to wear something sexy, but not too sexy. She didn't want him to think she was desperate. She fumbled through her closet and settled for a Stella McCarthy black strapless dress and some black Manolo Blahnik pumps. Her accessories of choice were a long black cameo necklace and a shiny black resin bangle.

It was too late for her to go to the hair dresser so she washed and set her own hair. Then she took a shower before sitting under the dryer. Looking at her phone reminded her that she needed to send Xavier a text with her address. When he didn't text her right back she started to get nervous. *I wonder if he changed his mind.* Just as the negative thoughts were taking over, her phone started to vibrate. It was a text message. When she saw his name and the words... *I got it*, she started to smile.

Shortly after eight, Reese was sitting in her living room waiting anxiously for Xavier to arrive. She was so nervous, her legs wouldn't stop shaking. To calm down, she poured herself a drink and took a deep breath. Minutes later, the doorbell rang. She sat her glass down, inhaled then exhaled slowly, checked her dress then walked over to the door. As soon as she opened it, he handed her two dozen red roses.

"Thank you. They're beautiful."

"You look stunning," he said, kissing her hand.

"You clean up pretty good yourself." She grinned widely.

"Are you ready?" Xavier asked.

"Yep. Just let me get my stuff."Reese grabbed her purse and her house keys. When they got to the door she set the alarm.

As soon as she walked outside and saw what he was driving she wanted to turn her ass around and go back into the house.

"Is that a police car?" Reese asked with a frown on her face.

"No! It's a loaner from one of my clients who provides police cars to the city. At least I took the radio out," he said laughing. "No seriously my Beemer is being serviced. We can walk if you like."

Reese smiled. "Don't be silly, "I'm fine."

Xavier walked to the passenger's side of the car and opened the door. When Reese got in, he closed the door. *Maybe he's a keeper.*

Reese and Xavier laughed and talked all the way to The French Room inside the luxurious Adolphus Hotel located in downtown Dallas. Reese looked around before getting out. She was a little embarrassed to be seen having a police car valet parked. As soon as they walked in, they were greeted by a young blond with huge breasts. *Look at this bitch!* Reese immediately looked at Xavier to see his reaction. He basically removed himself from the situation and let Reese handle all communication with the young woman. He got cool points for that. The young lady whose name was Misty grabbed two menus and took them to a quiet table in a corner.

The ambiance was very romantic. There were white candles, white linen tablecloths with pink carnation center pieces. Reese had been in Dallas for three years, but she had never been to that particular restaurant. She wondered if Eric hadn't brought her there because that's maybe a spot he would bring his whore since it was so convenient. Being that it was inside of a hotel. As soon as that thought entered her mind she wondered why the hell she was thinking about that loser when she had such a wonderful man right in front her. Within moments of their arrival, a waiter came over and asked for their drink orders.

"We'll take a bottle of your best champagne."

Feeling he maybe over stepped, he asked Reese if she was okay with his selection. Of course she didn't have a problem with it. Who would?

When the waiter brought back the Armand de Brignac champagne, he popped the cork and poured them each a glass. He then took their meal orders. As an appetizer, they decided to have a Heirloom Tomato Salad. Reese's choice for the main course was the Wild King Salmon. Xavier chose the Colorado Rack of Lamb. When the waiter left to go place their orders, Reese wanted to kick herself. Ordering seafood on the first date or during a business meeting was usually a no-no for her. Now she was going to have bad breath. What if he wanted to kiss her? *Oh well,* she thought to herself.

While they waited for their food Reese and Xavier took that moment to get to know one another a little better.

"So, have you ever been married?" she asked to see if he would slip up.

"You know you asked me that before, right."

"Oh I did?"

"Yes, you did. To answer your question, again. No, I've never been married. I've had the occasional girlfriend here and there," he said looking her straight in the eyes to let her know he was being a straight shooter. "My last girlfriend actually died in a car accident last year."

"I'm so sorry to hear that," she said, reaching across the table to place his hands into hers.

She quickly moved her hand back when the waiter bought them their salad.

"I think that's why I was so glad I met you. I've been so depressed since she died." He repositioned himself in his seat. "It was a very difficult time. She expressed to me and a few of her friends several times that if anything ever happened to her, she didn't want to be on life support. I tried to convey her wishes to her parents, but they didn't want to hear it. I felt so helpless." He hesitated a moment and with a somber tone said, "They were estranged. We ended up having to go to court and a judge ultimately agreed with me. That was the hardest thing I ever had to do. They still hate me till this day for it."

"Wow, that's so sad!" The waiter interrupted them again but just for a moment to place their food on the table. "I've been very

𝓑itter by DANETTE MAJETTE

depressed lately, too. I recently went through a divorce."

"That man has got to be the stupidest person alive. How could he leave a beautiful woman like you?"

"That's what I thought," she said letting out a little snicker. "I also have an eighteen year old daughter named Sydney who will be starting her first year at Clark Atlanta. I actually have to take her there in two more weeks to help her move into her dorm."

Xavier asked her to raise her glass for a toast. "Here's to new beginnings and new friends."

They clinked their glasses across the table then took a sip of champagne. Reese was glad she hadn't blown him off. All through dinner they kept grinning at each other like little kids. Two hours and a bottle of champagne later, they were finally finished eating and ready to leave.

The waiter came over and cleared their plates and asked if they wanted dessert. They declined. So Xavier was slipped the check. Like the perfect gentleman he'd been all night, Xavier reached in his wallet and placed an American Express card down to pay. Once the check was paid, the two left and decided to take a stroll to walk off their meals. They told the valet they would be back to pick up the car in about an hour.

They walked, talked, and laughed as they strolled under a half moonlight night. The weather was nice and people were everywhere, walking along the sidewalks. This was the first time in years Reese felt alive and she owed it to her new friend. Not only was Xavier fine, he was easy to talk to and seemed to have the same drive and ambition Reese had. Holding hands, Xavier pulled Reese in front of him and planted a kiss on her lips. His lips were so soft Reese didn't want him to stop. He held her close and slowly inched his hands down to her hips.

"I better stop before I kidnap you tonight."

"What if I want you to kidnap me?" she said, still sucking on his lips.

Xavier eyes began to widen. "You sure! I don't want you to think that's all I'm about."

"We're both adults," she said, leading him back to valet to pick up the car.

𝓑itter by DANETTE MAJETTE

● ● ● ● ● ● ● ● ● ● ● ● ● ● ● ● ● ● ● ●

Riding in the car headed back to her place, Reese was feeling extremely good. The alcohol had her in a state of relaxation and her body was at ease. As they cruised, Xavier glanced over at her in the passenger seat and watched as the street lights danced on her curves. He placed his hand on her thigh and gave it a slight squeeze, gesturing to her that he couldn't wait to see what was in store for him them when they got back home. She caught his slyness and seductively licked her lips. The combination of the liquor and the bumps in the road had her hormones on high. She reached over and placed her hands in his lap. Reese slowly rubbed her hand up and down his thigh until she felt the bulge in his pants grow. With her free hand, she lifted her dress and put her hands in her panties.

"Mmmm, I'm so horny."

Xavier looked over and watched her as she playfully fingered her pussy. "Oh shit," he exclaimed as he almost drove off the road, mesmerized by what was going on in the passenger seat next to him.

They both laughed hysterically.

"Watch the road now. I'm not going anywhere."

Reese smiled seductively then inserted her pointer and index finger into her pussy causing her back to arch. Meanwhile, she managed to free his dick from his jeans with her free hand. She started at the base of his dick and worked her way up to the head, simultaneously playing with her pussy. Hungry for more, she removed her hands from her panties and inserted fingers into his mouth.

"Suck all my juices off."

He obliged and the feeling of his thick, wet tongue caused a sensation she had never felt before run through her body, starting at her feet all the way up to her nipples. A moan escaped her lips and she looked down at his beautiful tool.

At this point, Xavier was rock hard, veins pulsating throughout his shaft. She licked his ear, softly kissed his neck, and without warning she reached down and devoured his dick in seconds. The sudden warmth on his dick caused him to swerve a little, but he quickly regained control of the car. She sucked on his head firmly taking in all of his premature juices. She proceeded to deep throat his dick as she massaged his balls. The tightness of her throat caused him to throw his head back and close his eyes. Remembering where he was, he quickly snapped back to reality and pushed the pedal to the floor.

Just as she was getting into it, he announced, "We're here."

Wasting little time, they both raced out of the car, into the house and up the stairs. Little did they know, Wayne was watching them secretly from his bedroom window. As soon as they hit the door, clothes were ripped off and thrown across the floor.

They were just about to take things to the next level when her doorbell rang.

Who the fuck is that? Reese thought.

"Umm...I'll be right back. I'm so sorry," she said, grabbing her robe.

"It's okay. Just hurry back," he said smiling.

Reese gave him another kiss and told him she would. She stomped angrily like a child out of the room. She had a gorgeous man in her bed ready to make love to her and someone was interrupting their mood.

When Reese opened the door, her eyes almost popped out of her head. "What the hell do you want?"

"I need to talk to you."

"Are you fucking kidding me? We don't have shit to talk about Wayne. You really need to get it through your damn head that the other day meant nothing to me." She got closer to him. "Look, no offense but it was just sex. To be honest with you...you just don't do it for me."

"I did it for you when I was fucking you."

She laughed. "Wayne, I hadn't had sex in months so anybody could've done what you did and I still would've thought it was the greatest. I was just really horny that day."

She gave him a pat on the chest and laughed as she started to close the door in his face. When Reese heard him kick the door

*B*itter by **DANETTE MAJETTE**

she started to open it up and curse his ass out but she was not about to keep Xavier waiting any longer than she already had.

As soon as Reese got back upstairs, Xavier quickly placed her on the edge of the bed. He wanted to express his gratification of the bomb head she'd just blessed him with. He placed her feet on his shoulders and slowly kissed up her inner thighs. Using his tongue, he traced a trail all the way up until he reached her beautiful pussy. He passionately tongue-kissed her clit, not missing a beat. The pattern between his lips and tongue sent a volt of electricity threw her body and she came instantly. Xavier softly bit her lips, and flicked her clit with his tongue as he finger fucked her. Her juices ran down his arm and this caused his dick to jump with excitement. No longer able to control his erection, he kissed his way back up her body, stopping at her breast, hungrily taking in her nipples. As he took her breast into his mouth, he entered her wet center. Her body shook uncontrollably as she came upon entry.

A growl escaped his lips, she felt so good wrapped around his dick. Love making was the last thing on her mind, "Fuck me, Daddy," she moaned and he obliged. He pounded her pussy until screams of passion escaped her lips. His hard cock felt good hitting her G-spot with each deep thrust. She clinched her pussy muscles each time he made contact. Feeling himself coming close to his climax, he pulled out and motioned for her to flip over. Head down, ass up, he plowed into her pussy as she thrust backwards at him. Reese grabbed and clawed at the sheets. It felt so good…and she had no control over her body. She came hard. Over and over again. All over his dick.

Xavier showed his wild side. He smacked her ass and then reached under to play with her clit. He wanted her to cum harder. He fucked her even harder and rubbed her clit until he felt her body tense up. This was his cue.

"Cum…with…me…baaaaaaby!"

As his last words escaped his lips, they both released in unison with shrills of passion. Her body convulsed, she collapsed, and he fell on top of her as his juices flowed out of her. Breathing deeply, they passed out and slept until the sun peered through the blinds.

Chapter 13

College life was about to start in a couple of days so Sydney and her mother were on their way to Atlanta to get her settled into her living quarters. As soon as they got off the plane, Reese's eyes began to water. Even though she and Sydney had been having problems, and she was still mad about her getting arrested, she was still her baby.

They walked up to the rental car counter. Reese gave them her reservation number and her credit card. The agent told them they would be bringing the car around in just a few minutes so they took a seat in the lobby.

"Well, this is it. You're about to be a college student. Are you excited?" Reese asked as she sat down in the hard chair.

"Yes, but I'm nervous. It was easy to make honor roll in middle and high school but this is going to be different."

"You'll be fine," Reese said, patting her back. "You'll be the first doctor in our family."

"Just great! Stress me out even more," Sydney said, rolling her eyes.

All at once it hit Reese that her baby was no longer a baby and now a young woman about to be on her own. She knew it was going to be a big adjustment for her because Sydney had always been spoiled. She had her own room with a king size bed, Jacuzzi bath tub, and a walk in closet big enough to make a spare bedroom.

Bitter by DANETTE MAJETTE

Now she was going to have to share a community bathroom, sleep on a twin size bed, and cram her clothes into a small closet.

The agent motioned to Reese that her car was in front of the door. They grabbed their luggage and packed it in the car. Although most of Sydney's stuff was shipped and already at her dorm, she and Reese found a Target so they could pick up a few more things, like towels, sheets, and personal hygiene items.

"Are you ready to go check out your room?" Reese asked her daughter as they left the store.

"I guess."

They drove about twelve miles before reaching the campus and when they did, Sydney's face lit up. This was the day she had been waiting for since she walked across the stage at her high school graduation. She just hoped she could live up to her mother's and Eric's expectations.

When they drove onto the campus of Clark Atlanta University, it was buzzing with students and faculty all ready for the start of the semester. The main campus consisted of 39 academic, administrative, and student support buildings spanning over 126 acres of land. It was huge and not too far from downtown Atlanta. The fact that it was accessible from all major highways made Reese feel good inside.

As they drove past the football field, they saw the players in a huddle, the band practicing, and the cheerleaders jumping up and down in front of the bleachers chanting with their pom-poms twirling.

"This school is so live. I can't wait!"

"Ummmm...let's not get too excited. You are here to learn."

"I know Ma, but this looks like so much fun."

"Why don't you try out for the cheerleading squad?"

"Not! Those days are so over. I had enough of it when I was younger."

Sydney had been there on a college tour but it was during the holidays so there weren't that many students around. After parking in front of the dorms, Reese and Sydney begun to unload Sydney's things. A couple of boys who were standing around asked if they needed help. Reese told them yes, and that she would compensate them for their time. Reese noticed one of them giving Sydney the eye. *At least he's in school unlike that bum she was with at home,* she thought. As soon as they walked into her dorm room, her roommate introduced herself.

"Hi. I'm Maya."

"Hi. I'm Sydney and this is my mother, Reese."

Reese told the guys they could just put the bags and Sydney's luggage on the bed then she gave them a twenty each. The roommate then told them that the boxes that were sitting on the floor belonged to her. Reese was a little confused because they had mailed three boxes but there were four. Sydney knelt down to see what was what. She started smiling when she saw Eric's name on one of them. She picked it up and sat it on the bed.

"Who sent you that?" Reese asked.

"Eric!"

Sydney tore the tape off with her key and started going through the box. The first thing she saw was an Ipad. She dug a little deeper and saw a Tiffany box. When she opened it she jumped up and down. It was a platinum bracelet with diamonds.

"Oh my God! I love it."

The only thing left was a card. When she opened it, a credit card fell out. She was so excited that she had her very own Visa credit card.

"Wow! Someone really loves you," Maya said impressed.

Seeing all the stuff Eric sent Sydney reminded Reese of the time when he would surprise her with lavish gifts. It was one of the things she loved about him. It didn't have to be a holiday or a special occasion for him to give her little trinkets. Of course, the gifts started to get few and far between and that's because he was showering someone else with gifts.

Sydney noticed the gloomy look on her mother's face.

"Are you mad because he sent me this stuff?"

"No, baby. I'm happy for you! Well let's get the rest of your stuff unpacked and make your bed before I go check into my room."

Reese looked at how happy her daughter was after getting

the package from Eric. She came to the realization that she had been too wrapped up in her own anger and pain to think about how the divorce affected Sydney.

While her mother was making her bed, Sydney hung her pictures on her side of the room. She hung all of them except the picture of Eric and Melanie. That would have to be hung after her mother left or she would never hear the end of it. On the other side of the room, her roommate was attempting to hook up her laptop and printer. Sydney and her mother wanted to laugh because the girl was just being so comical about not getting it to work. When she threw her hands up in exasperation, Reese told her to let her do it.

"Sweetie, I hope you're not majoring in computer technology," Reese said smiling.

"I'm not! I'm actually majoring in Biology."

"So am I!" Sydney said, thrilled that she would know someone in her classes. "I'm also going to minor in Chemistry."

Maya told her good luck. "One major is enough for me."

Once everything was set up and in its place, Sydney's roommate asked if she wanted to join her and a couple of girls she had just met in the student union. Sydney looked at her mother.

"Go ahead. I'm about to leave anyway."

"Okay…well at least let me walk you to the door."

They walked down the hall and exited the building. Trying to hold back her tears, Reese gave her daughter a big hug and told her to be careful. It seemed like all the problems they were having were so trivial now. They weren't the first mother and daughter to not get along and certainly wouldn't be the last. As her mother was walking toward her rental car, Sydney told her to wait a minute. She ran up to her and gave her another hug.

"I love you," Sydney said with tears in her eyes. "I'm really gonna miss you."

"I'm gonna miss you too, baby," Reese said, shedding tears herself.

Just then her cell rang as she walked away. There was heavy breathing on the phone.

"Hello," Reese said in a heavy tone. "Hello," she repeated.

*B*itter by DANETTE MAJETTE

Still nothing. Just breathing.

● ●

There was so much traffic on the way to the hotel which irritated Reese because she had to use the restroom and was hungry. Not to mention, she was still irritated by the anonymous caller. She wanted to pull over but she was only a few exits from her hotel. She used the time to check in with the station. Joi told her shit hit the fan as soon as she left.

"What the hell happened?" Reese asked.

"First, the police came to the station and questioned me about Angelo's death at the club. They want to talk to you too when you get back."

"Why are they questioning us? That was three weeks ago."

"Well, they knew we were with him and a witness told them about Lavar and Angelo getting into it over me. Then on top of all of that we've been getting all of this hate mail and complaints so management called Julian and basically ripped him a new one."

"I'm quite sure he took care of things."

"He took care of things alright! He threw your ass under the bus. He told them he was going to sit you down and have a long talk with you."

"That backstabbing muthafucka! He just did that because I won't go out with his ass!"

"I thought the same thing. He's probably going to call you later."

"Okay. Well, I can't deal with that shit right now. I'll deal with it when I get back because this could really hurt our chances of getting syndicated."

"Alright. Well, I'll try to keep things under control until then. Tell Sydney I love her."

Reese told her thanks and she would see her when she returned.

When she got to the Westin Peachtree Plaza hotel Reese checked in then took the elevator up to her room. After she opened the door, she threw her Louis Vuitton overnight bag on the brown

Bitter by DANETTE MAJETTE

colored sofa and looked around. "Not bad," she mumbled to herself. The room had two queen size beds with a beautiful caramel colored duvet cover and an oversized bathroom with six shower heads.

Reese waltzed over to the desk and looked inside the drawers for a menu. When she saw a bible, she wondered why all hotels had one in the drawers. She figured it was for the cheaters to pray for forgiveness after they do the deed.

She got her cell phone out of her purse and charged it because once again it was dead. Throwing the key on the table, she sat on the edge of the bed trying to decide what she wanted to eat. Once she knew what she wanted, she laid across the bed and started to daydream about her many nights with Xavier. It had been two weeks since her initial date, and the night she had multiple orgasms. Suddenly the room got hot. She broke away from her dream. Hot and bothered, she got undressed and took a shower.

The water from the shower was so relaxing. She could've stayed in there for hours but her stomach wouldn't let her. She needed something to eat, and desperately needed a drink. Reese dried her body, slipped into a pair of sweats and a tee shirt, then laid across the bed. Picking up the phone next to the bed she ordered room service. It was nice to finally do something for herself because her life was basically centered on her work.

It had been an hour and Reese was starting to get impatient because her room service still had not arrived. When the phone rang, Reese jumped. It was the front desk letting her know there was a problem in the kitchen so her order would be delayed.

"It's already been a damn hour. How much longer is it gonna take?"

The front desk told her it should be only a few minutes more and if there was anything they could do to compensate for the delay.

"Hell yeah! You need to send me up a free bottle of wine with my order because this shit is ridiculous. I feel like I'm at a damn Motel 6," she said, then slammed the phone down.

Not wanting to piss her off anymore. They agreed.

Finally, after waiting patiently for thirty minutes there was a knock at the door. Reese hopped off the bed and after looking through the peep hole, opened the door. The bellman bought the tray in and sat it on the desk. After signing the receipt, she went to her purse and got out a ten dollar bill to tip the young man. Even though she was hungry the first thing she did was open the bottle of wine. She smelled it, swished it around in the glass then took a gulp. She figured there was no sense in playing around with it.

Once she had eaten and had a few glasses of her wine she grabbed her cell phone and called Xavier.

"Hey baby! Is your daughter all settled in at school?"

"Yes she is."

"I should've gone with you."

"That's so sweet of you," she said.

She was really feeling Xavier. He was just what she needed in her life right now. She couldn't explain how he made her feel but every time they were around each other her stomach would flutter.

"Yeah, I'm torn about her leaving though. I'm happy because we've been fighting a lot lately, but I'm sad too because that's my only child. That's my baby girl."

"You know your daughter could be acting the way she does because she's spoiled. I mean not many kids can just go in with a check for the whole school year."

"You're right! That's the only good thing my ex did."

"You sound like you're still bitter. Are you still in love with him?"

"Of course not! Especially since I have you now," she said smiling. "I'm not gonna lie, it still hurts sometimes because I know I was a good wife and for him to treat me like that bothers me."

"Do you need anything? I have a couple of friends out there who owe me favors. They can get you whatever you need."

Reese was glad to know she could count on Xavier if she needed him. She was the one always in control, but she was glad to hand over that reign to him. She bit her lip when she started to feel her pussy get wet. She was about to indulge in some naughty phone sex with him when she heard her phone click. She looked at the screen and saw Julian's name. She was about to answer it just to curse him out but she just didn't feel like dealing with him tonight.

"Okay, I'll let you get some sleep so you don't miss your flight in the morning. I don't want to be apart from you another day."

"Don't worry, I don't want to be here another day without you either."

"Oh one more thing, make sure the door is locked and you're secure in your room."

Reese told him she would. Her phone clicked before she hung up with Xavier. She thought maybe it was Sydney, but when she looked at the screen Julian's name appeared again. *Why the fuck is he blowing up my phone?*

She told Xavier goodnight and gave him a smooch over the phone. He did the same. Just to be on the safe side, she got up and checked the door one last time. With her eyelids heavy from drinking the whole bottle of wine, she went into the bathroom, brushed her teeth and then climbed into bed.

The next morning, she got up early. She wanted to make sure she'd have enough time to make it to the airport in time for her nine fifteen flight back to Dallas. Reese arrived at the airport an hour an a half early. She dropped her car off then took the shuttle to the terminal and checked in. The bustling airport was filled with travelers. The security checkpoints only had minor delays so she still had an hour to spare so she stopped by Starbucks near her gate. She found a table and started munching on a bagel and drinking her coffee until they called for people to board the plane. She couldn't wait to get back to work and especially to Xavier.

Thirty minutes before lift off, they announced that her plane was boarding. She got up and got in line. She couldn't wait to get back to Dallas. She had been so focused on her work, there wasn't any room for nothing else until Xavier came along.

• •

As soon as the plane landed in Dallas, Reese turned her Blackberry Tour back on. She had several messages. Of course,

ℬitter by DANETTE MAJETTE

most of them were from Julian. Two were from Xavier and one was from Sydney just checking to see if she made it home safely. As soon as she exited the plane and walked into the terminal, Xavier was standing there with a big smile on his face and a dozen white roses. He handed her the flowers and gave her a kiss.

"What are you doing here?" Reese asked, giving him a big hug.

"I came to give you a ride home," he said, grabbing her bag. "You didn't think I was going to let some cab driver take my baby home did you?"

"How'd you know what time my flight landed? I never told you."

She smiled.

"I know everything," he told her with confidence.

They walked out to his new shiny BMW. *Now this is the kinda car I should be seen in.* Xavier opened the door and helped her in. He put her bag in the backseat and got in. After putting his seatbelt on, he drove out of the airport and headed to the freeway. Merging into the traffic, he headed to Reese's home so he could officially welcome her home.

Bitter by DANETTE MAJETTE

Chapter 14

It was Thursday night and after two days off, Reese was ready to get back to work. She enjoyed the time off, which she spent in bed with Xavier, but she had her mind on having her show syndicated. The only way that was going to happen was if she dedicated every waking moment to her show.

She stepped off the elevator with pep in her step. Being with Xavier was making her a new person but she couldn't display that on the air. She still had to keep up the theme of her show which was to give men hell. As soon as she walked into the booth, Joi jumped up and hugged her friend tightly.

"Girl, I missed you."

"I missed you, too," Reese said, putting her purse down on the floor.

Joi looked her up and down. "Ooohh...somebody glowing. Did you get you some?"

Reese smiled. "Two days in a row." They slapped hands.

"Girlllll," you better be glad Julian is off 'cause that nigga would be able to tell. It's written all over your face. And he woulda been sniffing your coochie like some hound dog right about now." Joi rubbed her girls shoulder. "So, tell me everything."

"Nah...we bout to go on the air. I'll tell you about it later."

"Oh, you are so wrong for that shit. Now I gotta sit through the whole show wondering."

*B*itter by DANETTE MAJETTE

"Don't worry. I'll give you all the juicy details after the show," Reese said, taking a seat and putting her head set on.

"Okay, but at least let me tell you about our latest hate mail. Some guy says he wants us both dead!"

The girls laughed, but inside were tired of the threats. They started the show off talking about all the hot new gossip. Then they played the new song called 'I Hope She Cheats On You With a Basketball Player' by Marsha Ambrosia.

"So, why do you think men cheat?" Reese asked. "Dallas, let me hear what you think."

"Well, before we take the first call I want to say something about men cheating," Joi added.

Reese laughed. "I know you do. You think we should take the high road?"

"All I have to say is if that muthafucka dishes it out then he should be able to take it," Joi said with anger.

As usual the phone lines lit up. Reese took the first call.

"Caller what's your name and tell us what's on your mind?"

"Dis is Antonio. Personally, I don't agree with this mentality that all men cheat. Men do sometimes give off a vibe that may seem that they are cheating on their spouse, but speaking from a man's point of view I feel that we are sometimes stereotyped. Most women tend to label all men as liars and cheaters, but all men are not like that."

"Is that so?" Joi asked.

"Yeah! Some men do care about their woman's feelings and the woman still sometimes blame a man for stuff that he has no idea about. If a woman blames a man for something that he has not done, that will make him want to go out and do it. Usually it's something that a woman done heard from one of her friends. I think the most important thing in a relationship is "TRUST". Without trust, the relationship will not last no matter how much two people love each other."

"Well, how the hell we supposed to TRUST ya'll when you lie to us about stupid shit? I mean, tell me," Reese said about to get in the guys ass.

"Man, I can see I'm not gonna win that battle. Ya'll got

ya'll minds made up."

"You right boo-boo go ahead and hang up cause we ain't buying that shit," Reese said. "Who's up next, Joi?"

"We got Mary on the line."

"It's interesting to hear a man's opinion on relationships. But to be honest, I do think that men get a bad rap and I personally feel that we have to stop looking at each other as either men or women but rather as people," Mary stated.

"What the hell is she talking about?" Reese whispered to Joi.

Joi couldn't stop laughing. "Reese, don't you do it!"

"Good-bye Mary Poppins, thanks for calling," Reese said, cutting Mary's call. Joi fell out of her chair onto the floor laughing. "You are so damn crazy, girl. Get yo' ass off the floor."

"I can't! Oh God it hurts," Joi said, holding her stomach.

Reese looked down at Joi and shook her head and said, "Where the hell did I get you from?"

Once the show was over, the owner of the station asked Reese to meet him in his office. Her first thought was she about to get fired because of the shit that was going on like the police visiting Joi, all the complaints, and massive amount of hate mail. Maybe all her ranting and raving was too much for him to handle. When she walked into the office, she took a seat across from him and waited while he finished up a call. She had no idea what this impromptu meeting was all about but she would soon find out.

As soon as Mr. Andrews got off the phone, he told Reese that he was aware of all the negative feedback her show was getting, but in spite of all that her ratings were through the roof. He explained that hate mail and complaints were common when it came to satellite radio because of all the freedom of expression and speech.

"You know people are always getting uptight about something you've said but I think you guys are doing a great job."

A sigh of relief came over her. "Thank you, Mr. Andrews, I appreciate that."

Reese had great respect for Mr. Andrews. He started out from a poor upbringing and worked his way up the ladder, now owning Reese's station, and several television stations. "As you know, one of the shows here will be syndicated. You and two other shows are up for consideration. Don't tell anyone I said this but I'm rooting for you."

"Thank you so much for your support."

"You're welcome. There's a catch though! I know this is short notice but the board will be meeting Monday morning to make a final decision. So you need to give a presentation stating why they should pick your show and what kind of numbers you expect this fiscal year."

Reese smiled. "Don't worry sir, I'll be ready."

This is what she had been waiting on for years. There was no way they were going to pick someone else over her. She had already done the ground work of her presentation in anticipation of this day.

Reese shook Mr. Andrew's hand before leaving his office and told him she would see him Monday morning. She ran back to the booth to share the news. Joi was so excited she suggested they go out and get drunk.

"Sorry, but I have plans."

"Oh shit! You get some new dick in your life and now you dissing me," Joi said, with her lips poked out.

"Girl, you know I love you but the presentation is due Monday morning…that's only three days away, so I need to get cracking. So you're going to have to do the show by yourself tomorrow. We'll celebrate afterwards."

"Alright whore!" Joi said in a playful tone.

"So, give me the details on what the police were asking you."

"Not much. I just told them that yes we were hanging out with Angelo but then he left to go to the bathroom and that's all I knew. It's not like I'm lying because that's what happened."

"Okay, I just have to make sure I tell them the exact same thing. Did they ask you if you think Lavar did it?"

"Of course they did, but I didn't actually see him do it. So whether or not I think he did it doesn't really matter."

"True."

Bitter by DANETTE MAJETTE

"I'm just sorry I got you involved in this mess," Joi said exhaling deeply.

"Please, I'm a big girl. I can handle the police when they come back. So what's up with Lavar? Has he calmed down?"

"Still lying and cheating," Joi said, grabbing her belongings. "You ready to go?"

"No, you go ahead. I need to make a phone call."

"Alright. I guess I won't see you this weekend, so I'll see you Monday."

Walking to her office all Reese could think about was how glad she was that Julian was off. If Joi figured out she had already slept with Xavier, he would've figured it out too. That was the last thing she needed to deal with. She sat behind her desk, picked up her cell phone and hit the speed dial for Xavier. After the fourth ring it went to voicemail. She wanted to tell him the good news herself so she didn't leave a message. Minutes later, he called her back.

"Hey Baby! How was your first day back at work?"

"It was great! I have some great news. My show is being considered for syndication."

"That's awesome. You deserve everything that's happening to you," Xavier replied.

"Thanks. I think so, too. I was wondering if we could spend some time together on Sunday instead of tonight. I have to give a presentation Monday morning so I need to work on it tomorrow and Saturday. I have to convince the big wigs that they should choose me so I gotta be on top of my game."

"No problem. I'm gonna miss you though."

"I'm gonna miss you too but we can still talk until then."

"Sounds good."

Reese hung up the phone and grabbed her purse. Just as she was walking out the door two detectives walked up and showed her their badges.

"Reese Kennedy. I'm Detective Knight and this is my partner Detective Allen. We were wondering if we could ask you a few questions about Angelo Martinez."

"Umm...sure have a seat," she said, pointing to the couch

in her office. She sat down and asked, "What's this all about?"

"We understand you were with the deceased when he was killed?" Detective Allen asked.

"No. I wasn't with him. I believe he was in the men's room," Reese said, annoyed that they were already playing mind games.

The detectives looked at one another. "I meant you were with him at the club," Detective Allen inquired.

"No, we weren't with him at the club. He was already there. We merely had a drink or two in the VIP section with him. He got up and went to the restroom. A few minutes later, they told everyone to leave the club."

"Did anything happen before he went into the restroom?" Allen shot back.

It was clear they already knew what happened between Lavar and Angelo so Reese confirmed that yes they did have words, but then Lavar left. When they asked Reese if she knew who might've killed Angelo, she told them no. They could tell from her nervous body language that she wasn't exactly telling the truth so they pressed harder.

"Do you think Miss. Franklin's boyfriend might have gotten angry about her being with another man?"

"I'm not sure. You gotta ask him."

"Lavar and his crew are pretty well-known in Dallas as being very ruthless and dangerous. It just seems a little odd that he would just back down from a man who is pushing up on his woman," Detective Knight added.

"It wasn't that serious detective," she responded.

"Well, what is serious is the fact that Mr. Martinez's death has started talk of retaliation within his community. The Untouchables are a very dangerous group also."

"Well, I'd love to hear all about it, detective, but I've told you about all I know. I really need to get home now."

The detectives thanked her for her time then left. As soon as they did, Reese let out a heavy sigh. *This shit is getting out of hand!* she thought as she grabbed her purse and headed out the door to go home.

Chapter 15

Sunday finally rolled around and Reese couldn't wait to see Xavier. She'd spent the last two days working hard on her presentation, hardly eating, no leisure at all, and barely bathing. She was ready to play a little now. She was so excited, she had already been dressed an hour before it was time for Xavier to pick her up. Dressed in a Tory Birch tiered tank, William Rast jeans, and BCBG strappy sandals, she waited for her man. Her makeup and hair were flawless. Reese managed to have her stylist make a house call. She had to pay a little bit more than normal but it was worth it. She needed to look her best for him.

Xavier rang the bell at five o'clock on the dot. Reese opened the door and greeted him with a wet kiss. He checked her out from head to toe and was very impressed. As usual, he was impeccably dressed in a Burberry Polo, Mek Jeans, and Bruno Magli shoes.

"I'm so glad to see you," she said, holding him tightly.

"You sure? I've been listening to your show and it seems you have it in for all men."

Reese chuckled. "You know that's just an act. I have a good man now but that's what my listeners like to hear."

"Okay. Just checking. I don't want to toot my own horn but I thought I was pretty good the last time we were together."

"Oh, you were daddy! And stop listening to my show."

𝓑itter by DANETTE MAJETTE

She grinned, then grabbed her bag, locked up, and continued out to Xavier's car.

Once outside, Reese knew trouble was headed her way as she watched how Wayne stared at her like she'd killed someone in his family. "So, are you gonna introduce us?" he asked, blocking her path to Xavier's car.

Xavier had already opened his car door, but hesitated to get inside. Reese made sure she kept a nonchalant facial expression as she responded.

"Oh sure, Xavier, this is my neighbor, Mr. Nichols." She changed her tone, quickly to a more condescending one. "Okay, so bye-bye. Have a great day. See ya later. Chow!"

This angered Wayne deeply. He had to make sure Xavier knew that he wasn't just a neighbor who'd borrowed sugar. She'd actually borrowed his dick and he wasn't having it.

"So, did you tell him about us?"

Reese reached for the door handle and Xavier's eyes crinkled.

"No, she didn't," Xavier interrupted. "Is there something I should know?"

"Yes," Reese said hurriedly. "He's crazy and not worth our time. I'll tell you all about it in the car. Let's go. Pleasseeeeee," her eyes begged.

Wayne had to get a few words in before they shut the door. "Oh my God Wayne...your dick feels so good," he taunted as he remembered the words Reese said to him as he was blowing her back out.

Within seconds Xavier had pulled from the curb and Reese pretended that nothing had just happened.

"So where are we eating at tonight?" Reese asked.

"I made us a reservation at Sullivan's."

"Oh good! I love their food."

Xavier thought about asking more questions about Mr. Nichols but decided against it. He knew he could find out on his own. He watched Reese closely as she applied some more lip gloss before getting into a conversation with her.

I don't mean to get into your business but I hear some of

the callers and they sound pretty mad at you," he said, turning in his seat towards her.

She looked over at him and smiled.

"They talk a lot of smack but I don't think anyone would actually try something with me."

Xavier disagreed but he told her that if she ever needed him to just call. She told him she would but she doubted it would be necessary.

When they pulled into the parking lot of Sullivan's, they could tell that it was packed. The wait was at least one hour. Reese was so glad Xavier had made reservations because there were a lot of people waiting to be seated. As soon as they walked in they were seated and handed food and bar menus. The waitress was this cute little college looking girl. She was energetic like she may have been a cheerleader.

"Hi! Welcome to Sullivan's. I'm Catherine and I'll be your server tonight! What can I get you guys to drink?"

Xavier did the ordering.

"I'll have a Devito Mojito and the lady will have a...lets see...maybe a Watermelon Martini," he said, looking at Reese to see if he was making a good choice.

Once Reese gave the thumbs up, the waitress smiled and said, "Okay, I'll be right back with your drinks."

While she was getting the drinks Xavier and Reese looked over the menu to see what they wanted to eat.

"What do you have a taste for baby?" Xavier asked.

"I'm not sure. How 'bout you?"

"I think I'm going to get the Porterhouse Steak and Horse-radish Mashed Potatoes."

"I'm gonna have the Prime Rib and Crème Spinach," Reese said, placing her menu on the table.

When the waitress came back with drinks in hand, they rattled off their dinner orders. Until their food came, they talked about work, Reese's trip, and what their goals were in life. Reese was surprised that they had so much in common. Having similar goals and aspirations was always a plus.

"Do you think you'll ever get married again?" Xavier

asked.

Reese had never really thought about it. She'd kept her feelings bottled up so long because she didn't want to ever feel that kind of pain again. Just having another relationship was a big step for her.

"I don't know. Do you ever plan on getting married?"

"Absolutely, if the right woman comes along."

He took a sip of his drink and winked his eye at Reese.

Smiling, Reese asked him if he wanted children. Xavier told her that if he did it would be fine and if it wasn't in the cards for him he was fine with that also. She was glad to hear that because she definitely wasn't having anymore children.

Their food finally arrived thirty minutes later. Catherine apologized for the delay. She explained that one of the cooks had called out of work so they were short staffed. Xavier told her they understood and for her not to worry about it. Reese looked across the table at Xavier and thought to herself how lucky she was to have bumped into him that day in the mall. He was obviously sent from heaven at the right time.

They ate, talked, and laughed. She learned a lot about Xavier like he drank his coffee black with one sugar, he liked to sleep on the left side of the bed, preferred his eggs over easy, and blue was his favorite color. Reese was having the time of her life, but what they were going to do after dinner is what she was most excited about.

They had several drinks before they left and were ready to get their freak on, so Xavier paid the check and then they left to go back to Reese's. They both had meetings in the morning so they couldn't hang out late like they normally did.

●●●●●●●●●●●●●●●●●●●●●

As soon as they got into the house, they were all over one another. Xavier promised her a night she wouldn't forget and she was looking forward to it. Reese told him she couldn't wait, but she needed just ten minutes to look over her presentation one last time. He told her okay. They went into her home office after mak-

𝓑itter by DANETTE MAJETTE

ing another drink.

Reese opened her laptop, booted it and went to her Powerpoint presentation. While she was looking over it, Xavier stood behind her massaging her shoulders.

"Hurry up! I need you," he said, kissing her on the neck.

"It's kinda hard to concentrate when you're distracting me."

He moved his way up her neck to her earlobe. He slipped his hand down to her breast cradling it gently. His touch shot through her body like electricity.

"You are not playing fair," she said. "Just give me one more minute."

She made a few minor changes then hit save.

"There, I'm all done. At least for now," she said, looking over her shoulder.

"You're not going to log off," Xavier asked.

She stood up said, "No. I want to look at it one more time before I go to sleep," she said, rubbing his arms up and down.

The first thing she noticed was the tattoo on his arm. She had been meaning to ask him since their first date what the inscription meant but she didn't want to pry. But now that their relationship was blooming she felt she had to right to know.

"There's something I've been curious about." She reached out and circled the small tattoo on his forearm. "What is Nes? Is that your ex-girlfriend?"

He wanted to evade the question but had already told her she could ask him anything.

"Yes. That's the one who passed away," he said with sadness in his eyes.

"I'm sorry. I know that was a very painful situation for you. So let's just change the subject."

"Thanks. I appreciate you understanding why I don't like to talk about that particular time in my life."

"I understand. I feel the same way about Eric."

"Well enough of that! I'll make us another drink and meet you up there," he said, kissing her on the lips.

He made them both Martinis, then walked upstairs with the

***B*itter by DANETTE MAJETTE**

drinks in hand. When he saw Reese spread across the bed naked, his dick got hard. Exchanging each other's alcohol scented breath, Reese and Xavier went at it like animals in heat. No longer having control over her actions, Reese aggressively ripped off his clothes. He could tell the alcohol was in control but he did not object.

Suddenly, there was a knock at the door.

"Ignore it baby," Reese said in between kisses.

She was extremely horny and needed to feel Xavier inside of her. The knocking got louder, and whoever was at the door, was not going away.

"Just answer it," Xavier responded, pulling away gently so that he could face her.

"Ugh, Okay," she grunted. "Grrr...somebody better be dead."

At that moment she thought about the detectives, hoping they weren't back for more questions. Then she thought about Wayne.

Her thoughts played ping pong as she realized that Xavier had grabbed Eric's old robe from her closet and was probably planning on greeting the visitor along with her. Reese jetted down the stairs. When she opened the door, she was shocked to see Julian just standing there with his hands in his pockets.

"What are you doing here?"

"Well you haven't answered your phone so I was worried."

Out of the blue, Xavier called out to Reese from the top of the stairs.

"Baby, you okay down there."

Julian looked away. He shot Reese a judgmental look. Reese could tell he was crushed. His silence spoke volumes. He was mad as hell, but his feelings were of no concern to her. After a long stare, he finally spoke.

"Did I catch you at a bad time?"

"Yes you did!"

With his face balled up, Julian had the nerve to ask, "Who was that?"

"None of your damn business! Now good night," she said, slamming the door in his face and returning to her naked lover.

Still standing at the door, Julian could feel everything in him tense up.

"Okay, fine... if that's how you want to play!" he grunted.

Reese kindly shut the door, hoping that was the end of that. As she walked back up the stairs, Reese was worried that by disrespecting Julian the way she did may have just messed up her chances of becoming syndicated.

Aggravated and wound up from what just transpired with Julian, Reese staggered back up the stairs, attitude on high. Sensing her tension and frustration, Xavier handed Reese who was already drunk, another drink straight on the rocks so it would have an immediate effect. She took no time in throwing it back. It did exactly what Xavier knew it would. Within seconds they were back at it.

Reese pushed him on his back onto the bed and grabbed an ice cube out of her emptied cup. She kissed him on his lips and the coolness made his dick jump. She proceeded to make a trail from his neck all the way down to his belly button, alternating between her tongue and the ice cube.

At this point, Xavier could not take it anymore and begged her, "Baby please, stop teasing me, I want to feel you," as he gripped her head.

"Don't touch me," she stated, swatting his hands.

With her mouth nice, cold, and wet Reese took his beautiful python into her mouth. He immediately grabbed hold of the sheets and let out a loud moan. This motivated her. She sucked his dick like a champion. It must have been the liquor because she deep throated his dick and ran her tongue across his balls at the same time, something she had no idea she was capable of doing. Xavier jerked with pleasure and grabbed Reese up by her shoulders. He simply couldn't take it anymore. Xavier roughly flipped her over onto her stomach and propped her ass up in the air.

"Arch your back, baby."

Reese obliged and prepared for his entry. She was caught off guard when she felt the warm sensation of his tongue from her pussy to the crack of her ass. It felt so good to her. He sucked on her clit and tongue fucked her until she came all over his face.

𝓑itter by DANETTE MAJETTE

"Mmmm mami," Xavier said as he sucked all of her cum out of her.

He was not finished though. Reese had gotten a little weak from the intensity of that orgasm, so he pulled her back up so that her ass was up enough to his liking. He then plunged into her with his rock hard dick and fucked her violently. Reese came over and over again all over his dick, she swore she passed out a few times and was awakened by Xavier hitting her G-spot so beautifully.

He smacked her ass, and moaned, "Ah shit, I'm about to cum."

Reese threw her ass back to match his every stroke as she reached under her and grabbed his balls to intensify his orgasm. Gripping her hips, Xavier exploded and buckled as the last of his nut escaped his balls. The effects of the alcohol and the multiple orgasms knocked Reese right out. Xavier nudged her and got a loud snore in return.

After a quick trip to the bathroom, Xavier nudged Reese again.

"Baby, I'll see myself out okay."

"Huh. What did you say?"

He repeated it again.

"Oh. Okay," she said, turning over and going back to sleep.

Chapter 16

Julian opened the door and walked into the dark foyer of his two story colonial home. He flipped the lights on and sat his Tumi briefcase onto the floor.

He loved living in his childhood, two-story home although the silence made him want to scream sometimes. The home had a beautifully landscaped front yard, fenced backyard, and two car garage. His mother made the home more of a showplace than a home. Each room was spacious, had a fireplace and high ceilings. It was located downtown so it was close to I-35, the Dart Rail, and Stevens Park Golf Course. Julian loved that because on his weekends off he liked to play golf or go sailing on his boat. He didn't have too many friends other than his friends at work. No one could bear to be around him because he was so competitive. Everything was a contest with him. He always had to show everyone he was better than them. He often thought of himself as 'the little engine that could'. Everything he ever committed to, he did with a competitive and goal oriented stance.

Julian headed into the kitchen and poked around in the refrigerator. There wasn't much to choose from, seeing as though he hated to go grocery shopping and hated cooking even more. Being a bachelor was so depressing for him. It wasn't like he didn't want to be in a relationship. He just couldn't have the one woman he wanted to be with. That was Reese. She stole his heart the first

*B*itter by DANETTE MAJETTE

time he laid eyes on her.

Grabbing the last bottle of Fiji water and an opened bag of chips from the cabinet, he went up to his spare bedroom that he'd turned into a home office. He took a seat behind his desk and turned on his computer. He fumbled through some mail as he waited for the computer to warm up. Most of them were bills so he sat them to the side.

After Julian threw a few chips in his mouth, he clicked on the Mozilla Firefox icon so he could check his emails. Most of them were from his family. That's how they usually communicated. He had three other siblings but none of them were close. It was something they inherited from their mother and father. Their parents weren't affectionate people. Julian could remember when he was younger how all the other kids in his class would get hugs from their parents when they did something good. His parents would just say good job and then go on as if it wasn't a big deal.

He took a sip of his water as he clicked on an attachment. He laughed when he saw his niece in her soccer uniform. She was the spitting image of his sister. He printed the pictures on photo paper and added them to his collection.

Tired and ready to hit the sack, he went into the bathroom to brush his teeth. He turned to leave the bathroom and stood looking at the 18x24 poster of Reese over his Bodega grey finish bed from Z Galleria. He often pictured her laying across his Hologram bedding, naked, posing like a video vixen. He knew the thoughts were bad but he couldn't help himself. He was just so in love with her. It bothered him how she had treated him at her house, but still…he loved her.

Undressed and laying back on his bed, he closed his eyes and fantasized of making love to Reese. He imagined her voluptuous lips on his rigid sword.

The coating of his spit made an excellent lubricant. He let his hand stray down to his thick package and gave it a firm squeeze. He began a steady rhythm of long strokes until a warm, thick spew blasted from the head of his dick. He groaned loudly as his body shivered from the intense pleasure. When he opened his eyes a massive amount of creamy goo was all over his hand.

Julian rested for awhile then headed to the shower. Clean and refreshed he returned to his bed and climbed in. It wasn't long before he was fast asleep and snoring loudly.

●●●●●●●●●●●●●●●●●●●●●●

Being in a loveless relationship was starting to take its toll on Joi. When she pulled up and saw Lavar's car in the parking lot, she wanted to turn around and go back to work. Her hate for him was growing more and more each day. People thought she was crazy for staying with him but they had no idea how mentally and physically abusive he could be. If he saw her talking to a guy, he would threaten to kill the guy. From the butcher at the supermarket to her male friend who owned a restaurant where she loved to eat. Everything was about how it looked for her to be seen talking to other men.

Before she started dating him, she had heard stories about him and none of them were good. The fact that he was out on bail for armed robbery and assault with a deadly weapon should have made her run in the opposite direction, but it didn't. Lavar was a very scary guy to everyone in the streets, but when he was around her he was the perfect gentleman. But just like that, he flipped the script on her.

When she walked in, Lavar was no where to be found. It didn't occur to her to see if his truck was in the parking lot. She noticed her bedroom door was closed and then sounds of laughter were heard coming from the other side. Easing the door open, she caught him off guard.

Sitting in a wife beater and boxer shorts, he jumped up.

"A'ight man, let me call you back."

Joi could clearly hear a woman's voice.

"You didn't have to get off the phone with your bitch on my account," she said, throwing her purse on the bed.

"Whatchu talkin' bout? That was Tony."

"Yeah right! You think you so slick but you're not."

"Look you keep sayin' I'm doin' dis and dat but you still here."

"Not for long!"

His nostrils flared.

"What you tryin' to say?" She ignored the tone in his voice. "You ain't neva leavin' me! You got that."

"I'm not going to be the one leaving. You are."

He walked slowly towards her in an intimidating manner. When she saw the intensity in his eyes her heart started to beat rapidly, but she didn't bat an eyelash. She wasn't about to let him know she was afraid of him. If she did, he would play on that. Instead she walked into the bathroom and got undressed. Wearing just her bra and a thong, she walked back into the room and pulled an oversized t-shirt out of her dresser.

She heard Lavar's footsteps on the hardwood floor as he walked up behind her. She knew he was staring at her ass so she tried to cover up as quick as she could. She felt his dick press up on her butt. It was hard as a rock.

"What's up wit some lovin'?" he said, when Joi turned around abruptly.

"Go fuck one of them chicks you be talking to!"

"I want to make love to you."

"Boy, get the hell out of here."

Without warning, he picked her up and threw her on the bed. Holding her down, he pulled his dick out and rammed it inside her. The pain made Joi shriek!

"Lavar get the fuck off me!" she yelled, beating her fist against his back.

"Stop actin' like you don't want some of dis dick," he said with a wicked smile as he went into the slick depths of her creamy tunnel.

"I'm not playing with your ass! Get off of me."

Her words turned into muffled grunts once he placed his hand over her mouth to shut her up. All she could do is make pathetic noises as he kept his hands in place. She squirmed and wiggled but she couldn't get him off of her. Fighting was useless. He was too strong and determined to get his way. With full force, he drilled his dick in and out of Joi's G-Spot. Within minutes he started wailing and his eyes started rolling in the back of his head as his juicy cum shot from his hole. Disgusted, Joi got up and gave him a dirty look. Lavar simply smiled, thoroughly pleased with himself as he grabbed his towel.

"You wanna take a shower together?" he asked.

Joi didn't respond. She grabbed a pair of jeans out of the closet, slipped her 'I'm that Bitch' wife beater on, and pulled her hair back. She snatched her rhinestone baseball cap off the dresser, slid her feet into a pair of flip flops, and rushed to the door. All she could think about was getting away from the most devious man she had ever met. "Where you goin'?"

Still silent, she grabbed her purse and keys. Before she could get to the door, Lavar grabbed her and turned her around. With his hands around her neck he said, "Let me tell yo' ass sumthin'. I been puttin' up wit yo' lil temper tantrums and yo' threats to leave but jus know that as soon as you do, you gonna start to see dead bodies poppin' up everywhere round you. Yo' mama…yo' pops…and specially dat bitch, Reese." He slowly released her. "Bitch, go head leave if you wanna."

Joi took two steps back and stopped as she examined the devious expression on Lavar's face. Defeated, she breathed heavily through her lips, and dropped her keys to the floor.

Lavar grinned wickedly. Within seconds, he'd returned to the bedroom and turned the shower on.

Joi sluggishly walked over to the couch and flopped down into the seat. Crying as she sat in hell, she could hear Lavar singing in the shower like nothing happened. She was positive he was bipolar or just plain evil. She had to get away from his clutches. One thing was sure. When she did leave, she was going to leave with a bang! She was going to inflict as much pain as he had throughout their relationship.

Bitter by DANETTE MAJETTE

Chapter 17

Reese woke up just an hour too late. Panicked and hung over, she called Joi and told her to let Mr. Andrews know she was on her way. When she hung up the phone, she jumped in and out of the shower so fast she still had suds on her body. She had already laid out her clothes the night before so she didn't have to figure out what she was going to wear. As she dressed hurriedly, her body felt so sluggish. It was as if she had been drugged.

Dressed sharply in a Rachel Roy black suit and her hair pulled back into a ponytail, she grabbed her laptop and purse and ran out of the door. At the first stoplight she reached she pulled out her makeup bag. She brushed on some foundation, applied eyeliner, and lip gloss all before the light changed. When it turned green, she sped down the street at top speed. It wasn't until she got in the parking lot of the station that she remembered that she had left her laptop out on her desk. *Awww...he's so sweet he logged off and put it in the bag for me last night.*

Practically running into the building, Reese bumped into several people trying to get to the conference room. As soon as she stepped off the elevator, Mr. Andrews asked her to meet him in his office.

"You can put your stuff down first," he said. He didn't seem too happy.

She ran to her office and threw her stuff on her desk. When

Bitter by DANETTE MAJETTE

Reese turned around she ran into to Joi.

"Can you get me a cup of coffee? I have the worst hangover ever." Reese was scrambling to get herself together. "I'll be back. I have to hurry to Mr. Andrews' office."

"I know I heard him."

Reese rushed off, leaving Joi in her office. Joi was sitting at Reese's desk when Julian walked in.

"Is she here yet?" he asked, showing his frustration.

"Yep, she's in with Mr. Andrews."

"That can't be good," he said about to take a seat.

"Hey, can you get her a cup of coffee before you get comfortable?"

"Sure," Julian said, running out of the office.

When he returned he had a cup of chamomile tea instead. He thought that would be a better choice for her under the circumstances. He knew she was probably nervous.

"Where's her presentation? I want to take a look at it."

"I guess it's in her bag."

She picked the bag up off the floor, pulled the laptop out, and turned it on. Joi wanted to make sure Reese would be ready to go when she got back in the office. She looked down at her watch.

"Shit! I need to go grab some paperwork," she said. "Tell her I'll be right back."

"Will do."

Joi rolled her eyes. "Can you be any whiter?" she said, walking out.

When Reese returned to her office, Julian was sitting at her desk looking at her laptop.

"What are you doing?"

"Nothing! I was just looking for your presentation," he said, getting up. "Here's some tea to calm your nerves sweetie."

As soon as he handed her the cup of tea she threw it up against the wall.

"I didn't ask for no damn tea! I asked for a fuckin' cup of coffee. I mean shit ya'll can't even get that right."

"Sweetie, I just thought it would be better for you."

"Well stop thinking! And stop calling me sweetie before I

really go off on your ass! Get it through your damn head. I am not your sweetie!"

Joi ran back in the office. "You're up!"

Reese rolled her eyes and walked out. When Joi saw the mess she asked Julian what happened. He was still in shock that Reese went off on him so he just shook his head and walked out.

Reese took a deep breath then walked into the conference with her head held high. She was ready to show them exactly why she should get the job. The atmosphere in the room was very upbeat.

Talking a good game was something Reese knew how to do very well but she was having a hard time concentrating. She was so hung over she had a headache and found herself stumbling as she walked around the room. Questions were being shot at her from every angle and she answered them but it took her a long time to get the answers out. You could tell Mr. Andrews and the other owners were a little embarrassed for her. When the numbers part of the meeting came up, she pulled out her laptop and hooked it up to the projector.

When Reese didn't see her Powerpoint slide show on her desktop she started to panic.

"Is everything okay, Reese?" Mr. Andrews asked.

"Yes sir."

After watching Reese fumble around looking for her presentation, Mr. Andrews pulled her to the side.

"What's going on?"

"Sir, I can't seem to find my slide show with all of my numbers and projections. I just had it last night."

"Do you think you saved it to your hard drive?"

"I checked. It's not there," she said, with tears forming in the corner of her eyes. "I can't believe this!" she wailed.

Mr. Andrews explained to the others what was going on and ended the meeting with a few words of his own. Reese could tell Mr. Andrews was embarrassed so she sat quietly in a corner still trying to figure out what happened. She couldn't believe this was happening to her. This was her big break and she'd fucked it up big time. As soon as the conference room was empty, Mr. Andrews sat down and said nothing for five minutes. He simply twitched his lips while in deep thought and continued to lock the fingers on one hand into the others. Out of the blue, he told Reese to take the rest of the day off.

"Off? The day? Ummmmm....I'll be fine. I just need to find out what happened."

"I can tell exactly what happened. See, I know a hangover when I see one." He stood up and looked out the window. "You probably had too much to drink last night and deleted it by accident." He turned to Reese, sticking his hand into his pants pocket. "You know I hear rumors all the time and I usually don't like to give them any thought, but after today I have to wonder if they're true."

Is this cocksucker calling me a drunk? she thought. He walked towards the door.

"Go home and get some rest. We'll see you tomorrow."

"But...Mr. Andrews..."

"Tomorrow, Reese," he ended.

As Mr. Andrews walked out, Joi was walking in.

"What happened?" Joi asked concerned.

Reese stood up. "I don't know. I couldn't find my presentation. I had it last night, Joi. I swear I did."

"Ahhhh, Sweetie. This is bad. Was anyone on your computer?"

"No. I was working on it after Xavier and I had dinner. Then we went upstairs. I had a few drinks and he left. He even packed it up for me before he left."

Her thoughts scanned through everything that had happened since last night. Then something hit her. She marched out of the office and past several partitions until she got to Julian's office. She didn't wait to be invited. She just flung the door open abruptly.

"Did you erase my presentation?"

He slid his chair back from his desk and stood up. With crinkled brows it was clear he was insulted.

"Why would I do something like that? Maybe you should ask your new boyfriend!"

She couldn't believe what she was hearing.

ℬitter by DANETTE MAJETTE

"Are you insane?" she said looking at him like he had two heads.

Reese knew she wouldn't get the truth out of him, but it all made sense. If she got the job she would have to leave the station and move to Chicago and she knew Julian wouldn't want her to leave.

"Look, I don't know how I can explain this any clearer for you. I don't feel the same way you do. We are just friends!" she said loudly.

She walked out of his office and headed to her car fuming. Once she was in her car, she fastened her seat belt. Without warning her emotions took over and she started crying. She needed someone to talk to so she called Xavier.

"Hey baby! How did it go?" he asked with enthusiasm.

Reese could barely talk. "Mannnnn, I can't believe this!" she cried out.

"Calm down and tell me what happened."

She calmed down enough to tell Xavier what took place in the meeting. He was so empathic. He tried convincing her that she still had a chance even without the presentation. She felt so guilty here he was being supportive and Julian was trying to blame him for it. *I know that muthafucka did it!* They talked for a few minutes, then ended the call with Xavier promising to come give her a massage when he got off of work.

•••••••••••••••••••••

Later that night, Joi went on the air, alone. She wanted to make sure her friend was well-represented so she planned on making sure they had a good show to keep their ratings up.

"What's up, Dallas? This is yo' girl, Joi. Reese has the night off, but I'm quite sure she's listening in. Tonight we're gonna do something a little different. I want ya'll to call in and just tell me what is on your mind tonight. What's going on good or bad?"

The phone lines started to light up like firecrackers. Joi answered the first call. "Hi, caller. What's your name and what's on your mind tonight?"

*B*itter by DANETTE MAJETTE

"Joi, this is Tawanna. I just wanted to say I know you and Reese catch a lot of flack from men because ya'll tellin' us how shiesty they can be but there are people out here like me who support and respect you."

"Tawanna girl, you just made my day. Me and Reese do have a lot of haters, but they can't do nothing with us girl. We are here to stay. Thank you for your call. Let's take another call," Joi said, hitting the answer call button. "Caller, what's your name and what's on your mind tonight?"

"Hi, Joi. This is Bambi. I just found out my husband has been cheating on me with this chick. He kept telling me she was his boy's girl. I knew something was up because she kept looking at me funny when I would come around her. I just didn't put it together until someone saw them hugged up together at a club. I don't know if I should forgive him or just leave."

"Honey, don't worry about it, just cheat with one of his friends. That's what I did. Fuck'em! They wanna play games, so show'em exactly how it's done. Eye for an eye."

"I have had my eye on one of his boys," the caller said laughing.

"Well go for it."

"Sounds good. Okay thanks!"

The rest of the night Joi took calls with just about everything from people cheating, to girls beefing with baby mama's. She had just shut down the show when she heard a loud commotion in the hallway. When she opened the door, she saw Lavar charging his way through the office.

"What the hell are you doing?" Joi asked with a fearful look on her face.

"Oh, so you fucked one of my boyz," he said, getting up in Joi's face.

Joi pushed him back.

"You better get the fuck out of my face." She picked up a pair of scissors off a desk near her and held them firmly in her hand. "Get up in my fuckin' face again and I'ma carve my initials in your chest, muthafucka."

Everyone was shocked and scared. So much so, no one

even tried to intervene. One lady did run to a phone to call security.

By this time, Julian was walking up.

"Hey Lavar man, you need to leave right now."

"Nigga don't act like you fuckin' know me," Lavar yelled.

"Ain't nobody got time for your bullshit. So just get the hell out of here before you get hurt," Joi said, still holding the scissors in her hand.

"Bitch, you ain't gonna do shit," he said, keeping his distance. "You think it's easy to get rid of me...huh...huh," he asked, waiting for a reply. "I'll see yo' ass dead befo' I let you leave me." He gave her a deadly stare before turning to leave.

By the time he got on one elevator, security was exiting from another. They rushed over and asked Joi if she was okay then suggested she call the police.

"Well, I think you should get a restraining order," Julian added.

"I don't need no damn restraining order! Ain't nobody scared of his sorry ass."

"Okay, well at least let me walk you to your car."

Joi reluctantly agreed. She went to the studio and grabbed her things and met Julian at the elevator.

Once they got off the elevators they could hear the screeching of tires behind them. It was Lavar in his Bronze Continental GT Speed Bentley. He pulled right up to them and stuck his Glock out of the window and said, "Get yo' ass home."

He scared the hell out of Joi and Julian. They both stood still until he drove away like a bat out of hell. They both breathed a sigh of relief when he left, but Joi knew it was far from over. She was used to his explosive, volatile behavior. Julian on the other hand, had never even been in a fist fight, let alone a gunfight.

"That guy should be locked up," Julian announced, wiping the sweat from his forehead.

"It ain't that easy. He'll find a way out or have someone just do his dirty work for him on the outside."

"I don't think you should go home. Why don't you go stay in a hotel or better yet go to Reese's for the night."

"No. I'll be fine," she said, hitting the unlock button on her

keychain and opening the door.
What the hell is she thinking? Julian thought.
"Well, at least call me and let me know you got home safe."
"Okay. I will."
Julian let out another fretful sigh before he closed her door. He waved goodbye and then caught the elevator back up to the station.

•••••••••••••••••••••

Not knowing what to expect when she got home, Joi drove home thinking about the argument she would have to have when she arrived. Hopefully, Lavar would be long gone. Then Joi paused…thinking, probably not.

It didn't take long for her to arrive at the condo. Hoping for the best, she took a deep breath before putting her key in the door. She turned the doorknob and walked in slowly. She hadn't even closed the door behind her when the hard smack to her face caught her off guard. She wiped her mouth and looked at her hand. When she saw he drew blood, she wigged out.

"Muthafucka," she yelled, jumping on him like a cat clawing and scratching Lavar like the baddest cat at a cat fight.

"Get the fuck out you bastard!"

"I ain't goin' nowhere. You ain't got nobody protectin' you now."

He grabbed Joi by the head and punched her in the face several times knocking her to the ground. As she fell she grabbed his wife beater ripping it off his body. Furious, he took the torn t-shirt and wrapped it around her neck.

"I'll fuckin' murda yo' ass in here," he shouted, as he choked her. When she started turning blue in the face he let her go. "You ain't gonna keep givin' me yo' ass to kiss bitch!"

Laying on the ground trying to catch her breath, Joi gasped and rolled around on the floor in pain. She had been laying there for about fifteen minutes as Lavar paced the floor yelling and screaming at the top of his lungs about how ungrateful she was.

"You always talkin' bout who I'm fuckin' and how I ain't

Bitter by DANETTE MAJETTE

no good but you still here spendin' my damn money!"

When she was able to get up, she grabbed her keys and hit the ADT panic button attached to her keychain.

When Lavar heard the alarm, he looked at Joi in disbelief.

"You callin' da po-po on me."

"Damn right!" she said, holding her neck.

"Shut up, bitch." He hit her again, "Now run tell dat!"

Lavar had to think fast because the police would be there in a matter of minutes. When the phone started to ring, they both looked at one another with wide eyes.

"I can't believe dis shit here."

"Nigga! What the fuck did you think I was gonna do? Let you sit here and beat the shit out of me all night."

Lavar was mad as hell. He had about ten guns in the condo.

He picked up the phone and told the ADT agent it was a false alarm.

"Okay sir we need your pass code please."

"6969."

"Sir, we still have to dispatch Dallas P.D. to you. They should be there soon."

"I said it was a false alarm," he said loudly.

"I know sir but that's standard procedure when a key chain device is set off."

"That's bullshit, but a'ight!"

As soon as he hung up, he told Joi to go over to the neighbor's condo next door until he got rid of the police. His plan was to tell the police he mistakenly hit the panic button trying to set the alarm. When she refused, he went ballistic.

"Look, yo' name is on da damn lease so if I go to jail you goin' too."

Joi knew what Lavar was saying was true so she grabbed her bag and went next door. Lavar cleaned up the mess they made, then went outside to wait for the cops. Standing in front of his car, he lit up a Black and Mild like nothing was wrong.

When the police finally pulled up five minutes later he walked over to the squad car and said, "Good evenin', officer! Well, it's actually good mornin'. It was my alarm dat went off."

*B*itter by DANETTE MAJETTE

"So, it was a false alarm."

"Yes sir. I was tryin' to set it and I hit da panic button instead."

"Okay, well I need your license. I still have to make a report."

"I understand," he said, pulling out his wallet and handing him his license.

The officer took Lavar's information down then handed it back to him.

Joi watched from her neighbor's window as Lavar worked his magic. Her first thought was to run outside and tell everything. But her second thought made more sense; just leave.

"You have a good night and watch what button you're hitting," the officer said to Lavar as he pulled off.

Laughing Lavar said, "Okay thanks!" He stopped to make eye contact with Joi who'd just taken two steps back from the window.

He had to make it look good so he got into his car and drove around the block until he was sure the cops were gone. *That bitch gonna pay for this shit! He told himself.*

Chapter 18

After the week from hell, Reese, Joi, and Julian all went out for a bite to eat before work. Something they didn't get to do that often. When they did get together, the Dallas Chop House was their spot. Although they had to work later they couldn't resist having a drink, to summarize all that had been going down; from Mr. Andrews comments about Reese, to the latest news about Lavar. Reese had a Vodka on the rocks while Joi sipped on an Apple Martini and Julian's wimpy ass had a virgin daiquiri.

Joi was a little self conscious about being out in public because you could still see the bruises on her face. Reese watched as Joi tried to hide her bruises with foundation. When Joi saw it wasn't really working she closed her compact and threw it in her purse.

"Why don't you just come stay with me?" Reese asked.

"I don't want to burden you. Besides he would be camped out at your house every night girl."

"Joi, you have to leave his crazy ass before it's too late. He's dangerous and I'm really worried about you being there with him."

"I know and I appreciate it but I have to do this my way. Don't worry Lavar is about to get just what he deserves," she said smiling.

Reese saw her plea was falling on deaf ears so she told Joi

she was giving her a week to leave or she was going to come pack her up herself. Reese was in the middle of chastising Joi for being so stubborn when she spotted Xavier. She got up from the table excitedly and rushed over to him. As soon as he saw her, his eyes lit up. He planted a wet one on her lips and gave her a big hug.

Sitting at the table watching the imaginary love of his life making out with another man almost sent Julian over the edge.

"Dang! Can that vein in the middle of your forehead get any bigger?" Joi teased Julian as he scanned every word that escaped Reese's lips.

"What are you doing here?" Reese inquired.

"I just finished up a meeting. Actually, I'm surprised to see you here, too. This is my favorite restaurant," Xavier remarked. "I was getting ready to order something to go when I spotted you."

"It's one of my favorites, too."

"Why don't you come join us?"

"Don't mind if I do."

Reese and Xavier waltzed back over to the table.

"Hope ya'll don't mind but I invited Xavier to join us."

Xavier pulled out Reese's chair as he greeted Joi and Julian. "Hello everyone."

Joi couldn't resist the urge to have a little fun at Julian's expense.

"Y'all make such a cute couple. Don't you think so?" she teased then looked at him.

Steam shot from his ears, "Yeah I guess," he said sulking.

"Thanks," Xavier said. "I think so, too."

Reese handed Xavier a menu so he could order.

"I don't need that, baby I already know what I want."

When he called her baby, Julian choked on his drink.

"You alright," Joi asked, hitting him in the back. Julian nodded.

After placing their orders, Joi bought up the subject of the missing presentation.

"I don't know what happened. It was there one minute and gone the next. It's really weird."

"Why you say that?" Joi asked.

"Because it should've at least been on my hard drive even if it wasn't on my desktop or in my documents folder. I'm telling you someone deleted it on purpose."

"Well, at least you have another chance to prove you're the best person for the job," Joi announced.

"Did you ever think maybe it just wasn't meant for you to leave?" Julian said.

Everyone got quiet and gave him a curious look.

"Excuse me, I need to go to the men's room," Julian said, pushing his seat back and getting up from the table.

"He's been acting really weird lately. You sure he didn't erase it," Joi said.

Xavier spoke firmly. "I was about to say the same thing. I just didn't want to over step my boundaries."

Reese shrugged her shoulders. "I don't know. But if he did, I'm going to jail cause I'm gonna kill his ass."

While Joi and Xavier made small talk, Reese thought about the comment Julian made. She wondered if he sabotaged her chance to get syndicated because he didn't want her to leave. When he came back to the table, she mentioned the lost presentation again. Of course, he denied any involvement in its mysterious disappearance. She didn't want to believe Julian would do something like that, but all the evidence was pointing in his direction.

Not wanting to waste another minute wondering if Julian did or didn't do it, Reese focused on Xavier.

"So handsome, you wanna have breakfast in the morning?" Reese asked, looking into Xavier's eyes.

"Absolutely!" he said, kissing her hand.

The waitress finally came with their food and as usual it was delicious. Julian was so occupied with watching what Reese and Xavier were doing that he didn't even eat. It was pure amusement to Joi. She kept looking at Julian, then laughing. This wasn't sitting too well with Julian who was not in the best of moods.

"So Reese said you're an investor," Julian said.

Xavier directed his attention to Julian and answered, "Yes, I am. What does your portfolio look like?"

"It was looking pretty good until I put my trust into this guy who was also an investor. You guys don't have a good reputation these days."

The comment sent steam through Reese. She knew exactly what Julian was insinuating. She started flipping on him but Xavier told her it was okay because what Julian said was a fair statement. There were a lot of investors who were taking money from their clients and using it for their own personal gain. He told her a perfect example of that was the case involving Joseph Blimline who was found guilty in a four hundred and eighty five million dollar oil and gas scheme. There were several other investors who have been found guilty of duping people out of their money using Ponzi schemes. Reese was still hot. She knew Julian was trying to disrespect Xavier on the down low and she wasn't having it so she gave him a dirty look."

"I see you know your stuff. Can I get one of your business cards?"

"Sure," Xavier said, reaching into his pocket and retrieving one.

"Hey, we better leave before we're late," Julian said, trying to get the attention off of himself.

He got the waitress' attention and asked for their check. She returned minutes later with it and placed it on the table. Xavier immediately leaned across the table and grabbed the ticket before Julian could get to it.

"I'll take care of that," Julian announced proudly.

"Nah, I got it!"

Xavier reached in his wallet, took out his Black Visa card and placed it and the ticket strategically in front of Julian.

Reese gave Julian a look like 'now what' as she kissed her man on the lips, thanking him. *Maybe now he'll get the message and leave me the fuck alone.*

Julian found this move to be a blatant attempt to embarrass him. He made a mental note to make sure Xavier didn't do it again. He was so upset he pushed his chair away from the table and left without saying anything. Joi and Reese were used to him acting up but this was a real bitch move. When he acted like that, they would just ignore him. Reacting to him would just be like feeding into his

Bitter by DANETTE MAJETTE

childishness.

As Joi reapplied her lip gloss, Reese and Xavier said their goodbyes. The smile on Reese's face was something Joi hadn't seen since she was married to Eric. Her friend was finally back to her old self. Joi stuck her Mac Spite colored lip gloss back in her purse and slid on her Fendi specs.

"Let's roll," she said, heading to the door, near her girl.

As they were all leaving, a man walked up to Xavier and gave him a manly hug.

"Hey, dude. How you doing?" the man asked.

"I'm doing good," Xavier answered nervously. The look on his face showed that he hadn't expected to see him, nor did he want to hold a conversation. "Good seeing you," Xavier added, trying to brush past, leaving Reese and Joi behind.

"Xavier, are you going to introduce us?" Reese stood in place with her hands on her hips.

Instead of introducing himself, the gentleman now looked at both Reese and Xavier strangely. Something just wasn't right, but it didn't seem as if Xavier was willing to explain.

"What shift are you on now?" the gentleman yelled out to Xavier over the loud talking crowd near the door.

"I'm actually still out on leave."

Reese's brows crinkled. Shift? What shift? She looked at Joi who shrugged her shoulders and gave that look that said, something is up. Reese remained in place waiting for Xavier to introduce her but he never did. Instead, he cut his conversation short with the guy and rushed her out of the restaurant, grabbing her by the arm. When they got to the car, Reese asked him who the guy was and what he was talking about.

"Oh! That was just a guy I used to work with a long time ago. I got hurt so I left. I didn't feel like going into details with him, that's all."

"Okay," she said with raised eye brows. "If you say so."

He quickly opened the passenger door to Joi's car. "You better hurry up before you're late. I'll call you later."

He got one more kiss in before the ladies drove off, headed to work for the night.

ℬitter by DANETTE MAJETTE

• • • • • • • • • • • • • • • • • • •

With only thirty minutes before they went on the air the girls hopped off the elevator at the station and went straight to the booth. Julian was there looking like someone had stolen his lunch money. Once again, the girls ignored him. To break the ice, he asked Reese how is it she is supposed to be such a man hater when she was dating one.

"Not that it's any of your damn business, but our relationship is in the trial stage. I might just hate his ass next week. You never know!"

"You don't have to get so defensive."

"I'm not being defensive. I'm losing my patience with your ass! You keep making all these little slick comments and I'm sick of it. My life is my life. Just worry about yourself from now on."

"Okay, calm down."

For the rest of the night, Julian sat behind his desk looking at some old station party pictures he and Reese had taken. He took his hand and rubbed it across her face and smiled. Then he began to get angry when he pictured Xavier with his hands all over her. He closed his eyes tightly as a pain rushed through his heart. He was getting tired of hiding his love for her, trapped deep inside but she could never know how he really felt. *What does he have that I don't? He can't love you half as much as I do,* he thought as he looked at a picture of her. He looked at a couple more pictures until he got to the one of Reese by herself wearing a tight little black dress. Her makeup made her skin look flawless, and her black strapped shoes made her ass sit up even higher. He gently kissed the picture and mouthed the words, "I love you."

It was a typical night on the show. People calling in ranting and raving because they didn't agree with what Reese and Joi had to say about relationships and particularly no good men. Then there were their loyal listeners who called in and supported them.

Joi was taking the lead tonight so the topic of the night was, "Why do people hate on you?"

"Caller, what's your name?"

"My name is JaKeith."

"JaKeith, why do you think people hate?" Reese asked.

"It's simple. Haters gon' hate."

They went to the next caller, who's name was Felicia. "I think it's because they need to bring down other people so they can bring themselves up."

"I agree with you. Jealousy is an ugly trait," Joi said.

One woman called in but she didn't want to give her name.

"Damn! Who you hiding from?" Joi said laughing.

"Nobody."

"Okay, nobody. Why do people hate?" Reese said teasing the woman.

"Because they are miserable and want to make others miserable."

"That's so true. Well, all of you out there hating on Joi and myself, you're only making us famous. So hate on!"

The girls took one last call.

"Caller, what's your name and why do you think people hate on you?" Reese asked.

"My name is Melanie. I think women hate because they're bitter bitches!"

Reese almost lost her mind. She couldn't believe Eric's little whore would have the audacity to call into her show and talk shit.

"Oh is that so, Melanie," Reese said, about to jump in her shit.

"Yes, it is! They can't keep their husbands satisfied anymore. So when they leave them for someone younger, more vibrant, and let's just say a little freakier in bed they can't handle it. Then they really get bitter when their children like us because we're more fun to be around."

"Well yes, Melanie, we're bitter and ya'll are whores!" Reese yelled to the top of her lungs. She stood up and banged her fist on the wooden booth. Immediately, the guy working the sound board knew trouble was coming.

"Well, that's what men like as long as we're whores for them!"

Joi saw the look in Reese's eyes that she had seen all too many times. She knew things were about to get ugly so she took her headset off and said, "Don't lose your job over this tramp. She ain't worth it."

When Reese kept going back and forth with Melanie, Joi took matters into her own hands by disconnecting Melanie's call. She then apologized to the listener's saying it was a technical glitch.

At the conclusion of the show, Reese threw her headset down.

"Can you believe that bitch?" Reese yelled.

"Girl, don't let her get to you. This is exactly what she wants. You got you a new man now and that's all that matters."

"You're right. Let's go to my office. I want to run some things by you."

"Alright," Joi said.

Walking out of the booth towards her office, Reese made a mental note to smack the shit out of Melanie the next time she saw her. Melanie disrespected her on the radio and all of Dallas heard it. There was no way Reese was about to let her get away with that.

When they got to Reese's office, the first thing Joi wanted to know was if she thought the scene at the restaurant with Xavier was odd. Joi positioned herself on the couch in Reese's office waiting for her response.

"Kinda, sorta," Reese said, taking a seat behind her desk. "Maybe the guy was just someone from his past that he doesn't like anymore."

"Umm...hmm...maybe. But enough small talk. How is he in bed?" Joi asked, sitting on the edge of the couch.

"Girl, I don't kiss and tell. I will tell you this though, I think he's a keeper."

"Oh shit!"

"How are things on your home front?" Reese asked.

"That bastard is still crazy as hell."

𝓑itter by DANETTE MAJETTE

"I still think you should've pressed charges against him for hitting you last week."

"I know, but what good would it have done. He would've been out before they served dinner," Joi said, sitting back on the couch. "I just want to let you know that if anything happens to me, he did it."

"Girl, don't talk like that."

"No, Reese, seriously. I think he might kill me. He's been so volatile and aggressive lately. He told me the other night he should get someone to murder my ass."

"What?" Reese got up from her seat. "Joi, this is serious. Look, how many times a day do we tell women to leave their abusive boyfriends and husbands?"

"You're right and I'm going to. I'm looking for my own place now."

"Come stay with me. Sydney's gone and I would love to have you there."

"Girl, you got a man now, and the last thing you need is a roommate."

"Joi, you're my best friend. I would never put a man before you."

"I know. If I don't find something by the end of the week, I'll consider your invitation."

There was a soft knock at the door interrupting them.

"Come in," Reese yelled.

Julian stuck his head his through the door.

"Can I come in?" he asked.

"Do we have a choice?" Joi said, rolling her eyes.

"What in the world would I do without your sense of humor?" he said, being snide. "I just wanted to apologize for earlier. I'm happy for you, but just be careful. He looks a little suspicious to me?"

"Boy, you want to get in her pants so everybody is gonna look suspicious to you."

Reese laughed and said, "I agree Julian! But I do accept the apology. Now leave!" she shouted, then picked up her cell to call Xavier.

Bitter by DANETTE MAJETTE

Chapter 19

It had been a good day for Reese. It was Friday and she was ready to enjoy her weekend. She and Xavier had dinner and then went to her house for a quickie. Amazingly, their love making was better every time they got together. They were attracted to one another not only physically but also mentally. She wanted to shout it to the world that she was in love but that's not what her fans wanted to hear. They loved the man eating Reese. It was kind of like how people felt about Mary J. Blige. When she was in pain she made some of her best music. Now that she was in love, no one wanted to hear anything she had to say.

So for now, Reese had to hold her tongue until she got another shot at getting her show syndicated. After that, she could tell the world that she was madly in love with Xavier.

Once Xavier left, Reese took a shower, got dressed and went to work. When she got there she didn't see Joi's car so she figured she must've been running late. She checked with the receptionist to see if Joi had called but she told her no. An uneasy feeling came over her, but it was still fifteen minutes before they went on air.

Reese started to get a little worried when Joi still wasn't there when the show was about to start. She couldn't just cancel the show so she went on the air by herself. All through the show, her mind was preoccupied, wondering what the hell happened to Joi. She kept texting her throughout, but never got a response.

The show seemed dryer than usual until one of the last callers called in asking if it was okay to cheat because his wife didn't know how to give a blowjob. Reese got annoyed and called the person all kinds of names. Soon, the show was about to end when the very last caller of the night asked where Joi was.

"She's a little under the weather, but she'll be back tomorrow."

"I hope she feels better," the caller said.

"Thank you, sweetie. That's it for tonight. Make sure y'all tune in tomorrow night because we're gonna be talking to Porn Star, Derrick Black. Apparently he's got thirteen inches below the waist and I can't wait to talk about it. Goodnight and God bless!"

Placing her headphones on the table, Reese immediately looked at her cell phone. It was so unlike Joi not to call her. She got up and jetted to Julian's office. As she walked pass several employees of the station she checked with them to see if maybe Joi called while she was on the air, but no one had heard from her. When she got to Julian's office she didn't bother knocking, she just walked in.

"Hey, did Joi call?"

"No, she didn't call you?" he asked, after sipping on his coffee.

Julian was really testing Reese's patience.

"If she had called me I wouldn't be in here asking your dumb ass," she said, pissed that he asked her such a stupid question.

She turned and left, slamming the door behind her. When she left Julian threw his coffee cup at the door. *That's your last time disrespecting me!* He thought.

Worried, Reese rushed to her car and headed to Joi's. Even if she couldn't get in touch with Reese, she would've at least called someone at the station. Something was definitely wrong and the first thing that came to Reese's mind was maybe she had gotten into it with Lavar.

When Reese arrived at Joi's condo she noticed her car was

still in her assigned parking spot. Pulling into a visitor spot, she looked around to see if Lavar's car was around but it wasn't. She hopped out and started towards the front door where she was immediately greeted by the doorman.

"Hello, Ms. Kennedy," he said with a smile.

"Hi, Bashi. Have you seen Joi today?"

"No ma'am, not since yesterday. She usually comes in around this time."

"I know but she didn't show up for work and no one has heard from her. I'm gonna just go in and check to see if she's sick or something."

"Okay. Well let me know because that doesn't sound like her."

Bashi had worked at Joi's condo since she moved there. He worked the eleven to seven shifts so he knew when she came in and out on her work nights. Reese rang the doorbell three times. When there was no response, she used the spare key Joi gave her in case of an emergency. She stuck her key in the door and unlocked it. She cracked it slightly and called out Joi's name. There was no answer so she walked in.

When she walked a little further into the condo she saw overturned furniture, broken glass, and blood everywhere. Icy chills rushed up her spine. She stood motionless. When she looked out the corner of her eye, she saw Joi sprawled out in a pool of blood—at least what was left of her.

"Oh my God! Oh no, oh no, oh no," Reese kept repeating, taking backward steps toward the wall. "Not Joi…nooooooooooo!" she cried out.

Joi's hair covered her face but Reese still knew it was her. She looked away quickly, trying not to take in the image she had already caught a glimpse of. The image was there, though and she couldn't get it out of her head.

Horrified, she ran out crying and screaming. "Somebody help me! Pleaseeeee, somebody!"

A few of Joi's neighbors came to their doors. They knew something was horribly wrong when they saw Reese hysterically running away from the condo. She ran around the corner to the front door and told Bashi to call the police. He did what she said as he tried to hold her up. She was so distraught she could barely stand on her own two feet. He sat her down in a chair then went to Joi's condo. When he opened the door, he smelt the scent of death. He knelt down by her body and checked her pulse. It was too late for paramedics. She was already dead.

Bashi got up and went back to the front to check on Reese who was in a state of shock. He tried to comfort her, but she was grief-stricken and her nerves were shot to hell.

By the time the police and homicide detectives got there, Reese was so out of it she barely remembered her name. Her eyes were red and her mascara was smudged. They had two officers stay with Reese while the others went into the condo to start their investigation.

A few of the officers who had been in the condo started to talk amongst themselves.

"Hey, doesn't this kind of remind you of that cop's wife's death," one of the officers whispered.

"Oh yeah! She was shot in the head and her throat was slashed, too."

"I wonder if it's a serial killer?"

"Could be."

They stopped talking when Reese turned her head sharply and gave them a curious look.

After being in the condo, a female detective came back out to the front to ask Reese a couple of questions.

"Ma'am, first of all I want to give you my sincerest condolences."

"Thank you," she said softly.

"What made you come over this early in the morning?"

"She didn't show up for work," she said sobbing.

The ringing of her phone made her jump. She took a deep breath and tried to compose herself before answering it.

"Hello."

"Hey, did you find Joi?" Julian asked.

"Yes." She broke down again. "I'm here at Joi's condo now. She-she-she-she's deaaaaad, Julian!"

*B*itter by DANETTE MAJETTE

You could hear Julian gasp before he spoke. "Are you alright?"

"No! My best friend is gone."

"I'm sorry. I'm on my way."

Reese pressed end and immediately phoned Xavier to tell him the bad news.

He responded just as expected. "I can't believe this. Where are you now?" he said in a fatherly tone.

"I'm at her condo right now but they want to question me at the police station."

Xavier could hear the pain in Reese's voice.

"I'll meet you at the condo."

"Thanks!"

When Xavier pulled up, he immediately rushed to Reese's side. Wearing black sweats and a baseball cap pulled down over his eyes he held her in his arms.

"Baby, are you okay?"

"Yeah…I just can't believe this is happening. She was just lying there with blood all over her."

"That had to be horrible for you," Xavier said.

"It's not something I'll ever forget."

Xavier hugged her tightly. As he was embracing her, she looked through the revolving doors and saw Lavar standing off by himself; he looked devastated. But everything in Reese told her he had something to do with it. Joi had just told her days before that she was scared of him and that he had been acting really crazy. Not only that, he had threatened her in front of the whole station the week before.

She broke away from Xavier and ran over to Lavar and smacked him in the face.

Xavier stood back making sure he didn't go near Lavar, but the officers quickly grabbed her and tried to pull her away from him.

"I know you did this. Your ass is gonna pay, you hear me," she said, taking large, fearful steps away from him. Xavier pulled her in a bear hug and told her calm down. "No! I'm not gonna calm down until they put some cuffs on his ass."

ℬitter by **DANETTE MAJETTE**

"Look, I didn't have nothin' to do wit dis," he yelled. "I'm fucked up ova dis shit too and you gonna come ova here wit dat bullshit." He stood so close to her she could feel his breath on her neck. "I loved her!" he yelled. "You not gonna blame dis shit on me, bitch!" He grabbed his head, kneeled down and started crying. "I'm gonna find out who did do it, though. I promise you dat!"

"Sweetie, listen to me!" Xavier held her face cupped in his hands. "I know you're upset but you can't go around making accusations. Let the police do their job. They'll find out who did this." He kissed her on the forehead. "I promise you they will find the person."

After taking several deep breaths, Reese finally calmed down. She was still upset but she didn't want to make matters worse.

A few minutes later, Julian arrived. You could tell he was distraught as well. He walked up to Reese and hugged her.

"I'm sorry it took me so long. I had to handle things at the station. When something like this happens, news travels fast so I just needed to brief everyone on how to handle any calls we're going to get. Everyone is in shock."

The lead detective on the case finally walked over and asked Reese and Lavar if they could come down to the station to answer some questions. They both agreed.

"Why don't you let Julian take you down to the station and I'll stay here and see if I can find out something," Xavier suggested.

Xavier began walking Reese to Julian's car, when the coroner's office wheeled Joi's body out in a black bag. Reese pushed Xavier out of the way, ran over and attempted to grab Joi's lifeless body. Xavier and Julian tried to hold her back, but she fought them with every ounce of strength she had left.

"Can she have a moment with her please?" Xavier asked.

When the coroners stepped to the side, Reese wrapped her arms around the black bag and cried. Xavier walked over and told her they needed to take Joi to the crime lab so they could find the evidence they need to catch her killer.

"C'mon, baby it's gonna be okay."

Although she was hurting, she knew the only way they would find out who killed Joi is to let them do their job. She backed away and went with Julian to his car so they could go down to the station. She was going to make sure they knew that Joi's murder had Lavar written all over it.

Xavier snooped around as the CSI team combed every inch of Joi's condo. He talked freely to the officers and lab specialist on scene for any information they would give. They found no forced entry so she had to have known her killer. Her throat was slit and she had been shot in the head at close range. There was no exit wound so the bullet was somewhere still in her skull. This would help forensics determine the type of gun used. As for what was used to cut her throat, they guessed it was some kind of hunting knife. No murder was perfect so the only question now was who and why did the person kill her.

Bitter by DANETTE MAJETTE

Chapter 20

It was well after six a.m. when the CSI team finally completed its investigation. By this time, Reese and Lavar were both sitting in separate interrogation rooms awaiting the detective to come in and interview them. In deep thought, Reese was still trying to figure out how she was going to go on in life without Joi. They were supposed to grow old together, but that wasn't going to happen now. At least she didn't have to break the bad news to Joi's parents. The police were at their home giving them the news. She really wanted it to come from her but with them needing to question her, she was afraid they would hear it on the news before she could tell them. Lavar on the other hand was worried they were going to suspect him of killing her after Reese's outburst at the scene.

With Julian holding her hand, Reese's head fell on the table as she wept. Julian looked at her. He had no idea how she was going to bounce back from the loss of Joi. He couldn't bring her back so all he could do for Reese was be there for her.

When the detective walked in Reese sat up. He was a balding middle aged man who had apparently eaten too many donuts.

"Hi. I'm Detective Hart. Can I get you something?" he asked nicely.

"No thanks." Reese wiped away her falling tears.

The detective pulled out his legal pad as he asked Julian to

*B*itter by DANETTE MAJETTE

step outside. Once the door closed, he began to write. He wanted to make sure he reviewed all the other details that he'd gathered thus far. Little did Reese know, that back at Joi's, Xavier had given the officers even more information. Hart needed to get on the case quickly because the first forty-eight hours were crucial to the investigation.

"When was the last time you saw your friend?" he said, looking over the rim of his glasses.

"The last time I saw her was at work Thursday night. We were at work from ten until two a.m."

"Is that the shift she usually worked?"

"Yes, Monday through Friday."

"Did you notice anything different about her that night?"

"No."

"Can you think of anyone who might want to hurt Joi?" Detective Hart asked.

"Well, a lot of men don't like our radio show, but I know who killed her. I'm sure of it! It was Lavar!" she shouted angrily.

She told him about the conversation they had about how crazy Lavar was acting and how Joi was scared he might try and do something to her.

"Ummm…" he mumbled as he wrote across the tablet. "What was their relationship like?"

"They argued all the time."

He scribbled a few words again then abruptly stood up. "Stay here for a few minutes while I go over to the other interrogation room."

●●●●●●●●●●●●●●●●●●●●

In the interrogation room across the hall from Reese, Lavar was being questioned by Detective Grant. He had been on the force for twenty years and a homicide detective for ten. The Dallas Police were very familiar with Lavar and his associates. They were as slick as they come. They would get arrested one day and be out the next. They didn't have a lot of physical evidence so they needed Lavar to slip up. The only way that was going to happen was to use a pro like Detective Hart, who was now ready to assist Grant.

"Mr. Knight, I'm Detective Hart. "I'm sure Detective Grant has already asked you some questions, but I have a few more."

"Yeah. Go 'head 'cause I'm getting' sick of dis shit already."

He started off by questioning Lavar about their fight and his threatening Joi at the station days before hoping to strike a nerve.

Lavar sat up tall in his chair. "Man, she had said on national radio dat she was cheatin' on me. Of course, I got upset but I was jus talkin' shit."

"And what about you pulling a gun out on her and…let's see." He looked at his notes. "Her producer… Julian Michaels."

"I ain't neva pull no gun out on dem. Somebody lyin' and I know it's dat bitch, Reese."

"No, actually, Mr. Micheals confirmed the story earlier."

"Dat's cuz she told him to say dat shit."

The detective looked at Lavar for a moment.

"I take it you don't care for Ms. Kennedy that much."

"Hell naw! I can't stand dat chick. She was always talkin' shit and tryin' to come tween me and Joi. You ask anybody in Dallas and they'll tell you she jus hate men period." He stopped to catch his face in the palm of his hands. Lavar was either putting up a good front or he was truly upset.

"How does she hate men when she has a boyfriend?" the detective said, tapping his pen on his notepad.

Lavar laughed slightly.

"Cause she's a fake! She's a maneater," he admitted with frustration.

Both detectives began firing questions off to Lavar. A murder like this in such a nice neighborhood was going to be the lead story in the news that morning so the police needed to have a suspect in custody to calm the fears of the community. They were hoping Lavar was their man.

"Where were you tonight around eight tonight?"

"I was at da gym from seven till bout nine. They got security cameras; jus go ask'em to let you see da tapes from last night."

The detective listened attentively, hoping he would have some inconsistency in his story, but there was none. If Lavar was lying, he was doing a good job at it. Hart wondered if he was questioning the right person. Lavar had motive, but without some kind of physical evidence tying him to the murder, they couldn't charge him with anything.

The Detective could see he was getting nowhere questioning Lavar. He could also tell by Lavar's attitude that he resented being brought in for questioning after he had just lost his girlfriend. Of course, it was possible Lavar was telling the truth and someone was setting him up. Detective Hart stopped the questioning when someone knocked on the interrogation room door. He stepped into the hall.

"Did his alibi check out?"

"Yeah, they said he was there the whole time," the officer said.

After having his alibi check out they had to let Lavar go. Detective Hart told him he was free to go but for him not to leave town.

"I told you I didn't kill her," he spat. "Stupid ass pigs holdin' me when her killa still out there. Find my girl's killer!" he shouted."

As Lavar was leaving so was Reese. He glared at her, but didn't say a word. The look he gave scared her a little. She wondered if she was next on his list.

• •

During the drive home Reese couldn't stop crying. The image of Joi's body wouldn't escape her mind. She'd come to grips with the fact that she wouldn't be seeing her friend ever again. By the time they got to Reese's house Xavier was there. Julian helped her out of the car but she could barely walk on her own. Julian was able to get her to the door. Then Xavier came over to handle things.

"I got it from here, man. Thanks."

Julian didn't respond. He simply turned back toward the

Bitter by DANETTE MAJETTE

car. Julian was a little miffed by the way Xavier was treating him. But this wasn't the time for a confrontation. They had just lost their friend and they were going to need everyone's help to get through it.

"Xavier picked Reese up and carried her to her bedroom. You want me to stay with you," he asked after he placed her gently on the bed.

"Yes. I don't wanna be alone. I'm scared."

"There's nothing to be scared of. I'm right here," he said, as he laid next to her and held her tight.

"I wish I could go to sleep and wake up and find this was all a crazy dream."

"I know you do. It's not gonna be easy but you will get through this and I'll be here for you day and night until that happens."

"Thank you. I don't know what I would do without you."

"And you never have to find out."

She fluffed her pillow, curled up in the fetal position and cried herself to sleep.

Bitter by DANETTE MAJETTE

Chapter 21

Days later, Reese found herself struggling to find the perfect outfit to wear to her best friend's funeral. She had already changed a dozen times. Yet, she couldn't seem to get it together because she was still in shock that her dear friend was gone. It all seemed so surreal. She was going through her closet when she came across a black Dana Buchman dress that Joi bought her for Christmas one year. Instantly, she started crying again. Horrendously.

The grief was unbearable. What was even more heart wrenching was helping Joi's parents plan the funeral. They chose the Golden Gate funeral home which was a very popular funeral home in the Dallas area to handle the service. They also had Joi outfitted in a white dress from the White House, Black Market store.

Reese went into her bathroom filled a glass with cold water, sipped it slowly then took a seat on her bed. She blew her nose loudly, wiped her tears, and tried to put on a brave face when Sydney waltzed into her room to check on her.

"Ma, you okay?" she asked.

"Yes. I'm fine." She hugged her daughter tightly. "Thanks for coming home. I know you were just getting settled into college life and then this happened."

They both took a seat on Reese's bed.

𝓑itter by DANETTE MAJETTE

"Joi was like an auntie to me so I had to come home."

"She was...wasn't she?" She rubbed Sydney on the back.

Reese's mind traveled back in time to the day she had Sydney and how Joi was in the delivery room with her through the whole fourteen hours of labor holding her hands and telling her to breathe. She even cut the umbilical cord and named her Sydney.

Reese jolted back to reality. She looked at her watch.

"I gotta finish getting ready."

"Me too," Sydney said, as she got up and walked out of her mother's room.

Looking through her jewelry case to find the right accessories, Reese's phone started to ring. She picked it up and saw Xavier's name on the screen.

"Hi," she said, after hitting the talk button.

"Hey baby. How are you doing?"

"I'm doing as well as to be expected."

"Well just know I'm here for you as long as you need me to be."

Xavier never ceased to amaze Reese. Not only had he been there for her day and night. He even opened his home to some of Joi's family members who lived out of town. The rest stayed in nearby hotels and with Joi's parents.

Xavier and Reese talked a few more minutes before she told him she needed to be leaving the house within twenty minutes.

Once they were dressed, Reese and Sydney headed over to the Franklin's. As they were pulling up, they saw fans lined up along the street with 'Rest in Peace' signs. Reese never knew there were so many people who loved Joi just from hearing her on the radio. She knew the sight was a comfort to Joi's parents. When Reese and Sydney walked in the home Joi grew up in, you could barely get in.

There were so many of their friends and family members there consoling her parents. As soon as they saw Reese they immediately went over and gave her a big hug. You could tell they hadn't been able to sleep either. Reese couldn't even imagine what they were going through. They were about to bury their only child. That in itself was gut wrenching. Of course, that was nothing compared to what they were about to endure when the time came for them to say their final goodbyes. They were all going to have to lean on one another to get through this horrific day.

When the funeral home arrived with the family cars, they all congregated in the living room to pray before they left for the church. Joi's cousin, who was a devout Christian, led the prayer. When she finished, everyone was in tears including Xavier who had just walked through the door before they all held hands to pray. He went over and introduced himself to Joi's parents then came over to Reese and held her in his arms. She tried holding back her tears. She had no idea how she was going to get through this devastating loss.

"It's okay to cry. Go ahead and let it out. Your friend's life was cut short but look at the quality of her life, and she had you as a friend, so that's worth a lot. Your friend would not want you to grieve too much. She would want you to be happy. I also believe that when someone has truly touched you, they never really leave when they pass on, and you will see them again. I am sure of it."

Reese wanted to tell Xavier to take those dark shades off, but decided against it. Some men didn't like to showcase their emotions, she thought.

The funeral home representatives interrupted all conversation when they made a loud announcement about the cars. They then walked the Franklin's to the first family car. Joi's mother insisted Reese and Sydney ride with them. Reese turned to Xavier who told her to go ahead.

"I'll be right behind you," he said, kissing her on the cheek.

Sydney watched how her mother smiled at him. She had only spent a couple of days with Xavier but in her eyes he seemed to be a good guy and she was happy that her mother had finally found happiness again.

During the drive to the church, Mrs. Franklin took the opportunity to tell Reese how much she appreciated her for helping plan the service and for being such a good friend to her daughter.

"You know, Joi would say to me all the time that had it not been for you taking her under your wings she probably wouldn't have gotten her job at the station," Mr. Franklin said.

"Yes, she would've. She was a natural," Reese said, tearing up again. "I don't know what I'm going to do without her," she said breaking down. Reese apologized.

"Honey, you don't have to apologize. We understand exactly how you feel," Mrs. Franklin said, patting her on the leg. "I know it's going to take some time but we all have a common purpose and that's to get through this ordeal and move on in life. And with God's help we will. I know that's what my daughter would want."

Hundreds of people crowded into Friendship-West Baptist Church to mourn Joi's death. The mourners filled the congregation hall to capacity, overflowing into an adjacent room and onto the sidewalk. Balcony seats were shared by other mourners and media members, who dangled cameras and microphones over the railing. Her death had generated a lot of attention. Not only were the Franklins and Reese mourning Joi's death, the whole Dallas community was. She was a great radio personality and those who knew Joi's voice on the air waves, say it's her wit they would remember the most.

The Franklin family along with Reese, Xavier and Sydney filled several rows at the front of the church. Joi's mother sobbed throughout the service. At times she rested her head upon her husband's shoulder. When Julian saw Xavier sitting with Reese and Joi's family he was hot under the collar. *I should be comforting her, not you. I've got to get rid of you and I will. All I need is a little time to come up with a brilliant plan.*

The service was at times solemn, punctuated by organ music, a resounding choir and pledges of support for Joi's parents. The owners of the radio station were in the audience and were thanked publicly for paying for the funeral. Several people got up and spoke about how positive Joi was about everything and how she kept people laughing all the time.

Before the eulogy, Reese was asked to say a few words about her best friend so she pulled the piece of paper out of her purse, walked up to the podium, and began to read.

"I still can't believe Joi is gone. I miss my best friend. I miss her so much." She took a deep breath and tried to compose

Bitter by DANETTE MAJETTE

herself enough to get through what she had written. "She always walked around with a huge smile on her face and people just absolutely adored the ground that she walked on. She was always there for me whenever I needed her and I could talk to her about any and everything. I don't even know how I'm going to exist without her. We were always together at work and on our days off. We would even text each other like teenagers all day long." She paused then let out a little snicker. "She was there when I had my daughter and she was my maid of honor when I got married. Right now I just feel hollow without her. I keep thinking I'll wake up from this nightmare and she will be right there like she has been all these years. It just wasn't enough time."

Reese stopped as a tear fell. The moment she began speaking again everyone could tell that talking was becoming more difficult. A breakdown was near. "Women like Joi always leave a little piece of themselves in the people they touch through their integrity, their honesty, their selflessness, and their joy." Her voice began to tremble as the tears now flowed. "That's where I think many of us will find our solace in the days to come. Joi left a lot of herself for us, she'll be missed immensely. But her character will be with us, pushing us to be better, for the rest of our lives."

By the time she finished, she was a complete mess. Reese walked down from the podium and on her way back to her seat she almost passed out but Xavier was there to catch her. Julian looked on with resentment. He hated the way Reese had completely changed her tune where men were concerned, all because of him. *And why does he have on those shades inside the church. Who is he hiding from?* He was so caught up in ways to get Xavier out of Reese's life that he missed most of the service. He finally got refocused on why he was in church anyway, when he saw people jumping up and down in their seats praising the lord.

At the end of Dr. Hanes eulogy, Joi's mother stood and walked over to her daughter's white, lacquered casket and placed her hand on it gently. It was such a touching moment. She was then handed a microphone. She wiped the tears from her eyes and began to speak.

"I would like to first thank you all for your prayers and offers of condolence. My daughter was beautiful, intelligent, and was always thinking of others. She has gone on so her battle is over, maybe she is even the lucky one in a way, because life can be very hard sometimes, and she graduated early without most of the suffering we go through. We will all graduate from this life eventually. Until then search for her in your memories, and she will be there smiling and waving to you, and that shall remain for the rest of your days, as will all the people that pass on before you. The pain will subside in due course, but until then, just take one day at a time, one step at a time, one breath at a time, one heartbeat at a time."

When Mrs. Franklin finished there wasn't a dry eye in the room. As she was sitting down the choir began to sing Joi's favorite song "Total Praise." When they sang "You are the source of my strength…you are the strength of my life", Reese and the Franklins were inconsolable. Joi would always sing that one part over and over again when she was having a bad day and especially when she going through a rough patch.

As soon as they finished the first verse, Lavar walked in sobbing. Everyone was in disbelief that he actually showed up at the funeral. Especially since word on the street was he did it or had someone do it. There were rumors that Joi was trying to leave him and he wasn't about to let her go. Another rumor was she threatened to go to the Feds and tell them everything about his drug business. It was also a possibility that her death was in retaliation for Angelo's death.

In true flamboyant fashion, Lavar walked up to Joi's casket and placed a photo of them together on her casket. Mrs. Franklin was incensed and Reese was just floored. *You arrogant son of a bitch!* She looked up at the ceiling and asked God to forgive her for that thought. Although she didn't have any proof that Lavar had something to do with Joi's death, she had a strong hunch. Mr. Franklin stood on his feet and buttoned his suit jacket. Everyone was on pins and needles in anticipation of what was about to happen.

His wife pulled at the tail of his coat for him to sit back down.

"It's gonna be okay," he whispered in her ear before walking up to Lavar.

By the time Lavar turned around Mr. Franklin was standing right in front of him. The choir kept singing like nothing was wrong but everyone else was holding their breath. They just knew Joi's father was about to kick him out.

Then out of the blue, Mr. Franklin grabbed him up pretty roughly and gave him a bear hug as he pounded on Lavar's back. He leaned in close to Lavar's ear and said, "Don't worry she's in God's hands now. But if I find out you had something to do with her death you're going to be in my hands."

He snatched Lavar up by the arm, walked up to one of Joi's aunt who was sitting directly in front of Joi's casket and asked her to move over. Then he pushed Lavar down in the pew and gave him a stern look. Mrs. Franklin was well aware of that look, she looked over at Reese and nodded. She had been married to her husband for thirty years so there wasn't anything she didn't know about him.

He was a man of few words and he believed in God. Of course, if God took too long taking care of someone, Mr. Franklin was known to take care of them himself and then ask for forgiveness later. Mrs. Franklin looked at her husband and let out a slight smile because she knew what that look meant, "I'm too classy to act up at my daughter's funeral but if you were the one who hurt my little girl I'm coming after you, my friend."

There weren't too many things Lavar was scared of but the tone and the calm demeanor Mr. Franklin was displaying made him a little uneasy. There he was sitting right smack dab in front of Joi's casket with all eyes on him. He sweated so nervously that he had to loosen up his tie.

When the service was over, the pallbearers who were all Joi's cousins rolled her casket to the front door of the church so everyone could view her body one last time as they were leaving. Her parents were in the front of the line. Her mother and father both kissed her cheek one last time. Mrs. Franklin pulled a locket out of her purse that she planned on giving Joi on her wedding day. She would never see that day now so she placed it in the side of the casket. The Franklins walked hand and hand sobbing, back to the family car. Reese was next. She placed a little memento in the casket also. It was a picture of them the first day they met in college. Joi always loved that picture. She also gave her a kiss on the cheek. Everyone else followed. As soon as she walked out, Reese was surprised to see Eric standing there talking to Sydney. Especially since he and Joi didn't get along too well. She and Xavier walked up to him. Reese introduced them, then Xavier with his eyes locked on Eric, flexed his muscles.

"I'll meet you by the car." Xavier kissed her on the cheek then walked away.

"Okay baby," Reese said.

Eric was a little taken aback because he wasn't even aware that their relationship was that serious. Then again, why would he. They could barely stand to be in the same room together let alone talk to one another.

Eric cleared his throat.

"Hey. I just wanted to convey my sympathies in person," he said, slipping his arms around her.

Memories of the days when they used to be together filtered Reese's mind as she closed her eyes and pressed her face into his neck.

"Thanks."

"Ummm...if you need anything just call me. Day or night," he emphasized.

"And just how is Melanie going to feel about that?"

He seemed a little hesitant about telling her the latest news about Melanie but he felt inclined to let her know.

"After that little stunt she pulled calling your show, I broke things off with her for now. She has a little maturing to do." He paused, then gave Reese a lustful look that she hadn't seen from him in years. "And I need to do a lil soul searching, too."

Her face tightened when she thought about how heartbroken she was when Eric left her for Melanie. Now he was standing before her acting as if he still had feelings for her. She knew it was only a matter of time before Eric would see Melanie for what she really was. She wanted to rub it in his face and any other time

𝓑itter by DANETTE MAJETTE

Reese would've, but she was too upset to enjoy the moment.

"Well, all I can say is good fucking riddance!"

Eric was surprised. He was sure Reese would've been jumping for joy.

"Well I need to go," she said.

"I'll call you next week to check on you," he replied, giving her another long hug.

Not wanting to read too much into his actions, she said, "Okay," and walked away.

It was now time to go lay Joi's body to rest at the Laureland Memorial Cemetery. This was the moment Reese dreaded because she knew that's when all the sorrow of losing Joi would flare up again. Just as Reese was about to get in the car, her emotions got the best of her. Just seeing Lavar standing at her casket with those phony tears made her lose it. As soon as he went over to his black Tahoe truck and opened the door, Reese quickly walked over to him as he was about to get in. She closed the door refusing to let him get in until she had her say.

"I'm not going to rest until you're behind bars where you belong."

She didn't care if people were staring at her, she needed to get it off her chest and she did. Some people thought it was a little tacky for her to make a scene at her friend's funeral but there were some who admired her gumption to stand up and do what they really wanted to do.

Lavar threw his jacket across his shoulder, and pointed his finger so close in Reese's face he could've poke her in the eye.

"Bitch, I'm not gon tell yo' ass again, I didn't have nuffin to do wit dis shit. I got a ten thousand dollar reward for anyone who can tell me who did kill Joi. What da fuck you doin' beside hurlin' accusations at me? You keep it up dey gonna be buryin' yo' ass next."

Xavier walked over and snatched Reese away from Lavar. "Go to the car, baby." Reese did as Xavier told her. He waited until she was out of listening distance before he said, "I better not ever see you stick your finger in my woman's face again! Do we have an understanding?" he asked sternly.

Bitter by DANETTE MAJETTE

"Nigga, do you know who da fuck I am?"

"Yea, I know exactly who the hell you are? But you don't know who I am, or what I'm capable of!" Xavier gritted his teeth just as he always did when he got angry. "You think you're bad...well, I think I'm badder. You got guns...guess what, I do, too. You got people...so do I. Need I say more, or do you get the point."

Lavar laughed. "You funny, partna. Let's see if you still think you bad when you balled up in someone's trunk." He stopped, then paused. His eyes squinted for moments while he thought deeply. "Aye..don't I know you from somewhere?"

Xavier shrugged off his comment, but said something that surprised Lavar completely. "Let's see if you feel the same way if Edna's found balled up in a trunk."

Lavar's laughing came to a screeching halt. His jaw dropped and mouth fell open.

Xavier grinned wickedly. He turned to make sure Reese, or no one else was in listening distance. "See, you fuck with me or my woman and my people are gonna fuck with that lovely mother of yours. You know the one who likes to go to Bingo on Tuesdays, lunch with her sister Rita on Thursdays and go to Concord Missionary Baptist Church of Sundays."

Lavar just stood there like his whole world had just been rocked. He looked deep into Xavier's face just wishing he would remove the shades. Somehow, he felt like he knew him; especially now that he revealed information about his mother.

"Yeah, I thought so," Xavier continued, before walking away with extra swagger.

Lavar watched as Xavier walked to his Beemer a couple of cars in front of him. He immediately got on his cell phone to call his contact at the Dallas police department. The guy was out to lunch so he left him a message.

"Yeah this me, I need you to call me back ASAP. I got a big problem on my hands."

Lavar definitely underestimated Xavier. He didn't like being caught off guard, but somehow Xavier was able to do just that. Lavar didn't understand how and why Xavier had all that information on his mother but he was sure as hell going to find out. He threw his sport coat in the passenger's seat of his truck and slid on his Roberto Cavalli sunglasses. *Who da fuck is this dude?* He thought to himself as he peeled down the street.

Bitter by DANETTE MAJETTE

Chapter 22

Back to real life, Reese returned to work after the demise of her co-host, and best friend. Although she was still torn, the reality was the 'Girlfriends' show couldn't host itself. Five days had passed since the funeral, and the show was already suffering because of her absence so Reese was determined to get things back in order. When she walked into the station she was surprised to see a memorial on the wall in Joi's honor. Seeing the memorial made her want to do something special for her friend. So she decided she would set-up a broadcasting scholarship.

Walking into the studio and seeing Joi's empty chair caused tears to fall instantly. How could someone take the life of such a sweet person? How could they take the only true friend Reese had, away from her? Hurt and anger overcame her simultaneously.

Gone in the physical, but not spiritual, Reese decided without it being known to dedicate today's topic to Joi. She felt like she could not save her friend, but she would make it her business to save another woman's life.

Wiping her fallen tears, Reese pulled herself together. She cued the engineer to start rolling and the show began. With as much excitement as she could muster up, which was not any at all, she got the show rolling.

"Good evening beautiful people, I have been gone for a while due to the loss of my sidekick Joi. I would like to thank you

𝓑itter by DANETTE MAJETTE

all for the letters and emails, the radio station and her family greatly appreciated it. In honor of Joi, we have to keep the ball rolling because that is what she would want us to do. With that said, the topic of discussion today is Domestic Violence and When Enough is Enough: Ladies, when is it time to pull the plug from these relationships with these sorry ass men who find joy in our pain? The phone lines went crazy immediately.

"First caller, what's your name hun?"

"Hi Reese, I'd rather keep my name confidential."

The woman on the other end sounded helpless and afraid of something and this enraged Reese. It reminded her of the tone of Joi's voice as she spoke to her on so many occasions after many nights of getting into fights with Lavar. Reese begged Joi to press charges and get his nothing ass off the streets but Joi insisted that everything would be fine. Still, Reese didn't push the caller to reveal her identity.

"Okay, that's fine sweetheart, what's on your mind?"

"Well, first I want to say that this topic hits very close to home." She paused. "Sorry, this makes me so emotional, but I've been asking myself the exact same question for the last five years and have yet to find an answer. Not only physically, but I've been emotionally ripped to shreds and I don't know how to get away." The caller broke down and her sniffles could be heard on air. Reese felt her pain and the rage inside of her rose to another level.

"Take your time, honey."

"I apologize. But I need help Reese, please help me."

"It's fine sweetheart. There are many women going through the exact same thing as you. Only difference is, you have finally reached out for help, which means that you have realized that a problem is present."

She glanced over sadly at Joi's empty chair once more, now it was time for Reese to unleash her feelings about men and their abusive ways.

"The problem we women have is that we give too much to these trifling men and they feel like once we give them our hearts that they have the power to do as they please to us. First thing is first, the answer to the question is, enough is enough the first time the sorry bastard puts his hands on you! They may apologize and say it will never happen again, but it always happens again. Men are incapable of change! They feed us lies and bullshit to make us stay after the first blow. You need to get up and out of this relationship, darling. If it's the fact that you don't have the funds or anywhere to go, there are plenty of woman's shelters out there willing to help. Stay on the line, sweetie, we'll have someone give you an agency to call who'll help you. I thank you for calling…next caller."

"Hello, Ms. Reese."

The sound of a man's voice sent chills up Reese's spine and sent her blood from a normal body temperature to a boiling point. She hated men. All men as of now were the scum of the earth. But she knew she had to let the man speak though.

"Yes, sir," she answered through clinched teeth. "What are your thoughts on the topic today?"

She could really care less about what the bastard thought or felt.

"Well, I feel like you can never really answer this question unless you know both sides of the story in every abusive case."

This answer pissed Reese off. How dare he fix his lips to say that stupid shit?

"So, basically what you are saying…I didn't catch your name…"

"Steve."

"Okay, Steve, is there a time when domestic abuse is plausible?"

"That's exactly what I'm saying. Women these days are just as abusive as we men can be. Sometimes these bitches ask for it. They disrespectful… like a man is just supposed to sit back and take it. That's some bullshit! You know what I'm saying?"

"No, I don't!" Reese fired back!

"It's time we men stop sitting back and letting women verbally bash us."

Reese blew a fuse. "The reason you bastards get bashed on the regular is because you ain't shit! Prime example, you're telling me that you have the authority to put your hands on a woman because she's disrespectful? Man... shut the fuck up and walk away! Who died and made you all God? There is no excuse for a man to put his hands on a woman! I'm pretty sure anytime we get disrespectful to you all, is because you all sit up here and think you can run us into the ground. Ole' unappreciative asses! We need to start beating asses out here to show ya'll that we are not to be fucked with!"

"Somebody needs to smack your ass around and put you in your place, bitch!"

He disconnected the phone line just as Reese was about to lay into his ass some more. With frustration and pain, Reese signaled for a commercial break, slammed her headset down, and sobbed uncontrollably as she gripped Joi's empty chair. As of now, she did not feel like she could go on with the show. It hurt too much. And she was scared, too. Always a threat, one after another...and then there was the thought of Lavar and his threats floating in the back of her head.

● ● ● ● ● ● ● ● ● ● ● ● ● ● ● ● ● ● ● ●

The next morning, Reese was scared out of her sleep by the sound of her doorbell. She had not been able to sleep after the way the show ended yesterday so she decided to take a few shots to help her get to sleep. She was mad as hell because she had just gotten into a good sleep.

"Who is it?" she screamed at the door impatiently.

She was not in the mood for anybody else and their "sorries." Sorry was not going to bring Joi back.

"It's me Xavier! Baby, open the door."

Panicked, Reese rushed to hide her liquor bottle. She didn't want Xavier to know she had been drinking. She blew her breath in her hand to see if the scent of alcohol was still present. She popped a mint and opened the front door, slowly.

"Hey baby," she said, greeting her man with a kiss.

Xavier could tell Reese had been crying, her eyes were swollen and trails of tears were left on her cheeks. He embraced her and kissed her on her forehead. He knew how hard Joi's death had been

Bitter by DANETTE MAJETTE

on Reese and he wanted her to know that he was there for her.

"What brings you over so early?" Reese asked, not looking at Xavier this time.

"It's actually two o'clock in the afternoon. I was worried because I hadn't heard from you today and I heard how the show went last night."

She ran her hands over her face and through her hair as she let out a deep sigh.

"Yeah that wasn't fun at all. But things will get better with time," she said. "At least that's what I keep telling myself," she mumbled.

"It will, baby," Xavier told her, looking deep into her eyes and planting his hand on her thigh to reassure her. Xavier took a deep breath and stated, "Joi's death has made me realize some things."

"What's that?" Reese questioned, still looking down at her hands.

He placed his hand under her chin so that she could look him in the eyes.

"It's made me realize that life is short and we should take advantage of every moment that we are alive."

"Mmm, what are you saying Xavier?" Reese asked impatiently.

She did not get the point behind his statement. As of now, all she wanted to do was have a drink, crawl back into bed, and cry herself to sleep.

"What I'm saying Reese is that I am so in love with you. Your eyes brighten my day, your touch makes me weak, and your smile makes my heart smile. Reese, I love you so much."

Staring at Xavier blankly, she had not expected him to say that. He was everything she had asked for in a man. But it was simple; she was still not over what Eric had done to her. Besides, in her heart she knew she still had feelings for Eric. Men always appeared to be so perfect, and at the drop of a dime they changed into these monsters. Look at what happened to Joi, she told herself.

*B*itter by DANETTE MAJETTE

● ●

The month of October was moving faster than usual and Reese felt like she couldn't quite keep up. With the announcement that Xavier made days ago, it was clear to her that his feelings for her were steadfast. She could tell that her not saying she loved him back kind of hurt his feelings, but she just had too much on her mind to think about being in love.

They sat around the dinner table having a typical day to day conversation when the phone rang. It was the first day in the past week that Reese had decided to cut the ringer on. She wanted to shut the outside world off as she mourned the loss of her friend.

"Hello," Reese answered.

"Hey. How are you doing?" Eric said through the phone.

"I'm okay. Thanks for asking." Reese appreciated the fact that Eric called to check on her but she wasn't in the mood to talk to anyone.

"Do you need anything? I could come over and bring you some food if you like."

Why is he suddenly being so nice to me?

"Eric, what's going on? Last month you couldn't stand my ass. Now all of a sudden you want to bring me food and check up on me."

He was silent for a moment.

"I guess I'm realizing what I lost. And now I want to see if I can get back what we once had."

"After everything you put me through. Are you kidding me with this bullshit?"

"I know…I know. I think I was just going through something."

Reese was no fool. She knew the only reason Eric wanted to get back with her is because he saw how happy she and Xavier were. She told him he would come crawling back to her and he laughed in her face. Now look at him.

"You know? Actually, you don't know! You don't know

how many nights I cried myself to sleep. How I couldn't eat or even get out of the bed to go to work. How Sydney would cry and blame herself for you leaving us. I have a good man in my life now so don't come at me with that bullshit!"

"Reese, I'm sorry, but if you give me a chance I swear I'll make it up to you."

She cut him off.

"Look, you made your bed ...now lie in it! I have a wonderful man who loves me. Why would I risk that for your wishy washy ass?"

"You know in your heart that he's just a substitution for me."

"Those days are over sweetie. I've moved on to bigger and better things. Now why don't you do the same."

Xavier tried not to make his eavesdropping apparent, but when he heard Reese say that to Eric, he couldn't help but smile.

Furious, Reese slammed the phone down and went to the fridge to take a shot of Bourbon. Eric had gotten her nerves all riled up and she needed to relax. Forget about him. She needed to contact the police to see if they had any information on Joi's case because knowing that her killer was still on the loose was tearing her up.

Bitter by DANETTE MAJETTE

Chapter 23

The weather was beginning to be so unpredictable. It would be sunny one day and rainy the next. Reese's weekend was great but it was now time to go back to work. The sky was clear even though it called for rain for the next two days. Reese spent most of the day cleaning and now was getting ready for work. As she dressed she sipped on a glass of Pinot Grigio wine. Once she was dressed she went downstairs to her office to catch up on some bills. Since Joi's death they just hadn't been a priority.

With another three hours before she had to be at work, she sat behind her desk and shuffled through the piles of mail that hadn't been touched yet. "Bill…Bill…Bill," she said, placing the envelopes one by one to the side. Most of it was fan mail from work she had brought home. She wasn't strong enough to read them yet. Reese knew they were letters about how they missed Joi and how they were praying for her so she threw them in a box. One particular letter caught her attention. It was addressed with this very weird handwriting and no return address. She went into her drawer and grabbed her letter opener. When she opened the letter she was shocked at it contents.

__Bitch, you keep runnin round tellin lies on me they gon fin yo ass in a gabage bag cut up in lil pices. I only gon tell you dis one mo time think im playin try me__

Besides the horrible handwriting, she could tell from the

Bitter by DANETTE MAJETTE

obvious misspelling of words that it was Lavar's drop out ass. She was not about to give him the last word so she hopped in her car and went to work.

● ●

With paper and pen in hand, Julian sat behind his desk scribbling little pictures of a family. The mother was Reese. The father was himself and the baby was Julian Jr. This is what he wanted. What he desired. He was willing to do almost anything to make it happen. There was a dark side to Julian that no one knew or even cared about. He was just some nerdy man who tried to fit in some of the office cliques, but no one wanted him around.

He sat for minutes talking to the picture as if he expected it to talk back to him. The phone rang, jolting his attention from the picture.

"Yes, this is Julian," he said clearing his voice.

The caller told Julian that he had a visitor.

"Okay, I'll be right there," he said frustrated.

He slammed the receiver down and proceeded to leave. As soon as he opened the door he ran right into the visitor.

"What the hell are you doing here?" He looked out of the door to see if anyone noticed the man coming in. "I told you I would meet you later!"

The man who looked like he just walked in off the street told him that he was paid to do a job and he did it.

"I found out something very important. I just thought you might want to know right away."

"I'm quite sure it could've waited until later."

"Yeah, but I just thought I'd drop by anyway," he said, taking a seat on Julian's couch.

The scruffy looking white man with a potbelly hanging over sloppy jeans and a dirty shirt handed Julian a manila looking envelope. Julian ripped through the tape, pulled out its contents, and began to read.

"His name isn't Xavier?" Julian asked shocked.

"Nope!"

"I knew he was a fraud." He walked back over to his desk. "How did you get this?"

"Umm…it's best you not know that. I had to bend a few rules to get the information." the man said.

Julian looked at him with raised eyebrows. He knew he was taking a chance working with the man but he didn't have anyone else who would do what he needed done.

"I can't go to Reese with just this though. I need something more concrete. Did you find out his real name?"

"No. Not yet but things are coming along. I should know more in a few days. Of course, I need some more cash," he said, crossing his legs.

"I'm sure you do. I have to expose this guy like yesterday."

"Okay…well things will happen quicker if you just make sure I have what I need to do the job," he said, holding his hand out.

Julian reached in his back pocket and pulled out his wallet. He counted out five crisp hundred bills and handed it to him. The guy slipped the money in his pocket and started rambling on about something, but there was no time for all that. Julian motioned for him to get up.

"Now, get out of here before someone comes in here."

"It's not like anyone knows who I am."

"I don't care. Get out of here."

The guy got up and started towards the door. Julian told him to wait and let him make sure the coast was clear. He stuck his head out of the door. When he didn't see anyone he pushed the guy out the door. Just as he was trying to slip the guy out without anyone seeing him, Reese walked up.

"Hey," Julian said with his voice quivering nervously. "I thought you were on the air," he said, shaking off the surprise of her impromptu visit.

"Not yet. I still have a few minutes before I go on," she said with her eyes fixed on the man.

The first thing she noticed about him was the kind of shirt he had on. *Who the hell wears a Redskins shirt in Dallas?*

"Ohh…umm…okay. Well…I'll be right back I just need to

walk him to the elevator," Julian said, scratching the back of his head.

He pushed the guy down the hall and told Reese to go in. Reese watched as Julian walked down the hall towards the elevator. Every now and then he would turn around and look at her. *What is he up to,* she thought.

She went into his office, took a seat, and waited for him to return. She was standing over by his desk looking out the window when she saw Joi's face smiling at her. It took her back to times they all would be in Julian's office cutting up. They had so much fun back then but those days were over.

She waited a few more minutes then decided she would just talk to Julian later. As she turned to leave, she spotted the picture Julian had drawn.

"What the fuck?" she said. Reese picked the picture up off the desk and examined it. "He's really losing it!"

When she heard his voice in the hallway she quickly put the picture back on the desk and ran over to the leather couch in his office and took a seat. She knew he would be very embarrassed if he knew she had seen the picture.

"Hey Reese," Julian said, walking into the office. "What can I do for you?"

"Ummm...I came to ask you something but I forgot what it was." She looked at her watch. "Oh...I have to go," she said leaving.

She couldn't get out of there quick enough. Julian's weird behavior was definitely alarming to Reese and she wasn't sure what to do about it. If she confronted him he would deny it or lie, so she just left it alone.

When Reese got to the booth she took a quick sip of Vodka she had mixed in her bottle of Coke Cola. She was already a little tipsy but she needed something to take the edge off so she could get through tonight's show. *If Lavar thinks he scaring me he's dead wrong!* She thought as she waited for her cue to start the show. Not one to back down from a fight, she opened up her show commenting on the letter.

"Welcome to Girl Talk," she said slurring. "So, let me just

start off the show by asking you how many of you have been bullied or if you were or are a bully." She got closer to the mic. "It just so happens that I'm being bullied right now by a man who has no scruples and is a menace to society. He thinks he's going to scare me off the air, but that shit ain't gonna happen. Dallas, let me hear from you."

The phones started lighting up.

"Caller, what's your name and were you bullied or a bully?"

"This is Gary and I've been both."

"Both!" Reese replied.

"Yep. I used to get bullied a lot when I was young because I was small. I started eating a lot and pumping weights so by the time I got to high school I was pretty big. I started bullying the same dudes who used to bully me."

"Too too funny, Gary. Thanks for calling in."

The next caller had their radio up too loud.

"Look, you need to turn that shit down!"

The woman apologized and then cut it down before Reese got to her comment. When they did she asked her name.

"Hi, this is Lynn and I was bullied. I wore these thick glasses growing up and people would call me names and play little pranks on me. It really hurt and I think that's why I had problems with self-esteem."

"So, did you get them back?"

"I did in a way. I wear contacts now and I write books for a living. I have a Facebook page and a lot of the people who used to call me names send me friend requests. At first I wouldn't accept them but then I thought, let me see what he or she looks like now. Let's just say I got the last laugh because none of them are aging as gracefully as I am. I don't want to toot my own horn but I looks damn good at forty, Reese."

"That's what I'm talking about, girlfriend," Reese said. She pulled the letter out and looked at it. "I just want to say to my bully I know who you are. You're not fooling anyone and just know your days of walking the street a free man will be ending really soon."

Reese was about to take another call when the engineer

*B*itter by DANETTE MAJETTE

shut down the switchboard and told her the owner wanted to see her immediately.

"He couldn't wait until the muthafuckin' show was over?"

"I guess not," the engineer said looking confused.

"What the fuck is so important he got to interrupt my damn show?"

"I don't know. He didn't say."

Frustrated, she took her headset off and went down the hall to Mr. Andrews' office. When she walked in he was sitting behind his desk on his computer. He looked over the rims of his glasses and said, "Reese, we have a big problem."

He turned the computer monitor in her direction so she could see the leading story of the day. When she saw a picture of herself helping the little girl she almost ran over with the caption, *Radio Talk Show Host Almost Kills Young Girl While Drinking and Driving,* her heart dropped.

"This is all over the internet." He turned the monitor back around. "This is going to be on every news channel and gossip website and I can't ignore it. I told you your drinking was going to get you in a world of trouble."

"Mr. Andrews', I swear I wasn't drinking and driving that day. I was driving down the street and the little girl darted out in front of me."

"Well, there was a woman there who said you reeked of alcohol." He threw his eyeglasses on the desk. "I'm sorry but I'm going to have to let you go. We can't afford to get caught up in a scandal when were trying to get some of our shows syndicated."

"What do you mean you have to let me go?" She started getting angry and very agitated. "I'm getting fired over some bullshit ass amateur video!"

"Reese calm down."

"Don't tell me to calm down. I have the highest ratings here. Plus, I've given this station everything I got and you're telling me you have to let me go," she said, standing on her feet.

He felt sorry for Reese but he couldn't risk her going out and doing something to damage the reputation of a company he spent most of his life building. Terminating her was difficult for

Mr. Andrews even though the circumstances for his decision were right.

"I know that and I understand how you feel but I have no choice."

He tried to thank her for all her years of service and wished her well but she lost it before he could finish. Scared, Mr. Andrews called security.

"I ain't scared of them muthafuckas!" she said, ripping the phone out of the wall.

She took her hand and ran it across his desk sending everything flying all over the place and a cup of hot coffee in his lap. She then lifted the small desk and flung it on him. Some of the employees could here the commotion from the other side and stunned to hear Reese cursing and yelling like she was crazy. Minutes later, the door flew open.

"Reese! Stop it!" the security officer yelled trying to put her in a bear hug.

"Get your damn hands off of me," she screamed, as she kicked and fought them.

Mr. Andrews couldn't believe what he was seeing. He knew she wasn't going to take getting fired well, but he never imagined this kind of reaction from her.

"Get her out of here," he demanded.

Security did as they were told and escort her out of the office. They did however let her collect her belongings before they escorted her out of the building. While in her office they took all of her keys, computer pass cards, ID badge, corporate credit cards and anything else that had been previously assigned in order to access the building and its contents before she left.

When Mr. Andrew's assistant came in with towels to dry his pants off, he asked that she reassign the evening shows until he could hire a replacement to take over Reese's show.

As Reese was being led out by security, Julian was walking up.

"Hey what's going on?" he asked as they waited for the elevator.

"Mr. Andrews' bitch ass just fired me!"

"For what?"

"I don't even feel like talking about it right now. I'll call you later."

Julian was in shock. Then it hit him that he wouldn't be seeing Reese everyday like he had for the past couple of years. *Now what am I going to do?* He thought.

"Hey I'm really going to miss you around here." His tone was very somber. "First Joi...now you."

Reese grabbed his face and said, "I know!"

This was the moment Julian had been waiting on for years. He got so excited he kissed her right on the lips. Appalled, she yelled at him.

"I told your ass before it ain't that kind of party. I don't like you like that!"

Julian's feelings were deeply hurt and it showed through his stunned expression. When he looked around and saw several of their co-workers laughing at him he was embarrassed and angry. He couldn't believe how she had yelled at him causing a scene.

The elevator door opened and Reese got on. Julian turned and went to his office with his tail between his legs. He rushed to his office and slammed the door. Pacing the floor in his office, he cursed at himself for being so stupid. Now the whole office was going to be talking about how he kissed her and she blew him off. He tried to think of a way to spin the situation so he wouldn't look like a complete ass but there wasn't a way. He played his hand and loss.

He took a seat and palmed his face with his hands. Sliding his hands down his face he looked up and the first thing he saw was a picture of him, Reese, and Joi. He picked it up and threw it across the room at the wall.

"One of these days!"

• •

By the time Reese got home it was one thirty a.m. There was an accident right outside of the station that closed down one lane. She wasted no time getting out of her clothes when she got

*B*itter by DANETTE MAJETTE

into the house. Nor, did she waste anytime making a drink. She seemed to be drinking even more now that Joi wasn't there to stop her. She made a gin and tonic and sat at her dining room table on her laptop.

Clicking away on the keyboard, she looked up the amateur video that was shot of her almost hitting the little girl. She couldn't believe she was linked to a scandal. She couldn't believe the comments people were making either. They acted as though she ran the girl down in the middle of the street and left her for dead.

Sipping on her drink, she picked up her cell phone and dialed Xavier. The phone rang several times before Xavier finally picked up.

"Hey baby. How was your day?" he asked.

"It has been the day from hell!"

"Why, what happened?"

Hesitant about telling Xavier about Julian she just told him it was just a bad day for her. He kept pressing her specific details, so she told him the truth. Mostly, because she was fed up with Julian's fatal attraction behavior. Xavier was livid.

"Baby, I hate to say this but I think that man is very unstable."

"I can't believe he's acting like this. And he's getting worse," she said.

"I wouldn't be surprised if he's the one behind the letter, the lost presentation, and the phone call you said you got while you were taping the show."

"He was there when I got the phone call."

"Was he actually standing there?" Xavier asked.

"Come to think of it, he came in afterwards." She was silent for a while. "I don't think it's Julian. I think it's Lavar."

"They both have a beef with you so it could be either one of them. My money's on Julian. The more he scares you the more you'll have to be comforted and he's hoping that he can be the man to do that."

What Xavier said made sense but she still thought it was Lavar behind all the craziness.

"I also got fired today!"

Bitter by DANETTE MAJETTE

"What?"

She repeated herself and then went into the details of her termination.

"What are you going to do now?" he asked.

"I have no idea but right now I need some sleep."

Exhausted from the day's events, Reese told Xavier she would call him when she got up.

"Okay baby."

She hung up and then went and made herself a cup of tea to take up to her room. Reese was finding it hard to sleep that night. Between Julian's kiss, Joi's death, and her getting fired, her mind was on overload. She tossed and turned for three hours trying to drift off. Reluctantly, she got up and took the sleeping pills Xavier had left on her dresser. For the next fifteen minutes she stared at the ceiling, wide-awake. By the time she finally got to sleep, the street lights were going off.

Chapter 24

Passing time as she awaited Xavier's arrival, Reese sat at her dining room table flipping through the newspaper, reading the local news articles, not really processing them. When her cell phone rang she thought it was Xavier calling to cancel. Seeing the words 'private caller' irritated her. *Who the fuck is calling me from a blocked number?* She exhaled then answered the phone.

"You're gonna pay for ruining my relationship with Eric!" Melanie yelled.

Reese couldn't believe Melanie was being so brave.

"Bitch, you ruined your own relationship. So don't blame me!"

"No, it was you. You just kept poisoning Eric's mind."

"Look, you're a whore. I already knew it, now he does, too. Now call my phone again and I'm going to break your damn face when I see you!" Reese said.

She was so heated she had to take a shot of Vodka to calm down. She was not in the mood for Melanie's bullshit. Especially after losing her best friend and her dream job.

After getting into it with Melanie, Reese focused on Joi's murder. She felt if the police weren't going to get the evidence they needed to arrest Lavar she would. She was researching information on her laptop when she noticed a dark shadow go past the window. It was a man with a mask looking at her through her bay

𝓑itter by DANETTE MAJETTE

window. She thought she was seeing things at first. But when the figure moved, she hopped up out of her chair and turned the lights off. She stood up against the wall in a panic. She slowly leaned over to see if the figure was still there but it was gone. She was starting to think she had too much to drink until someone started jiggling the handle on her door. She was on the opposite side of the house and needed to get to her ADT alarm system so that she could call for help, but she was afraid if she ran past the window, the person would kick in the door and grab her before she could get to the alarm.

Reese needed to buy some time so she started yelling and screaming, "I have a gun! And I will not hesitate to shoot your ass!" at the top of her lungs.

When the person stopped messing with the door knob she ran over to alarm system. She was about to hit the panic button when she heard a man's voice.

"Reese, it's me!"

She quickly turned around. "Xavier, is that you?"

"Yes, open the door!"

Her nerves were so bad she could barely unlock the door. She flung it open and jumped into his arms. "There was man standing outside my window and then he tried to open the door."

"Baby, I didn't see anyone out there when I pulled up."

"Are you sure?"

"Yes, but I can go check if it would make you feel better."

"No…no. You don't have to do that." She closed the door and went over and poured a glass of gin straight. "I've been so tired lately maybe my mind is playing tricks on me."

Reese thought maybe her imagination was working overtime. But even with Xavier there with her now, she still couldn't shake the feeling that someone may have been watching her. *I wonder if it was Wayne,* she wondered.

"You've been through a lot lately, maybe you need to just get away for a little while."

"Maybe you're right," she said enjoying her drink.

Sliding his hands from her waist to the middle of her back he held her tight. He took a step back and told her how sexy she looked. It was nothing overly suggestive or clingy. It was just enough to show off her hourglass figure. His sinful grin made her body temperature rise.

"I'm feeling better already," she said.

"Just wait until we get back here tonight. I'm going to make you feel like you've died and gone to heaven."

Xavier was a good guy with a bad boy edge which made him even more attractive in Reese's eyes. Collecting her purse, Reese led the way to the door.

"So, where are we going tonight?"

"It's a surprise," Xavier responded.

"Thank God, I like surprises," she said, locking the door.

• •

When they got Downtown, Xavier found a spot on the street close to the restaurant. He got out of the car and went around to the passenger's side and opened the door for Reese. Dakota's Patio was one of the most romantic dining spots in Dallas. Reese always wanted to try Dakota's but she never got the chance.

The restaurant was decorated with a hand-cut Italian Carrera marble floor in a basket weave pattern, dark wood paneling, brown leather, marble trim and New Orleans style brass gas lamps. The large French doors allowed sunlight to stream through, giving the dining room warmth and light.

Once they were seated and had time to look over their menus they placed their orders. Reese decided to try something different so she ordered the Sea Scallops. Xavier had the Colorado Lamb Chop. They both had a glass of white wine.

There was very little conversation while they waited for their food. Reese was often staring off into space.

"Heeellloooo," Xavier said, waving his hand in front of her face.

She jumped. "I'm sorry baby. What did you say?"

"Are you alright?" Xavier asked, grabbing Reese's hand. "You seem a little distracted?"

"Yeah, I just keep thinking about earlier. I swear someone

was trying to get in my house. And then Melanie called and threatened me about Eric."

"Melanie?"

"Yeah. She blames me for Eric leaving her."

"Wow. That's crazy. Well I'm going to stay with you tonight just in case. If anything ever happened to you I would never be able to forgive myself."

"I really appreciate you being there for me these past few weeks?"

"You don't have to thank me. It's been my pleasure," he said, kissing her hand.

The server brought their food out to their table and the food looked as delectable as Reese had imagined.

In between bites, Xavier and Reese exchanged naughty looks with one another. Reese would pick up a scallop and eat it sensuously, exaggerating the motion of wrapping her full lips around the fork. Xavier reached over the table, "You got a little something right there," as he slowly ran his finger down the side of her mouth. Reese started to giggle. She looked up and noticed someone.

"Hey, that's the detective working on Joi's case. I see he got a young one, too," she said, shaking her head. "Come on let's go see if they have any new evidence."

"You go ahead. I need to use the men's room."

"I'll wait for you."

"No! You go ahead," he said, kissing her. Xavier headed to men's room as Reese made her way over to Detective Hart.

"Good evening, detective. I don't know if you remember me."

"I do. Ms. Kennedy, right?"

"Yes."

"This is my daughter Amelia."

"Hi," Reese said, shaking her hand. "Sorry for interrupting your evening, but I was wondering if you had any new evidence on my friend's case. I've been calling your department almost everyday. Someone took my information and assured me it would be given to the right person. But I haven't heard from anyone."

𝓑itter by DANETTE MAJETTE

"We've been swamped but there's no new information as of yet, I'm afraid. I'll be sure to let you know when we do. Lavar's alibi checked out so he's no longer a suspect. He's not our killer. It was someone else."

The hostess told the detective his table was ready so he told Reese to have a nice evening and walked off. Reese was pissed. He just left her standing there. He acted like he could care less about Joi's case.

Storming off, Reese met Xavier back at their table.

"What did he say?" Xavier asked.

"Nothing! It was like I was bugging him."

"Well, you kind of were. He's off duty."

"I guess," she said.

The romantic ambience was getting Reese and Xavier in the mood, so they finished up their meals. Dessert could wait until they got back to the house.

They stopped the waitress and asked for the check. They were waiting for her return when Reese's phone began buzzing. When she saw the 404 area code she knew it was someone from Atlanta. Anxious, she picked it up hoping it was Sydney. Reese had been trying to call her for several days and she hadn't answered her phone. She was disappointed and scared when she realized it was Sydney's roommate.

"Ms. Kennedy, this is Maya."

"Hi Maya. Have you talked to Sydney?"

"No ma'am. We have the same classes and she hasn't been to class either. I'm getting really worried. This isn't like her. She didn't even show up to our mandatory dorm meeting."

"Okay. I'm going to see if her step-father has heard from her. If he hasn't then I'm going to call the school tomorrow because this is not like her at all."

"I agree. I've tried to get some answers but they just keep brushing me off."

"Thanks, Maya. I'll take it from here. If you hear anything, let me know."

"I will."

By the time Reese got off the phone, Xavier had paid the

Bitter by DANETTE MAJETTE

check and was ready to take her home.

Walking quickly, Xavier and Reese talked about what she should do about Sydney. They were crossing the street to get to the car when a black truck came racing down the street towards them. It all happened so fast Reese's body just froze, but thanks to Xavier's quick reflexes he was able to grab her and move her out of the truck's path. The driver hit several cars before continuing down the business street filled with tourists and people out taking a walk. After making sure Reese was okay he jumped up to see if he could get the license plate number. The truck was too far down the street for him to see the plates. Distressed and out of breath, he helped Reese to her feet and pushed her hair out of her face.

"Are you guys okay?" a cop who just happened to be driving by asked.

"Yes, I'm fine. Xavier how about you? You fell pretty hard."

"I'm okay. You were my only concern."

Grabbing his radio, he called it in to the station to see if they could catch the driver on one of the cross streets.

"This is Unit 428. I just had a suspect attempt to run down a couple in front of Dakota's. Vehicle is a black SUV heading east bound on Akard Street."

Another squad car came up. The officers took their statements. There wasn't much to tell really. But it was just a precaution in the event they found the truck. One of the cop's who looked like he was fresh out of high school, asked Xavier if he was able to get the license plate. He told him he couldn't see it.

Reese was still shaken and her knees felt weak. She was angry more than anything. Her first thought was the driver must've been drunk, but Xavier told her that the truck was going straight until it came up on them, which leads him to believe that the driver was aiming for them.

The other cop asked her if she knew of anyone who would want to see her hurt. Reese laughed and said sarcastically, "Yeah…half of Dallas." The officers were trying to decide if Reese was serious or just kidding with them. She explained, "I used to be a radio talk show host so I had a lot of fans but most of them hated me. Earlier tonight my ex-husband's girlfriend called and threatened me and then there's my best friend's boyfriend who has it in for me. So, there's no telling who it was."

"Well, not liking someone is no reason to run them down," the younger officer said.

"I agree." Reese said, rubbing the dirt off of her dress.

Her knees were a little scraped but when she saw that her expensive dress was ripped she threw her hands up in the air out of frustration.

"What's wrong?" Xavier asked.

Reese was too ashamed to let him know she was pissed about her dress after he had risked his life for her. So she told him it was nothing. After getting Reese's information, the cops left. They told her if they came up with anything they would be giving her a call.

Wanting to get home, Reese and Xavier told the cop thank you for all his help.

"You sure you don't need an ambulance," the cop asked.

"No. I'm fine. I just want to go home."

Holding hands they walked across the street, headed to the car.

"You sure you alright," Xavier asked.

Reese smiled. It was nice to have someone concerned about how she felt again. "I'm sure."

• •

The only thing Reese could think of was getting a drink as soon she walked through the door.

"What a night?" she said, pouring the Patron in a shot glass. She threw it back. "You want one," she asked.

"No, I would rather have something else if you know what I mean."

"Okay, just let me call Eric to see if he's heard from Sydney, and I'll see what I can do about that."

Xavier was incensed, but he understood.

She quickly placed her call and when Eric answered the

*B*itter by DANETTE MAJETTE

phone she asked him about Sydney. When he told her he hadn't heard from Sydney in a while she became concerned because she always called him. They talked a few moments more then hung up.

"What did he say?" Xavier asked.

"He said he's sure she's okay. She probably just stayed out with some friends."

"Now you believe in Eric," he said firmly.

"Not really, but it makes sense."

"Okay," he said leaving it at that. "Well, let's go upstairs so I can help you relax," he said with a slight grin.

Her sheets were scattered about because she didn't feel like making her bed. She fell back onto the bed and watched as he yanked his shirt over his head. When he finished undressing, he started to undress her, mindful of her injuries. He grabbed his thoroughly erect dick and said, "Open your legs and let daddy in."

She parted her legs widely and waited for him to ease into her. As they kissed, he fondled her breasts and she ran her hands down his spine. She pulled him closer as he drove his hips in and out touching every hidden spot within her walls.

"Ooohhh…baby…harder!"

Although Xavier was pleasing her she couldn't get her mind off of Sydney. She had never gone this long without calling her or Eric. Even though she was trying to assure herself everything was fine she couldn't ignore that feeling in the pit of her stomach that something was terribly wrong. Xavier rocking his pelvis against hers so forcefully made her focus her attention back on their lovemaking. She grabbed his shoulders and picked up the rhythm he set. The speed and force of his thrusts made Reese cry out as an orgasmic spasm shook her body.

"Mmm…yeah…ooohh yeeaahhh…I'm coming," he yelled, as he pumped faster and harder.

It wasn't long before Xavier's dick wilted and slipped from her twat with a plop. When they finished, they laid there with their bodies intertwined, too tired to move. Reese was utterly satisfied emotionally and definitely physically.

Chapter 25

Sitting in a hotel room, Lavar was trying to figure out what his next move should be. He couldn't go back to the condo because they were renovating it and he'd just about had enough of the police dragging him down to the station every other day. It was hurting his business and a lot of his associates were shying away from him because of all the media press and the police tailing him. He was the bad guy even though he had an air-tight alibi.

Yes, he and Joi had their problems but he would never have killed her. He'd gotten several tips but they never led to anything. Most of them were people just trying to get their hands on the reward money.

Grabbing the receiver, Lavar dialed nine for an outside line, then his friend who worked at the police station. When the guy answered he started in on him.

"Yo! What da fuck you doin' man? When we met up, I told you how bad I need this info," Lavar yelled.

"Calm down, I been trying to get that for you."

"Don't tell me to calm da fuck down. I got da pigs on my every move and this nigga knows bout me, but I don't know bout him. Start talkin' muthafucka!"

"He's going by the name Xavier Miller. He's supposed to be some kind of investor. But that's all a lie. Xavier Miller no longer exists. He's dead."

Bitter by **DANETTE MAJETTE**

"Well, who the hell is this nigga?"

When his friend told him who Xavier really was Lavar started laughing hysterically.

"That dumb ass broad don't even know who she fuckin'. That's what she gets."

Now all Lavar had to do is find out why Xavier was impersonating someone else. He knew too much about Lavar and his family so it was obvious Xavier's plan had something to do with him also.

Lavar hung up before the guy could say anything else. He got dressed and went down to the restaurant for breakfast. He was just finishing up his eggs, bacon, pancakes, home fries, and grits when he got a call from someone claiming he had some information about who killed Joi. He took a gulp of his orange juice and sprinted out to his car.

●●●●●●●●●●●●●●●●●●●●●

Later that same day, Reese and Xavier met up at her house for lunch. She wasn't really in the mood to do anything because she still hadn't heard from Sydney. She checked with her cell phone carrier and found out that Sydney hadn't made any outgoing calls lately. She was really starting to panic now because her daughter stayed on the phone. If she wasn't talking, she was texting. So where was she?

When Xavier walked in, he could tell she was preoccupied. She was sitting at the kitchen table frantically calling Sydney's school and some of her friends.

"Still no word from Syd," he said, kissing her on the cheek.

"No. Something is definitely wrong."

"Baby, let's not jump to conclusions. Maybe she just went away for a little while."

"In the middle of her first semester? No she wouldn't do that."

She got up and poured herself a drink. "She would've called me and let me know she was going somewhere."

"Well, maybe she thought you wouldn't let her go, so she

went thinking she would be back before anyone noticed."

"Xavier, I know my daughter, she would never do anything like that without letting me know first," she said, sipping on her vodka.

"Baby, everything is going to be okay. She'll call soon."

"I don't know. I just have a bad feeling about this."

They continued to have small talk for awhile.

"So, what do you have planned today?" Xavier asked.

"As soon as I shower I'm getting dressed and going down to the police station. I want to know if they have any leads about Joi's death and I want to find out about filing a missing person's report."

"You're not going let this rest are you?"

"No! If it were me Joi would be at that police station everyday until they found my killer. I've been calling and they keep telling me there's no updates on her case. I still think Lavar had something to do with it. What the hell do they need to arrest him? He threatened her right in front of everyone at the station."

"I would go with you but I have to meet with a potential investor later today."

"I'll be fine. Don't worry."

"I just don't want you to get your hopes up."

"Too late."

Reese wasn't trying to hear what Xavier was saying. If it was the last thing she did she was going to make sure Lavar paid for what he did to her best friend.

Once Reese got into the shower, Xavier went down to the basement and watched television until Reese got dressed. When she was ready he walked her out to her car. As usual, Wayne was gawking at her from his window. She sucked her teeth and tried to ignore his deadly stare. *That dude has some serious issues!* She thought.

"I'll give you a call later tonight," Reese said, giving Xavier a smooch on the lips.

"I would like that. Remember what I said about not getting your hopes up. You don't want to keep going down there pressing them to make an arrest and end up messing up their case."

"Okay! Okay! I won't," she said as she got in her car.

Xavier got in his car and went home so he could get ready for his meeting.

On the way to the station, she called Sydney. When she still didn't pick up she started to cry. She knew her baby was in trouble and she needed to get to her. She called Eric and asked him what she should do. He told her that since she was already going to be at the station she needed to see how she could file a missing person report. Eric in the meantime was going to fly out to Atlanta to speak to someone at the college.

The police station was loud and crowded. They had just busted a gambling spot so almost every officer was booking someone. It was an election year and the Mayor promised the city he would crack down on crime. Reese was sure that would be the key to getting Joi's murder solved. She was trying to be patient with the police but if they didn't make an arrest soon she was going straight to the Mayor herself.

She walked up to the desk sergeant and asked to speak to Detective Hart. The sergeant picked up the phone and dialed Hart's extension.

"You have a woman here who needs to see you." The sergeant pulled the phone away from his ear. "What's your name, Ma'am?"

"Reese Kennedy."

He repeated Reese's name to detective Hart then hung up the phone and told Reese to have a seat.

"He'll be out shortly."

Reese spun around and took a seat. She sat her Valentino purse down in the chair next to her. She quickly picked it up and sat it in her lap when a guy who looked like he had just walked in off the street sat next to her purse. She didn't think he would be dumb enough to steal her purse in a police station, but then again it wouldn't surprise her if he tried. The recession was hitting everyone and even sane people were doing things they never thought they would do to make ends meet.

While Reese waited for Detective Hart she tried to call Sydney again but it went straight to voicemail. Her legs started to

Bitter by DANETTE MAJETTE

shake. She felt so helpless. It was driving her insane not knowing where her daughter was. Just as tears started to fall from her eyes, Detective walked out.

"Hello, Ms. Kennedy. Are you okay?" he asked, grabbing her hand.

"Yes…yes. I'm just having a rough day."

"Sorry I kept you waiting. I needed to finish up a report."

He asked her to follow him to his office near the rear of the station. After asking her if she wanted anything to drink he pulled out the file on Joi's case and opened it.

"Has there been any new evidence?" Reese asked.

"I'm afraid not."

"I'm telling you Lavar did it!"

"We checked out his alibi and it's air tight. So someone else must've done it. As I told you before we've cleared him as a suspect and a person of interest."

"No, it was him! I'm telling you! If he didn't do it himself he's sure as hell behind it. Look at this," she said, pulling the letter out of her purse. "He killed her and now he's stalking me. He's trying to shut me up, but it ain't gonna work."

"Ms. Kennedy, we can't just arrest him on hearsay. We need something that would stand up in court like an eye witness. Look, we were able to obtain the bullet from Miss Franklin's brain so we do know what kind of weapon was used. Trust me we're doing everything we can to solve this. Whoever did this covered their tracks very carefully." He sat back in his chair and closed the folder. "Do you think it was a fan or one of her friends?"

"I doubt it! Detective Hart, I know it was Lavar. He's a dope dealer so it wouldn't be hard for him to get someone to verify an alibi for him."

"Be that as it may. We need the weapon that was actually used in her murder if we're gonna tie him to it."

Detective Hart was well aware of Lavar's criminal activities. He just didn't understand what a woman like Joi was doing getting involved with him. Reese explained to him that whoever killed Joi was now after her. She told him about almost getting run over by a truck the same color as Lavar's and someone trying to

Bitter by DANETTE MAJETTE

break into her house.

"Can I get police protection?" Reese asked.

He told her he couldn't justify giving her round the clock protection but he would ask the officers to keep a look out when they're in her neighborhood. She told him okay.

"Detective Hart, can I ask you a question unrelated to this case?"

"Sure."

"I haven't heard from my daughter in days. She attends college in Atlanta but she hasn't been to class, hasn't called any of her friends and she hasn't used her credit cards. It's like she just vanished. Everyone thinks she just took off and went somewhere but I know her and she wouldn't be that irresponsible."

"Is she maybe over a boyfriend's house?"

"I don't think she even has a boyfriend. Well, not one that I know of."

"You know when kids leave the nest they tend to go a little wild. It's like they've been freed from jail sorta speaking."

"Not my daughter. I mean she had all the freedom she wanted when she was here. She's traveled all over the country so there's not too much she would want to do that she hasn't already done."

"I see," he said, rubbing his head.

"How long does a person have to be missing before you can file a report?"

"At least 48 hours."

"Can I file it here?"

"No. You need to go there."

Frustrated, Reese told Detective Hart thanks for all of his help then left the station. She needed to get home and wait for Eric's call to see if he found out anything before she hopped on the next flight.

Sitting in her car, she pulled out her cell phone and called Xavier. When he answered she told him that Lavar had been cleared, and that the police were no closer to solving Joi's murder than they were the night she was killed.

"Exactly what do they think he's going to do…confess to

her murder?" She started to cry. "He did it! I know he did it!"

"See, this is why I didn't want you to go down there. I just finished my meeting so I'm on my way over."

"No, I'm okay. Besides I'm on my way to the cemetery."

"Okay, well I'll meet you there."

"I appreciate the offer but this is something I need to do alone."

"I understand. Call me when you get home."

Reese told him she would, then she disconnected the call.

# Bitter by DANETTE MAJETTE

Chapter 26

It was everywhere. The living room couch and the floor were covered with it. Even her kitchen table, was painted red. Holes were punched in the screen of her 60-inch television and the computer monitor was smashed. It got even worse as she went upstairs. Family pictures were slashed and the walls were dented. In her bedroom, eggs splattered the walls and oil had been dumped on the floor along with her clothes. Her mattress was slashed, a mirror was smashed and the bed overturned.

Reese's home was a wreck when she returned from running errands. It was unrecognizable. It was one of those things she couldn't wrap her mind around. The fact that someone had come into her home and destroyed her personal property made her want to kill someone. The first thing she did was call the police. While she was waiting for the police to arrive she walked around to see if anything was stolen. Ironically nothing appeared to be missing. *Why the hell would someone break in and do all this without taking anything?*

She looked at her caller ID to see if ADT had called, but it only showed a missed call from an unknown number at noon which she suspected was to see if someone was home. It was starting to look like the break in was personal. Someone was definitely after her but why and more importantly who. Then she had a sinking suspicion the culprit was Lavar or Melanie. She quickly called

Xavier and asked him to stop at Home Depot and pick up new locks for her.

"What happened?" Xavier asked.

"Someone broke into my house," she said boiling mad.

"What! Did they take anything?"

"No! That's what's so crazy bout this whole thing."

"Let me run to the store then I'll be right over."

"Okay. Thanks."

When the police arrived to investigate they were shocked by what they saw. It was just that bad.

"Ma'am, were any of your belongings stolen?" one of the officers asked.

"Not that I can tell," Reese answered looking around.

An officer who was looking around in her yard for clues said the vandal climbed over the wall in the backyard and entered the house by kicking in the patio door. When she went over to the alarm it was deactivated. She was sure she had set it before she left.

When the police were finished gathering evidence, an officer gave Reese a copy of the report number for her insurance company. He also advised her to be careful because he didn't think the break in was a random act. That was the last thing she needed to hear but at least he was being honest with her.

On the brink of a breakdown, Reese poured herself a shot of Hennessey and threw it back. She wasn't sure how much more she could take. There were too many things happening lately. She was beginning to think her life may be in jeopardy. Breaking into her home was too close for comfort.

As the police were leaving, Xavier was driving up. When he walked in he was speechless.

"Somebody really has it in for you!"

"That's the same thing I thought. They didn't even take anything. They just trashed the place."

"I don't think you should stay here tonight. We'll change the locks then you're coming over to my place. We can come back tomorrow and clean up."

Xavier tossed his keys on a nearby coffee table and then

*B*itter by DANETTE MAJETTE

tore through the plastic that covered the door locks.

"Baby, do you have a screw driver."

Reese was too distracted by the photo of two young boys on his key chain to answer him. *Who are they?* When she tried to get a good look at the photo he jumped up.

"Never mind, I have one in the car," he said with a smile.

He retrieved his keys and walked outside.

As soon as Xavier came back in, he threw his keys on the table again and started to change the locks this time. This time the photo was gone. *What the fuck is that all about?* She was about to confront him about it but she was too upset to get into it with him. Instead she went upstairs to pack an overnight bag. A lot of her clothes were damaged, so she just threw a pair of sweats and a t-shirt in a bag along with some toiletries. She wanted an excuse to go shopping but she didn't need this kind. With her Burberry duffle bag in hand she went back downstairs.

"Good timing. I just finished," Xavier said. "This one is for the front door and this one is for the patio door," he said, handing her the keys. He kept a set for himself.

Before leaving, Reese checked the alarm to make sure it was set this time. She even made Xavier check behind her. When he went over for a look, it came back to her. *I did set the alarm so how was it disarmed.* She started to doubt herself again because she had a drink before she left. *Maybe I just thought I did.*

●●●●●●●●●●●●●●●●●●●●●●

On the way to his house, they had stopped for take out at a local restaurant not far from his Harbor Glen subdivision. Reese loved his home. This was her first time spending the night because when she was working their schedules always conflicted. It was so cozy and spacious. It was two times the size of her townhouse, minutes from the major highways, and close to shopping and entertainment areas including Lone Star Park and Six Flags. The brick home had four bedrooms, two and a half bathrooms, a two car garage, family room, game room, a huge master bedroom, and an office.

𝓑itter by DANETTE MAJETTE

As soon as they got into the house, Reese kicked off her shoes and started to pace the floor. This was truly the day from hell for her. Eric had called with several updates but none of them were with any real news on Sydney's whereabouts. She flopped on his couch and threw her head back while Xavier warmed their food up. She then started calling several of Sydney's friends in Atlanta and in Dallas to see if they had heard from her. Reese was so pissed that her daughter had been missing for days and the school never even called to notify her. She wanted desperately to go to Atlanta but Eric told her that he had to go to Atlanta to take care of some pressing business so he would be there anyway. He also wanted her to stay just in case Sydney showed up back in Dallas.

"Why is this happening to me?"

"I know you're upset baby, but the insurance company can replace all the materials things, just be glad you weren't there. There's no telling what would've happened if you were at home when this happened. And as far as Sydney goes, she'll turn up. She probably met a boy and is spending time with him" he said, handing her the plate of food.

"I'm not hungry," she said, putting the plate down. "I'm worried sick about my little girl. I just don't understand what's going on. Who's doing all this shit?"

"Baby, I know you're worried but you haven't really eaten in days. You have to keep up your strength."

Reese ignored Xavier. Eating was not what she needed. She needed her daughter to call and say she was alright.

"I know you think it's Lavar or Melanie, but I think it's one of your fans." He took a fork full of his broccoli and rice then stuffed it in his mouth. "Maybe it's someone who maybe called into your show and you pissed them off."

"No. It's someone who's close to me," she said, pushing her food around on her plate.

"Well, the only people close to you lately have been me and Julian. I almost got killed with you so that leaves Julian."

"But why?" she said, taking a small bite of her Orange Chicken.

"Do you even need to ask yourself that? You know as well I

do he's obsessed with you and he's bitter because of our relationship."

"Maybe you're right," she said.

"I am. Now let's just enjoy our night. Tomorrow we'll go to your place and clean up, then I'm going to have a little chat with Julian."

"Oh no! You leave Julian to me."

Xavier could see how tense Reese was so he told her to come go with him upstairs so he could give her a massage.

"Baby, I'm not really in the mood."

"Don't worry, I'll do all the work."

When they got upstairs, Xavier tossed the covers off the bed and laid her down on the mattress. She braced herself for another wild ride of lovemaking. He pressed the head of his shaft into her slick opening, teasing her.

"Is this what you want?" he asked.

She didn't answer. Instead she pushed him off of her and said, "I'm sorry. I can't do this. I'm worried about Sydney."

"Alright," he said.

Reese could tell by the way he got up off the bed that he was pissed.

"I'm going to take a shower."

She couldn't believe he was getting upset with her. She thought of all people he would understand but apparently he didn't.

"Xavier, look, my daughter is missing. So I'm sorry if making love to you isn't my main concern."

"It's okay. I'm cool," he said, walking away. He pulled a towel out of the closet in his massive bathroom and turned on the water.

Reese laid back down. While Xavier was in the shower, she had a brainstorm. She was always curious about this one particular room Xavier never seemed to go in when she was around. When she was sure he in the shower she quietly went into the room to snoop around. There was a mahogany desk, an executive chair, a few pictures of Xavier, and college degrees on the walls. It appeared to be just another office so she didn't understand why he was secretive about it. She went over to desk and opened it. There were the usual files and miscellaneous paperwork that seemed to deal with his job. One thing did stick out though, a picture of a woman and two young boys hidden in back of the desk. The boys were the spitting image of Xavier. *Is this bastard married?* As she dug deeper into the desk she found several pictures of the boys but not the woman. She grabbed the family picture and raced out of the room on fire. Her hair was flying everywhere and her pulse was elevated as she rushed into the shower to confront him.

"Xavier!" she yelled, sliding the curtain back.

"Who the hell is this?" she said, sticking the picture in his face. Her eyes looked wild. "Did you hear me?"

He was completely caught off guard. So he didn't answer right away. Furious, she stormed out and started getting her stuff together. He grabbed his towel and stepped out of the shower.

"Yes! I heard you. Now hear me!" he said, following her as he wrapped the towel around his waist. "You just had your home burglarized right. How did that make you feel? I'll tell you! You felt violated. So why would you go and do the same thing to me?" He slid on some boxers he got out of his drawer. "That woman is my sister and the boys are my nephews."

Reese turned around quickly.

"What sister? You never mentioned having a sister before," she said, dragging her hands through her hair.

"I know, but that's because we don't get along. I haven't seen her in about five years."

"Well what about the picture on the keychain?"

"What keychain?"

"Your keychain! You had a picture of two boys on it when you first came into my house tonight, but when you left to get the screwdriver and came back in it was gone."

"I must've lost it but those were my nephews. The same boys in that picture!"

Embarrassed, Reese took a seat on the bed. They had been dating for months and he never mentioned anything about his family, only his deceased girlfriend. Even if they didn't get along, he still should have told her he had a sister. He never even talked about his nephews. It seemed he was really fond of them because

Bitter by DANETTE MAJETTE

there were several pictures of them in the desk. Reese stared at Xavier for several minutes. Something just wasn't sitting right with her. Then she started to think about it. They had been all around the city together and she was spending the night at his house so he couldn't be married. Of course, the fact he didn't wear a ring on his finger meant nothing. In her mind, men were so slick they could be married and a woman wouldn't even know. For now she decided to take his word for it, but there was still some doubt lingering in the wings. If he was lying, she knew it would only be a matter of time before he was exposed.

Just in case Reese didn't believe him, Xavier slipped his arms around her waist, lowered his mouth to hers and kissed her. She rested her hands on his naked chest.

"You need to believe in me," he said, trying to reassure her that she was the only woman for him.

He seemed so sincere and since she didn't have any reason not to trust him she said, "I do."

Bitter by DANETTE MAJETTE

Chapter 27

Lavar was in the mood for some soul food for lunch so he went to Thelma's Kitchen. Thelma's was a hometown favorite that had relocated from Centennial Park to Sweet Auburn.

"Hey, Lavar. I ain't seen you in a long time," Princess said.

"Yeah. I been real busy."

"I was sorry to hear bout Joi."

Lavar stared at her moment then said, "Thanks."

"So whatcha havin' today," she said, pulling out her pen.

He gave Princess his order then made a few phone calls. Money was coming in real slow because of all of the unwanted police attention. He needed to stack his money back up but it was getting hard to do that. Most of the people who usually bought weight from him were scared to even come around him. It didn't help that he was so occupied with finding Joi's killer and investigating Xavier.

When Princess brought his pork chops, macaroni and cheese, collard greens, and sweet potato pie, Lavar couldn't wait to dig in. He took a forkful of macaroni and stuffed it in mouth. *This what the fuck I'm talkin' bout!* He thought.

He was enjoying his food when his phone rang.

"What?" he yelled irritated that he was being bothered during his delicious meal.

"Hey, it's me," the man said. "You know the guy you had

Bitter by DANETTE MAJETTE

me check out?"

"Yeah. What about him?"

"I found out he has a P.O. Box."

"Okay hold on, let me get a pen."

Lavar yelled for Princess to come over so he could borrow her pen. She handed him the pen and her order book.

"Aight, what's the address?"

He wrote the address down and handed the pen back to her. He told the guy thanks and jetted from the restaurant after paying his check and leaving a huge tip.

Sitting behind the wheel of his Bentley he put the address in his GPS, and took off. He was determined to find out what Xavier was up to. As he drove to the post office he thought about Joi. No matter what anyone else thought, he loved her in spite of the dirt he did. She was his rock. He had his fun in the streets but home was with Joi. She took care of all of his finances and kept the bills straight. That's something he would never trust the bitches in the streets to do. Nor would they even be able to.

Lavar drove to the post office and parked across the street out of sight and waited to see if Xavier would show. While he waited he conducted some business. After waiting for hours, Lavar decided to leave and just have someone else stake out the post office. He was way too busy to sit around waiting on someone who might not even show up there.

He turned the ignition and put the car in gear. As soon as he pulled out he noticed a man drive up in a BMW. He drove past to get a good look at the man. Wearing glasses didn't fool Lavar. He knew it was Xavier when he got out of the car and walked up to the door of the post office. Xavier was so busy on his phone he didn't even notice Lavar scoping him out. This made it easy for Lavar to follow him without being noticed. He whipped his Bentley around and waited for him to come back out. Five minutes later, Xavier returned to his car with a stack of envelopes. He jumped in his car and sped off. He made a few stops then drove to the southern Dallas area to Lou Foote airport, an abandoned airfield off Hwy 77.

"What the fuck is this nigga doin' here?" Lavar mumbled.

He parked in front of an old warehouse and walked down to the area where Xavier was. He watched as Xavier unloaded a rolled up carpet from his car.

Lavar had done a lot of killings in his life so he knew exactly what he was carrying.

I wonder who's body that is. Lavar thought.

Once Xavier was inside, Lavar went up to get a closer look. He was caught off guard when Xavier flung the door open. Strapped with his Glock, Lavar walked over to him and laughed.

"So we meet again," he said.

"You know you're really beginning to be a pain in my ass," Xavier said, walking back into the warehouse.

Lavar followed him in. He looked around and asked Xavier what he was up to.

"I did a little investigating and I found out that you aren't who you said you are. As a matter of fact, I know who you really are."

"Is that so?"

"Yeah it is." He folded his hands across his chest. "I wonder what Reese is gonna say when she find out she's been fuckin' a fake."

Xavier walked closer to Lavar.

"She doesn't have to find out. Face it. You don't like her so if we work together we can both take her down."

"Naw. I work alone," Lavar said with cold eyes.

Xavier told him either he worked with him or he didn't work at all. Lavar refused again sending Xavier into a blind rage. They argued for a few moments before Lavar abruptly stopped and dropped his jaw when he saw a pair of shoes that looked familiar to him. He had the sneakers custom designed for Joi but she said they were too small for her. He walked over to the balled up rug. Standing so he could keep an eye on Xavier, he pulled the rug back and was stunned by what he saw.

"Muthafucka! You killed Sydney?" he asked.

Xavier answered with a shot to the chest. Lavar was still standing and trying to shoot back as he moved towards Xavier, so he shot him again.

*B*itter by DANETTE MAJETTE

When his body fell blood gushed rapidly from his body. Xavier stood over him and said, "You should've come on board with me." He stepped back and took a minute to think. Then he had an idea. He wiped his fingerprints off the gun and placed it in Lavar's hand as he moaned and groaned until he lost consciousness. Then he grabbed the rug and laid it down on the ground in plan view.

"You just made my job a lot easier," he yelled to an unconscious Lavar as he walked out of the warehouse and got into his car.

Chapter 28

It was nine in the morning and Reese was waiting for Eric to come over. His plane had landed at eight thirty that morning and he told her he would come straight over from the airport. She had been up all night drinking and calling people to see if they had heard from Sydney. She even had to curse few people out because they were acting like she was getting on their nerves due to the fact she had called them so many times. She didn't give a fuck! Her daughter was missing and if she had to call their ass all night she would. Somebody was going to tell her something.

She needed to sober up so she made herself a cup of coffee and went over to her laptop to see if Sydney had been on her Facebook or Twitter pages. She took the picture of Joi off the refrigerator.

"God, I wish you were here with me. I don't know what to do."

She felt herself about to tear up so she quickly grabbed a napkin. As she wiped her eyes, her phone started ringing. She started to just let it go straight to voicemail but when she saw it was Xavier she answered it.

"Hey, baby. Any word on Sydney?"

"No, but Eric's on his way over. He just landed."

"How's your house looking? Are they on track?"

"Yes. I think so. They would probably be finished but I

don't let them work when I'm not home."

"That's understandable. Especially since they haven't found out who's been stalking you."

The fact that she was actually being stalked blew Reese's mind, she couldn't fathom what they could possibly be getting out of it. Today of course wasn't the day to even think about it. She had to focus on the task at hand and that was finding her daughter.

"Oh, baby I gotta go. I need to keep my phone lines free," she said.

"Well, call me and let me know what you found out."

"Okay."

"I love you."

"I love you, too."

While she waited on Eric, Reese went up to her daughter's room wishing she were there. The room was decorated in Victoria Secret Pink dorm merchandise. She had pictures of her friends and Reese on the walls. The shelves were filled with books, stuffed animals, and trophies from her cheerleading days. The only thing missing was her favorite girl. There were no words to express how she felt. She didn't even think it was possible to miss someone that much. Distraught, she walked over to Sydney's bed and laid across it. Holding Sydney's pillow tight and sniffing her American Eagle perfume Reese cried her eyes out.

"I want my baby…I want my baby," she shouted over and over again.

Thirty minutes later, Eric drove up. He sat in the car for a few moments to try and get himself together. His mind drifted back to when Sydney was a little girl and how she loved to dance and sing around the house. In his mind, he recalled every time he ran a boy away from the house, how she would run up his credit cards buying designer clothes, and always said 'Daddy you're the greatest'. Tears began to fall from his eyes. He quickly wiped his face when he saw that Reese had opened the door and was standing in the doorway. He took a deep breath and tried to regain his composure.

Reese's adrenaline was pumping, when she saw Eric walking up with his head hung low. The look on face made her knees buckle. She slid to the floor and started bellowing.

"No...it's not what you think!"

Reese grabbed his face. "Is she okay?"

"I don't know. C'mon lets go inside and talk."

Eric told Reese that there still wasn't any activity on her credit card, she still hadn't shown up for her classes and the most disturbing news was her cell phone had been found in the woods behind the dorms.

"It doesn't look good, but we're not going to give up hope," he said.

"I can't take this. I don't know if she's safe. I haven't heard anything from her nor have any of her close friends. What if the person who's been stalking me has her?"

"We can look into that possibility but right now we need to stay positive and just keep focused. That's what's going to get us through this," he said embracing her.

"So, what do we do now?"

"We have to fly back to Atlanta so you can file a police report. They wouldn't let me do it because I'm not her biological father. Then we're going to hit the pavement until we find her. Clark Atlanta has lots of volunteers already canvassing the campus looking for her."

She started crying and couldn't stop. She missed Sydney and wanted her home.

Eric stayed with her for awhile then told her was going to his office just to check in and let them know he would be leaving for a few days. He promised her they would find Sydney then left.

• •

Rage consumed him. The thought of Reese and Xavier playing house was driving him insane. He pictured Xavier ducked taped and hog tied. He stood up, pushed his chair back and began pacing the floor. He needed to think this through. He sat back down at his desk and picked up the receiver and placed a call.

"Hey, this is Julian. We need to meet."

"Dude, I was just about to call you. I got the information

Bitter by DANETTE MAJETTE

you've been waiting on."

The person on the other end told him that he was available now, so Julian left work to meet him in a nearby park. Sitting on a bench reading a newspaper, Julian acted as though he didn't know who the man sitting next to him was.

"Take a look at this," the man said, handing him some papers.

When he looked at the papers, his eyes almost popped out of his head.

"Oh my God! I have to get to Reese and tell her. I need you to find out his real name." Julian said, jumping up.

"What about my money?"

Julian sighed, rolled his eyes and reached in his wallet.

"Take this and I'll give you the rest later. I have to go."

Julian jumped in his car and headed to Reese's house, but when he got there she wasn't home. He tried several times to call her on her cell phone but it kept going to voicemail. *Damn her battery must be dead again.* He drove around Dallas looking for her but was unsuccessful. *Now what am I going to do? I have to find her before he gets to her,* he thought as he sat in his car trying to figure out where she could be.

Chapter 29

Reese struggled getting down the stairs with her bags. Just as she was about to sit her bags down, she felt someone grab her from behind. She screamed and started swinging.

"Whoa! Baby, it's me."

"Xavier! You scared me half death!"

"I'm sorry. I was just trying to surprise you," he said, holding his jaw. "Wow, you pack a mean punch."

"How did you get in?"

"The door was open."

"Shit, I must've forgotten to lock it when Eric left."

"What's up with all the bags?"

"I have to go out to Atlanta to look for Sydney."

"Oh, when are you leaving?"

"We're flying out tomorrow morning."

"We?"

"Yes, Eric and I," she said, leading him to the living room. They took a seat on the couch and began to talk. "Do you think you can go with us?" she said, holding his hand.

"If you want me to I can. Just let me tie up a few loose ends around here." He got up to leave.

"You're leaving?" Reese questioned.

"Yes. Don't worry, I'll be back. We'll go to Atlanta and we'll find your daughter and bring her back home."

*B*itter by DANETTE MAJETTE

Hearing him say those words to her made her chest tighten. He was such a wonderful man and there was no denying she'd had fallen in love again.

"Okay."

She walked him to the door, kissed him and told him thank you.

With a shot in one hand and a glass of wine in another, Reese went up to her room to try to find some recent pictures of Sydney. Taking a seat on the bed to gather her thoughts her cell phone rang.

"Reese! Thank God I got to you," Julian yelled out of breath. "I've been looking all over for you."

"Julian, what do you want?"

"Xavier isn't who he says he is. Xavier isn't even his real name."

"Really and how do you know that?"

"You remember the guy that was in my office that day? He's a private investigator I hired to do a background check on Xavier. He told me that Xavier Miller is dead. He died twenty years ago."

"Well, you're mistaken! You're unbelievable you know that. You'll do anything to try to come between us won't you! I can't believe you went behind my back and checked out my man without even talking to me first."

"I know and I'm sorry but something wasn't right with him."

"No! Something ain't right with you. My daughter is missing and muthafucka you calling me with this bullshit!" Reese blew a fuse. "How can you be so damn insensitive?"

"I'm sorry, I didn't know."

"Shut the fuck up! I don't want to hear it. You're obsessed and frankly a little on the psychotic side. I don't ever want to talk to you again. Do you understand me? Don't call me or come over here or I'm going to call the police."

Julian knew the only way he was going to convince Reese that he was telling her the truth was to get some more proof that Xavier was playing her. He vowed to work day and night until he did. There was no way he was letting the love of his life get hurt by this man.

● ●

Later that night, Xavier planned an impromptu dinner party. He needed to put a plan in action quick. Especially since Reese was leaving town. He knew it was only a matter of time before she found out the truth about him. When his guests arrived, he instructed the bartenders to make sure they kept everyone's drinks full. If he was going to pull this off he needed everyone there to be tipsy. He walked around the room to make sure everyone was having a good time. Most of his guests were just meeting him for the first time even though he had lived in the neighborhood for awhile. They thought it was little strange that he would invite them to his going away party, but they weren't about to pass up on free food and booze.

One of Xavier's neighbors wanted to ask him about some of the investments he had for him.

"Hey, I can't seem to find any information on that company overseas you bought stock in for me?" the man said.

"That's because it's listed under a subsidiary company."

"Oh okay. I thought there was a reasonable explanation," he said, patting Xavier on the back.

Another man there was wondering if Xavier was on the up and up because he hadn't received any profits yet from an investment he had made with Xavier six months ago. When he tried to confront Xavier about it, Xavier told him no shop talk tonight.

"Don't worry. We'll talk about it in the morning," Xavier said, handing the man another glass of champagne. "Come on, everyone drink up!" he announced.

Once he saw everyone mingling and a little tipsy, he told a few of them he had to go in his office for a very important conference call. He told them it would only take a about an hour but for them to keep drinking and eating and he would be right back to join them. He went into his home office and pulled out a CD and put it in his CD player. He made sure the door was locked, hit play on the player, scooped up his belongings then slipped out the back door of his office.

• •

While Reese packed her clothes, she sipped on a glass of Rose'. While going through her closet she found a pair of shoes she borrowed from Joi to wear to a wedding.

"I guess you were right. I did have them."

When she dug in the back of her closet she found a pastel colored box with a pink ribbon attached on top of it. She started to cry. She opened the box and pulled out the pictures. One by one she looked at the photos. It brought back so many memories of her and Joi in college. They were inseparable back then. Reese could always count on Joi for anything. Joi was an only child who grew up in a middle class home so she was beyond spoiled. Her parents always sent her money and she had access to their credit cards. Reese didn't have that luxury so Joi would always give her money for food and buy her clothes when she needed them. Joi was popular and never missed a party. On the flip side Reese was the smart one. She promised Joi that if she ever got into broadcasting she would bring her along for the ride. It was a promise she kept.

Time was flying by so fast, Reese didn't even realize she had been sitting in her closet looking at old photos for an hour. She still had a few things left to do so she took a quick shower, blow-dried her hair, and pulled it back into a ponytail. Trying to keep busy, she grabbed a bottle of wine and went down to the basement. She had neglected boxes and boxes of fan mail so she wanted to read and reply to some of them. A lot of her fans were sad that she was off the air and wanted to let her know they still loved her. A few vowed not to listen to the station anymore. They even staged protests to get her re-hired but Mr. Andrews wouldn't bulge. Especially after she basically attacked him in his office.

She started sifting through the mail when she noticed one letter was old and turning colors. It had the word important written on the bottom right hand corner and post marked a year earlier. *Where did this come from?* She thought. She opened it and started

Bitter by DANETTE MAJETTE

reading the contents. The woman's name on the letter however was Vanessa Carr. It basically said thank you and how she had taken Reese's advice. *What the hell was my advice?*

Reese was beginning to wonder what this woman's connection to her was. Sure, she had given her advice of some sort, but she has given thousands of people advice. She also wondered if Vanessa's case had been solved so she grabbed her laptop. She logged onto the internet and put the woman's name in the search engine. She clicked on the newspaper article of the Vanessa's death and read it but there was no photo. She then clicked on a video link about Vanessa Carr and watched the broadcast of the case. At the end of the video there was a photo of the Vanessa and her two sons. The sons were now being raised by the maternal grandmother because the father was a Dallas Detective who worked long hours.

She kept looking at the picture because it looked so familiar. She dug deeper. *If her husband was a police officer there should be a picture of him somewhere.* She googled the officer's name. There were several articles about him making arrests but no pictures. She then googled his name and put the word 'picture'. Her heart dropped when the picture came up. When she zoomed in, she almost passed out. Reese gasped and held her hand over her mouth. She couldn't believe what she was seeing. It was definitely him. In the picture, however, he had dreads. Then it all started to come together. She remembered exactly where she had seen the photo. *What the fuck?* She cringed then remembered what Julian had told her. She started to get sick. It was a sinking feeling like riding an elevator and having it quickly drop several floors. How could she been so clueless? It's Xavier!

Bitter by DANETTE MAJETTE

Chapter 30

Dressed in all black like he was going on a special ops assignment, Xavier made his way to the rental car that was parked down the street from his home without being seen. He opened the door and threw his duffel bag in the passenger's seat. Once he started the engine and pulled off he didn't look back. He was focused on getting to Reese's house. This was the final curtain. The day he had been waiting on for a year. He didn't think he could pull it off but Reese's vulnerability made it a piece of cake. As he drove, he kept watching the clock. He had exactly fifty-two minutes to get in and out and be back at his home before anyone noticed he was missing. With one hand on the steering wheel, he opened the duffel bag to make sure he had everything he needed. A gun, duck tape, and a computer typed suicide note.

With no one else to turn to, Reese called Eric and asked him to come over quickly. She wanted to make sure she was right before she confronted Xavier. Until Eric got there she paced the floor and kept looking out the window. At that moment, she realized she hadn't seen Wayne in weeks. Strange but nothing she needed to worry about. Finally, when Eric pulled up she immediately deactivated the alarm and opened the door.

"What's going on?" he asked, rushing into the house.

"Thanks for coming over. I didn't know what to do. Look at this," she said, turning her laptop in his direction so he could see the picture.

He read the article and was shocked. "Why did he lie to you?"

"I don't know!"

"I think we need to go to the police station and see what they can tell us because clearly he changed his identity for a reason."

"Why? What does he want from me?"

"I don't know but let's go find out," he said, grabbing her by the hand.

She broke away to grab her keys and purse then met him at the door.

After parking the rental car that resembled Julian's car, Xavier who was armed with a .357 Magnum quickly made his way to Reese's front door. He was just about to use the spare key he had to open the door when he bumped right into Reese and Eric.

He pushed them both back inside and made them go to the living room. Eric started pleading with Xavier to let them go. This irritated him so he hit Eric with blunt force in the head with the butt of his gun. Reese ran to her house phone to call the police but the line was dead. She threw it on the floor and then grabbed her cell phone. As usual, the battery was dead. Attempting to flee, she ran for the back door but Xavier caught her. He pinned her up to the door.

"So, it was you," she said.

She bit his arm, giving her the chance to run again but she tripped over some of the equipment the contractor left. He picked her up by her hair and covered her mouth. With his gun pointed at her head he said, "Shhhhhh...be a good girl okay and you won't get hurt."

He slowly lowered his hand from her mouth then pushed her down onto the couch. He took a seat next to her. Reese was so terrified. She had no idea what he was going to do to her. She knew if she wanted to make it out of this alive, she was going to have to comply with his demands.

"What do you want from me?" she asked on the brink of tears.

He slid the gun up and down the side of her face.

"I want you to pay for what you did, bitch!"

Reese was completely puzzled. She had no idea what he was talking about so she tried to dig deeper.

"Okay just talk to me. What did I do?"

"I'm not on your show bitch! I don't need to talk about shit!"

He was starting to grow angry.

"Okay…okay, please just calm down. You're scaring me," she whispered.

They were both caught off guard when Julian came running into the house.

"Reese! Reese, I have to talk to you about Xavier!" he said, rushing into the living room.

Xavier quickly grabbed Reese around the neck and pointed the gun at her head. He wasn't expecting Julian to come there. He had to rearrange his plan.

"Come in and sit your dorky ass down or you can watch the love of your life get her brains blown out."

"Don't you dare hurt her!" Julian said.

"Shut the fuck up! I'm giving the orders around here."

Moving very slowly, Julian sat in the chair across from them. When he looked out the corner of his eye he saw Eric lying on the floor bleeding. Xavier ordered Reese to go sit next to Julian. Sitting back on the sofa, Xavier looked at Reese with contempt.

"You know I was happy until you opened your big ass mouth." Reese was clearly confused. "That's right, I was married with two beautiful boys and then poof… it was all gone." He looked at Julian. "You already knew that though, didn't you," Julian remained silent. "How'd you figure it out Sherlock?"

"I hired a private detective," Julian said, glaring at him.

"I don't understand what your marriage has to do with me," Reese said, feeling like she was in the twilight zone.

"Of course, you don't understand. You never take responsibility for any of the marriages or relationships you break up." He started hitting himself on the side of his head with the gun. "See, everyone thinks it was just a random act of violence." He started laughing. "I waited for about six months before making my move then I killed her." He crossed his legs and started shaking his foot. "That bitch thought she was going to divorce me, take my kids and go be with another man…I don't think so!" Reese flinched when he pointed the gun at her. "She called into your show and you and that bitch Joi told her to leave me. Leave me!" he yelled. "You told her that if she loved someone else then go be with that person." He became even more enraged just talking about it. "Did you ever think about my feelings? And what about my boys? They need their father, but you didn't care about any of that. All you cared about was your fucking ratings!" His voice was filled with bitterness. Xavier's eyes were fixed on Reese as tears fell down her face. She couldn't believe her relationship with him was all a plan to get back at her. "I mean give yourself some credit too. I thought it was going to be hard to get you into to bed, but you practically threw yourself at me," he said laughing. "I followed you and watched you for months then I made my move in Neiman's. I seriously thought you were gonna just brush me off considering how you hated men. Those hormones of yours just couldn't resist me though. Could they?"

"You dirty bastard!"

"Shut the fuck up!" he said, pointing the gun at her.

"Look, just let her go, you can keep me," Julian pleaded.

"Shut up! You have to go, too. See, I stopped by that dump you call a house and planted some evidence. Yeah… they're newspaper clippings and pictures of Reese all over your place so it was gonna look like you killed her. But there's been a change of plans. Now it has to look like a murder-slash-suicide."

Xavier was tapping the gun on his knee and rocking back and forth on the sofa by this time. He was like a man possessed. Reese and Julian had no idea what he was going to do next. All they knew was if they wanted to get out of there alive they were going to have to act fast before he became fully unglued.

"You're not going to get away with this, you know that

𝓑itter by DANETTE MAJETTE

right," Julian said, trying to reason with him. "No one will ever believe I would kill her or myself for that matter."

Xavier sat on the edge of the sofa.

"I beg to differ. See, I have an airtight alibi and you my friend are obsessed with her. Everyone knows that. That's why you killed her. You couldn't handle her being with me so you lost it!" he said.

"Xavier…I'm sorry!"

"Awww…shut up. You're not sorry. You enjoyed every minute of it. Just like I enjoyed killing my wife and your sidekick." He reached into his pocket and pulled out a college class ring. "You remember this. I think you have one just like it."

"You killed Joi?" Reese said in tears.

"You killed Joi?" he said mocking her. "Yeah…she had to pay just like you're gonna pay. As luck would have it her drug dealing boyfriend threatened her in front of everyone so that made him the perfect target." He started cracking up. "That poor sap. Everyone's been giving him hell and he didn't even do it. Let's see, your lost presentation, the attempted run down at the restaurant, the vandalism here, the letters, and the phone calls were all my handy work."

He started laughing hysterically.

"Oh, and I can't forget Wayne Nichols who you fucked and thought I wouldn't find out.! Got him, too!"

"Oh my God!" Reese shrieked then covered her mouth.

"I had so much fun watching you squirm…bitch!" he looked at her with contempt. "Oh wait it gets better…I killed that brat of yours too!"

Reese immediately started shaking her head.

"What? No! Not my baby!" she yelled and screamed.

"Yes! Yes! I slit the little bitch's throat."

Reese's body shut down. She sat in shock, barely able to breathe. She couldn't believe her daughter was actually dead. Killed by a man she was in love with. Reese began to cry out in agony, caring nothing about her own life.

"Well, you two love birds say goodbye," he said, cocking the gun.

Bitter by DANETTE MAJETTE

When Julian jumped up, the gun went off. He and Xavier started fighting for the gun. In the midst of the fight, the gun went off again.

Chapter 31

Tied up to a chair with duct tape over her mouth, Reese tried to free herself. She was crying and hysterical as Xavier pointed the gun at her and played Russian Roulette. Julian was unconscious and lying on the floor bleeding. She could see her life flashing before her and there was nothing she could do. This isn't how she imagined she would die.

With her eyes, she begged and pleaded for him to spare her life even though he had already killed before with no regret. He cocked the gun again and pointed it straight at her chest. Smiling, he pulled the trigger.

Her body jerked as she yelled out, "Help me."

"It's okay. You're safe," Eric said comforting Reese. "You were just dreaming. We're safe now."

She looked around the hospital room and realized that it was a dream. At least part of it was. Xavier had indeed shot her but only in the shoulder. Julian suffered a flesh wound to his forearm. He was bandaged and released but he refused to leave Reese's side.

"Welcome back sleeping beauty," Julian said, sitting on the other side of her bed.

They survived thanks to the grungy private investigator. He had spoken to Julian before he headed over to Reese's to tell her about Xavier. After calling Julian several times and getting no answer he called the police. Once Xavier shot Reese and Julian, he

*B*itter by DANETTE MAJETTE

heard the sirens and slipped out the back.

Julian told Reese what happened after she was unconscious. She couldn't believe she had been so naïve. She couldn't believe what happened to her daughter. She got sick thinking about her daughter out there somewhere dead. Finally, the identity of Joi's killer and her stalker had been revealed and it stunned everyone. Reese was shocked and hurt the most.

"This is all my fault," she said, crying. "My daughter, best friend and Wayne are all dead because of me."

"Hey, it's not your fault," Julian said, rubbing her hand. "He had us all fooled."

"He didn't have you fooled. You told me he looked suspicious," She wiped her face. "I should've listened to you."

"My baby is gone. What am I going to do without her?" she cried.

"Stop it...I'm not going to let you do this to yourself," Eric said. "Aaron Carr is a sick man."

"Did they catch him?" Reese asked.

"No, but they will. There's an APB out for him. Don't worry. There's a guard outside your door so he can't hurt you anymore," Julian assured.

Julian tried to tell a few of his corny jokes to try and cheer Reese up but it didn't work.

"Well...I guess I have to bring in the big guns," he said.

"What are you talking about?"

"I'm going to go down to the cafeteria and get you some cookies. If I remember correctly you love chocolate chip cookies."

Reese smiled. "You know me so well."

They were interrupted by the shift nurse who came in and inserted a syringe filled with pain medicine into Reese's IV. She told Reese that her medicine would be kicking in at any moment then she left the room. When Reese started talking out of her head, Eric and Julian went down to get her the cookies.

"We'll be right back. You get some rest," Eric said.

"Oooohhh...taaayy," she mumbled, dosing off.

He laughed. "I need to get some of this stuff to take home," he said, as he kissed her on the forehead.

Julian was a little jealous, but he knew he was fighting a loosing battle if Eric wanted Reese back. He was her first real love and he saw how devastated she was when they split up. He was so glad she was alive and knew it was going to be hard for her to bounce back from this. The horror of being shot by a mad man was going to be nothing compared to the guilt she would feel for the rest of her life that she was sleeping with the enemy. Aaron aka Xavier had killed her daughter, best friend, Wayne and terrorized her for months. She was going to need some happiness in her life and if Eric could do that than he would support them. That's if she even wanted him back. He wasn't throwing in the towel, he was just going to wait and let things play out.

Walking to the elevator, Julian smiled. *Maybe there's a chance for us to get together after all.* As they stepped on the elevator, a man with a baseball hat pulled down over his head stepped off the elevator next to him. Julian had an eerie feeling so he held the elevator door open and watched the man walk down the hall. When the man walked past Reese's room he let the door go. He was a bit paranoid and who could blame him after everything that had taken place. As they were riding the elevator down to the first floor the man doubled back. He slipped past the guard who was busy flirting with a nurse and entered Reese's room. She was a little groggy so she thought she was dreaming when she saw the man's face. Paralyzed with fear she couldn't even yell for help. He grabbed a pillow from the back of her head and said, "Bye, bitch!" He was about to smother her to death when he heard a click. He quickly turned around.

"Not dis time muthafucka!" Lavar said, pointing his nine millimeter at Xavier's head.